The Disgrace T

DEE PALMER

Disgraceful
A Disgrace Trilogy Novel - Book 2
Copyright © 2016 Dee Palmer
Published by Dee Palmer

ISBN-13:978-1539106869
ISBN-10:1539106861

Editor : Ekatatina Sayanova at RedQuill Editing Services
Cover Judi Perkins at Concierge Literary Promotions
Formatting: Champagne Formats

Warning: ADULT CONTENT 18+ This story is on the filthy side of smut and isn't suitable for those who don't enjoy graphic descriptions that are erotic in nature, but for those that do, enjoy ;)

For free stories sign up to my Newsletter on the contact page at www. deepalmerwriter.com (Promise No Spam)
or go here
http://eepurl.com/biZ6g1

FREE BOOK
Never a Choice
First In the Choices Trilogy
(But no cliffy…So can be read as a standalone:))

Other Books by Dee

The Choices Trilogy
Never a Choice
Always a Choice
The Only Choice

Never 1.5 (A Valentine Novella)

Ethan's Fall
(Can be read as a stand-alone)

Disgrace

DEDICATION

Tess…
Yes, I am dedicating this book to my beautiful dog…
She was the heart of our family, she was loved, so very much,
every single day.
and I will miss her

Every Single Day.

ONE

Sam

HE PROPOSED. I CAN'T BELIEVE HE PROPOSED. I TWIST THE ring that feels oddly comfortable on my engagement finger. As a new piece of jewelry to me, it shouldn't feel so good, but it does. It's perfect. I exhale a deep breath and stroke the smooth surface, mesmerised by the early morning light catching the stone, reflecting brilliant shards of light across the room. *He does like me in diamonds.* The largest Asscher cut stone I have seen outside of a Bond Street jeweler is surrounded by a halo of baguette diamonds and set in an Art Deco pattern on a platinum band. It's stunningly beautiful, and I can't imagine how much it must have cost. I lift my hand to the equally expensive collar that I haven't removed since I made a show of putting it on at the club last night. What did I do to deserve all this? What did I do to deserve Jason?

He is curled up on his side facing my empty space. The shadow that darkens one side of the room covers his face. I couldn't sleep but have been watching him from the chair at the end of his bed—our bed, I suppose, since I moved in a few months ago, and definitely our bed now that I am going to be his wife. The covers have dropped or more likely were pushed down to his hips, more shadow hiding more deliciousness. We both sleep naked, him because he gets so hot, and me because every night he peels off each attempt I have made at covering up. I tried to argue that I don't generate heat like he does, and I need my PJs to ward off the cold, but there really is no need. All the warmth I desire is afforded by his strong arms and firm body holding me each night, or at least until I wriggle free.

"Penny for them?" His deep voice makes me jump. His voice has an edge of sleep-induced gravelly roughness, and his stretch and groan are more reflective of his semiconscious state.

"I'm sorry. I didn't mean to wake you." I keep my voice quiet, which is ridiculous now that we are both awake.

"Your body isn't next to mine, and that always wakes me." He shifts so his torso is now bathed in the silvery glow of the moonlight through the gap in the curtains. His face is pale, but his eyes look sharp and clear. His gaze is searching.

"Not straight away, though. I've been sitting here for a while." I tuck my toes under the edge of the throw, which I have draped over my shoulders.

"And I've been awake for a while."

"Really?"

"Yes." His lips curl in a sexy grin.

"You've been watching me this whole time?" A pleasant ache starts to tingle between my legs at the thought.

"Yes." His tone is as flat as his answers are brief.

"Why?"

"Because I can." His smile spreads, and I feel a warm glow ignite deep in my chest. He curls his finger, and I move without hesitation, not from his silent command but from the innate draw I feel to him. I crawl onto the bed, and he sits up so I am kneeling beside him. He rests his back against the headboard. "Now tell me what has you a million miles away when you should only ever be right here." He takes my hand and places it on his firm chest. His skin is smooth and warm, and I can feel the strong, heavy beat of his heart beneath my fingertips.

"You proposed." My throat feels dry, and I swallow loudly in the quiet of the room.

"I did." His hand covers mine and holds it firmly. "And you said yes."

"I did." My voice waivers, and I try to avert my eyes, but he dips to maintain the contact.

"You did. Is that cold feet already, Sam?" His tone is light, but his expression is anything but jovial. His thick brows knit together with concern.

"Did you really mean it, Jason?" I meet his gaze and search for any signs of regret. There are none, and his words only confirm his feelings.

"You think for some reason I would ask the question if I didn't?"

"But marriage, Jason? That's a huge commitment. I believe marriage is for life," I tell him in all earnestness.

"I would hope you did." He laughs lightly, but my smile is tentative at best.

"But for us, Jason…is that even viable?" I can't hide the anxiousness in my voice. I didn't realize how much I had been holding in until I started to talk. Now all I can feel is a huge wave of uncertainty and a sense of my own doom. I don't deserve this.

"I don't understand." His voice is calm and filled with concern.

"Just four weeks ago we were having a four-way with your brother and my best friend, and you're going to be happy with a normal missionary marriage until death do us part?" I squeal at the sudden speed with which he has pushed me flat and pinned me to the bed with his full weight. His legs wedge between and ease mine wide. I can feel his instant heat and solid erection at my entrance. A gentle roll of my hips makes us both moan, but he clears his throat with a sharp cough.

"Sam, I want you as my wife. I have never wanted anyone the way I want you. I never saw myself getting married, but being with you, I can't see that there is any other life for me." His lips cover mine in a gentle, possessive kiss, sweet and soft. "We don't have to do this tomorrow. For now, I'll take you any way I can, but understand this…I want you as my wife. Our happy ever after is inevitable, and the marriage bit is probably the only normal thing about our relationship." Before I can utter a single word, his lips consume mine once more, this time with an unhindered urgency that steals my breath. His tongue traces the seam of my lips and dives inside, swirling and drawing my bottom lip into his mouth. He sucks hard, and I can feel the painful pull of blood into the full swollen tissue before he lets it pop from his mouth. "We have our own *normal,* beautiful, and our marriage will be everything we want it to be. And very much until death do us part." His smile is a perfect mix of striking and salacious. I find I am just as speechless at his perfect words as I am breathless from his weight. "And there is nothing wrong with missionary." He grinds his hips. I feel his thick cock spread my soaking silken folds, and I get that deep tingle of anticipation. With one deep, firm thrust, he sinks inside me— hard. He is so unbelievably solid and impressively large that he hits the very end of me and makes me gasp. He pulls back, a wicked grin etched at the corners of his smile. "It's a classic for a reason." He pitches up on his elbows, but the majority of his weight covers my body. I close my eyes and relish the feeling. My muscles start to twitch around his cock as he holds himself firm and immobile. I open my eyes to meet his intense, fiery gaze.

"You are having doubts." His voice is low and stern, but the gentle rotation of his hips is more than a little distracting to the seriousness of his statement.

"Mmm…that feels so good, Jason." I sigh.

"Yes, it does. You are having doubts." He repeats both his statement and his heavenly hip action. I swallow thickly and watch as his eyes darken, and the tiny muscles inside me begin rippling like crazy along his erection.

"Not about us…not about how I feel about you." The pitch in my voice is remarkably level, but the words are breathy and strained.

"Good." He pushes deeper, and I lose all cognisant thought until he draws back just a little. "That is all that matters, Sam. Everything else is detail…we will deal with the detail together as husband and wife." I had been gripping his taut shoulder muscles, and I slide my hands down his back and flex them wide to take a good grasp of his fine backside in each hand. The way his defined muscles contract under my hands with each thrust and drive is the sexiest fucking thing. I sink my nails into his skin to secure my hold.

"Some of those details are pretty fucking big, and we've not exactly sat down and discussed the future." This feels so good, why the fuck am I bringing up this subject now?

"What details?" Oh God, he just grinds with the perfect pressure that makes my clit pulse like a needy bundle of aching nerves and it drives me crazy.

"Please, Jason." I try to shift down and tilt to get a little bit more friction, just where I need him, but he sinks like a dead weight preventing any further movement on my part.

Stupid dumb ass, you deserved that, Sam. You couldn't just wait and have this conversation in the morning?

"What details, Sam? What specifically about our future do you wish to discuss?" I can see the muscles in his jaw clench with effort, controlling his temper or his libido, I can't quite tell. His face is stern and his voice is calm.

"I don't want to discuss any of it now. *Now*, I just want to come," I grind out through a fake and frustrated smile.

"And if you tell me what details, I might let you." His tone is a perfect mix of lightly mocking and threatening.

I let out a defeated puff of air. His face is impassive, and he has now frozen all orgasm-inducing movement. I can't exactly think straight, but I know him well enough to understand he is more than capable of keeping me hanging until he gets his answers.

"My house for one," I call out.

"What about your house?" He raises a curious brow.

"Do I sell it? Am I living here permanently?" He chuckles, a deep throaty rumble I can feel in my chest and much lower.

"You're getting riled over this? You're adorable. Yes, you are living with me permanently. That's what husbands and wives do; they live together. I couldn't care less where that is—here or at your place is not important. Sell your house, or don't; that's your decision, beautiful." He shifts a little, just enough to send a wave of tingles from my clit to every waiting nerve in my body. I stifle a whimper. "What else you got that's troubling you?"

"Babies," I blurt out, but my tone is more like an accusation.

"What about babies?" His words come out slower and with more caution. His brows pinch together to form a dark, almost-touching line.

"Well, we've never talked about them and that's a pretty big detail to leave unmentioned, don't you think?"

"I don't want children, so it honestly didn't cross my mind, but since it is a detail you have clearly considered, tell me, Sam, do you want children?" His tone is soft, but I feel like an ice blast has frozen my heart at his stark revelation.

"I…I don't know…maybe one day." I swallow the lump in my throat and try to push his heavy body away as I fight to take in my next breath.

"Hey, Sam, look at me." His stern tone draws my gaze. My nose tingles, and I feel stupid and exposed that this has upset so. Of course, he wouldn't want children. Too domesticated for someone like the kinky owner of London's elite sex club, and certainly not with someone like me.

"It's fine…I understand." I dig my nails into his biceps to get him to move, but he doesn't budge at all.

"You clearly don't." He arches a brow, and I can see his lips start to curl with amusement, which fires my blood with irritation, and I struggle like a wild animal to get free. He grabs my flailing arms and pins them high above my head. He pushes his hips harder onto mine, and I swear I can feel him swell inside me. "You're making me painfully hard, Sam. It is very distracting, and we need to clear this up before it gets silly."

"Silly?" I snap, my tone piqued. I'm incredulous at his flippancy. He narrows his eyes, and his dark stare makes me bite my tongue. He looks deadly serious.

"I have never wanted children, and that hasn't changed. What has changed is you. You are my world, and I will do anything in my power to make you happy. If that means having a dozen children, then I will *happily* be your baby daddy." All tension has left his face despite his serious tone. His smile is breathtakingly beautiful.

"Oh." I mouth the word, because he's once more rendered me speechless.

"Oh…happy now?" He nudges my nose with his.

"You won't get bored?" I hate that the doubts just keep bubbling up.

"What?" He shakes his head a little.

"There aren't many married members at the club, Jason. I don't think it's what normal couples do. I worry the whole domestic nature of marriage is going to be a huge turn off." I try to shrug, but my arms are still stretched taut.

"Actually, there are several married members. And what have I said about our 'normal'? We make our own rules, beautiful, and as long as you belong to me, nothing else matters." He gazes at me for endless seconds that feel like hours. I didn't realise I was holding so much tension, but his words wash over me and seep into my soul, making me a pliant, gooey mess.

He rolls his hips, and I can feel every inch of his considerable length slide in and out at a gloriously languid pace. His eyes darken and his brows crinkle with concentration.

"Any other details you want to discuss?" His deep voice drops an octave, and the roughness sends a tingle of shivers across my skin. I shake my head and tilt my hips at an inviting angle that makes him groan. "Words, Sam, I need to hear your words. I need to know you are happy."

"I am, and in about five short moves, I will be euphoric." He growls and drops his weight to stop me from moving against him.

"Sam." His tone is reprimanding, but the last thing I want to do is extend this conversation.

"I am very happy, Jason. I have no other details to discuss other than I would very much like to finish what you started." I try fruitlessly to grind a little pleasure from his body.

"You love me?" His question makes me stop. His deep chocolate eyes shine with flecks of gold, but there is hesitation in his voice that breaks my heart. I hope to god that I haven't made him doubt that I do.

"With all my heart, Jason. I'm sorry, but I struggle to believe I deserve this happy ending. I can't help looking for the catch." I rush to try and explain my destructive doubts.

"No catch, beautiful…our happy ending is just a little different. It's just you and me and our very own kinky ever after."

"I like the sound of that." I let out a sigh that is captured by his eager mouth over mine. His tongue takes possession, and we duel with sensual strokes and urgent kissing that leaves us both breathless. "Now, fuck me like you hate me." I cry out when I manage to catch my breath. His eyes light, and his smile turns from warm to wicked in a flash.

"With pleasure."

"Oh good god, Leon, what is that smell?" I instantly slap my hand to my nose when I step into the kitchen of my old apartment. The detritus on every surface looks days, possibly weeks old. Take out boxes and half-eaten meals congealed and decomposed on every plate I owned. Stacks of glasses…and is that a vase he has used for beer? "Jesus, Leon, I'm surprised someone hasn't called environmental health."

"Do you want a coffee?" Leon ignores my comment and runs his hand through his long dark hair. He does, at least, have the decency to look embarrassed.

"In what, Leon?" I wave my hand at the array of dirty cups.

"It's six in the morning, Sam. I wasn't expecting visitors." He picks up one of the fresher dirty cups and starts to rinse it under the tap. I push him to the side, flick the tap to boiling hot, and squeeze a large dollop of washing liquid in the bowl already crammed to bursting. Once the bowl is full and soaking the dried-on, stained crockery, I open the cupboard and pick out a large black sack. I hand it to Leon with a scowl.

"Maid's day off." He tries to joke but bites his lip shut at my thunderous glare.

Thirty minutes is all it takes to clear the surfaces, load the dishwasher, and clean up enough to make us both a fresh cup of coffee.

"Seriously, Leon, you can't live like this." My tone is sharp. It's not as if I used to clean up after him when we lived together. He had always been the tidy one. "Get a cleaner if you can't be arsed—"

"I miss you." His words stop me dead, and I soften inside and out. I step up to him and wrap my arms tight around his trim but naked waist. It's been four weeks since we became more than best friends, along with Jason's twin brother, Will. The most amazing night of my life not just because…well, it was my number one fantasy, but because I became *me* again. Richard had very nearly succeeded in destroying me, with kidnapping, torture, and murder. Even being saved wasn't enough to bring me back to my old self. The physical scars healed, but I didn't know how to heal the scars inside. Jason did…he saved me.

Leon and I have seen each other since then, and it's not been at all awkward, but I had no idea he felt like this about me moving out.

"Oh Leon, sweetie." I nestle against his chest and draw in a deep sniff of his manly overnight smell. "I miss you too, but you are always welcome to come over. There's a spare room, and I know Jason wouldn't mind."

"I think he would." His arms hold me a little tighter when I start to move away. "Besides, the last thing I need is to be listening to your marathon fuck-a-thons. Jason's like the fucking Energizer Bunny." He kisses the top of my head and releases his hold. I sniff out a laugh.

"He really is. But you and me...we're okay, right? You're not saying it's the last thing you need because you want something to happen between us, right?" My voice raises a touch high with worry.

"I definitely want something to happen with us...but I mean *all* of us. I can't get that night out of my head." He drags his hand roughly down his face, and I hear the sound of his morning stubble scratching his palm. "But no, we're cool, babe, you know that." He ruffles my hair in its already messy bun. "I just miss you being here, and seeing you with Jason. Damn." He lets out a heavy sigh. "I'm happy for you, babe. Your relationship just made me realise how lucky Jason is in finding someone like you. I mean you love that kinky shit; you both do, and I don't know if I'll ever find someone who gets me like that." He shrugs, but the genuine sadness in his eyes tugs at my heart.

"And to think just this morning I was worried that Jason would be bored once we got married and become all domesticated," I joke.

"Boring is not the word I would ever use to describe you two, and it's just a piece of paper, babe. It doesn't change who you are. It just changes your last name...if you want that. Besides that little display you did last night was more of a binding ceremony in our world."

"So why propose at all?"

"Maybe he doesn't think that way. Maybe for him, this lifestyle is just play. The fun and games are great, but now he's found the real deal, and under all that kink, he is Mr Traditional, after all, just like you." He bops me playfully on the nose, and I frown.

"What are you talking about? I love the kink." I balk at his accusation.

"I know you do, Sam, but I also know you hide behind it. It's easy to turn your back on an ideal if you think you'd never get the chance of experiencing it. But that is exactly what you have with Jason. You, my darling, have the whole fucking package."

"Maybe, but it doesn't stop the doubts," I murmur aloud.

"Doubts?"

"I struggle with happily ever afters, Leon, and he doesn't want kids." I throw that in like an unsubstantiated criminal charge.

"Um, not to state the bloody obvious, but you don't want kids, either. You have that three-year implant thingy because you're scared of forgetting pills, so I don't think you can hold that against the guy," he challenges me. "Did you change your mind?"

"No. Well, maybe, I don't know. I never thought I would be in a position to consider it. When Richard got me pregnant, I was terrified. When I lost the baby, I was devastated; that's why I have the implant. My experience of the whole thing was not something I would wish on my worst enemy. But I love Jason; I want a real life with him, and that might involve children." I shift under his soft but intense gaze.

"And you think he feels any different? Because I will bet my arse he doesn't. And as for not deserving a happily ever after, fuck that bullshit! That's your mother talking if ever I heard a put-down." He steps up to me and holds my chin firmly, his eyes searing right through me. "Don't let her ruin this for you, Sam. You deserve to be loved. You deserve him." Although he grits his teeth slightly with that last word, I get a warm feeling from the sentiment and sincerity of his words.

"Thank you, Leon. I've missed you, too." I lean up to kiss his cheek. "Do you have time for breakfast? If you have eggs, I could whisk up something scrambled?"

"You cook now?" His eyes widen with shock.

"Jason's been teaching me," I offer shyly.

"Maybe I will come for a sleepover if a cooked breakfast is on the menu. There are eggs in the cupboard, and I think there is a loaf in the bread bin, but don't quote me on that." He turns to leave. "I'll grab a quick shower," he shouts over his shoulder and disappears into the hallway.

Fifteen minutes later, Leon appears in a crisp white shirt, tie, and elegant three-piece navy suit. He scrubs up well even if his face is still unshaven, and his hair is damp. I plate up the glossy eggs and split the last slice of toast between us. I pour him a fresh black coffee and slide onto the stool beside him.

"No work today?" Leon's appraising glance at my casual skinny jeans, oversized scoop neck cable knit sweater, and some flashy five-inch suede ankle boots might be a giveaway.

"Day off. It's why I'm here. I am hoping I left my passport here." Leon raises a brow, waiting for me to elaborate, which I happily do. "We're going on a weekend break, but I don't know where. It's a surprise and very last minute." I can't hide the excitement in my voice, and it's clearly contagious as Leon returns my beaming smile.

"If you kept it in your room, it will be safe. Out here…not so much." He grimaces as his eyes take in the bombsight that used to resemble my living room. I jump off the stool and go to check if what he has said about my room is true. I have moved most of my stuff to Jason's over the last few months, but I had left a few things. I shake off the likely notion that this in itself is evidence of my reservations. This is stupid. I don't need to keep my room here. I don't live here anymore. I fish my passport out of my bedside drawer and return to the kitchen. Leon has washed the dishes and is just wiping the counter. He flashes a knowing smile.

"There are two bedrooms empty now, Leon, you should get a flatmate to share." His smile widens.

"You gonna move the rest of your stuff over to Jason's then?" He purses his lips, trying to suppress his grin.

"I am as soon as I get back." I nod my affirmation.

"Then perhaps I will. I could use some company. Maybe some twins would be fun, don't you think?" He bites his lip flat, and I feel my cheeks heat with instant fire. I throw the nearest thing at hand, which lucky for him is a cushion.

"Jackass." I narrow my eyes, but he catches the cushion and barks out a deep chuckle.

"So no repeat performance on the horizon...you know we have Valentine's Day in a few weeks, hmm?" He wriggles his dark brows suggestively.

"You're incorrigible."

"I really am. But I didn't hear a no," he teases.

"That's the thing with fantasies, Leon. They are like favourite places or moments in time. The shine and brilliance of the experience you can never recreate, and going back is always a disappointment."

"By that token, fucking Jason would lose its lustre, no?" He challenges my hypothesis.

"Ah...you have me there, my friend, because that just gets better and better." I pat Leon on his cheek. "And it is never a disappointment."

I return to Jason's place just as he is loading the boot of his car with our bags.

"Perfect timing, beautiful. Are you ready?" He sweeps his arms around my waist and covers my lips with his before I get the chance to answer. His soft lips taste of sweetness and bitter coffee. My body melds to his, and my hands fist the collar of his jacket, holding him tight to me. I can't get enough of the way he makes me crave him, every touch, every taste. He's addictive, and I'm a blissfully happy addict. He releases my lips but holds me steady as I sway, a little giddy from the kiss.

"I am." I wave my passport. "Where are we going?"

"Amsterdam."

Jason

IHIT THE ACCELERATOR JUST OUTSIDE OF CALAIS. THE motorway is pretty clear, and at this time in the morning, we should make the journey through Belgium and up to the north of the Netherlands in less than four hours. Sam has kicked her fuck-me heels into the foot well and has her fluffy sock-clad feet resting on the dashboard. Her head is resting on her shoulder, and a mass of dark hair has fallen to partially obscure her face. My fingers twitch to stroke the hair away and reveal her flawless skin; even the tiny scar on her cheekbone is perfection. It's a permanent reminder that she is a survivor. She glows with strength that, every day, I am humbled to witness. With extra effort, I still my hand and let her sleep. Today was a surprise early start after an action-packed and seriously interrupted night's sleep. I guess I should be tired too, but I'm anything but. We fucked like we were both possessed, and that is exactly what she does. She possesses me when she comes apart in my hands and surrenders everything she is; at that moment, she is at her most vulnerable, most beautiful, and that's why she fucking owns me.

She's crazy if she thinks anything is going to change the way I feel about her, but she's right that marriage is a big deal. I love that she made the display at the club with my collar in front of everyone but, even if she hadn't, it would never be enough for me, not now. She changed all that. I only invited Will and Leon to join us at the club on Christmas Day because I thought it was the only way to bring her back to me. I am so fucking glad it did, but there is no way I could share her again, and for someone like me, that is a *massive* fucking deal. I sound more like Daniel than I do myself. But with Sam? I. Don't. Share.

I know she's mine, and there is no hurry to get married. I want her to have the perfect day, and that takes time, but I also want her to realise that nothing has to change. That's what this weekend is about. After she fell asleep, I went online and arranged this trip to the sex capital of Europe. The legalised drugs aren't of interest, but because of the liberal laws regarding the sex trade, some of the private clubs are...*special.*

"Mmm," she moans and arches her body into a decent stretch given the confines of the R8 interior. "Are we there yet?" She yawns and pulls her legs into her chest, wrapping her arms around her knees and shifting onto her side to face me.

"What are you...four?" I mock.

"I didn't say 'Are we there yet, Dad?'" She pouts and wrinkles her nose. She has soft pink lines on her face, crumpled skin from a heavy head against her shoulder. Her tongue darts out to wet her lips, and it's all I can do to keep from swerving off the road. She looks edible.

"Oh beautiful, you can call me *Daddy* if you want, but I'm always gonna prefer Sir." My voice drips with sensual meaning.

"I prefer Sir." Her sultry, soft tone feels like a direct hit in my balls. I push my head back into the headrest and straighten my arms; my fingers tighten on the wheel, a subtle, instant reaction that makes her giggle. I try to shift in my seat to ease the painful ache from my now rock-hard cock.

"Sorry." She sucks in her lips and fails to look even vaguely apologetic.

"No, you're not." I groan when her hand reaches over and rubs the material stretched taut over my shaft.

"Not remotely, but I am more than happy to help." She slips the seatbelt over her head so it is only wrapped across her waist, and she slinks across the center of the car, like a super sexy feline. I lift my left arm to make room. Christ, my balls feel like they are ready to explode, and she hasn't even loosened my buckle. Oh, now she has…shit!

"Sam, I really don't think this is a good idea." My voice catches, and I try to swallow the sudden dryness in my mouth.

"Really? I think this is a great idea. Besides…" Her warm breath sears the fibers on my pants; her head hovers as she deftly releases my erection into her waiting hand. "Breakfast is the most important meal of the day."

"Holy. Fucking shiiii…Ah! Oh yes that…do that again!" I swallow back a choking cough and let the most amazing feeling radiate through my body unchecked. She has her fist tight around the base, but her mouth covers the engorged end, and she swallows me down like I really am the best meal of the day. I can feel the muscles in her throat, and I fight the urge to jerk my hips forward. The back of her head keeps nudging the bottom of the steering wheel as it is. Her tongue does this thing where she slides and wraps it around my shaft, all the while drawing me deeper into her mouth, until I am touching the back of her throat. She pauses only to catch a breath before she swallows me deeper. *God, this feels fucking amazing.* I know I'm not all in; her hand is taking over where her mouth is physically unable... at least at this angle.

I am counting backward in Italian just to try and not think about losing control. But when she releases my cock, and her lips instantly wrap around one of my balls, I swerve the car onto the hard shoulder and into the police only waiting area. I'd rather get arrested than die, and she is fucking killing me here. Her head pops up, and I slip from her swollen lips.

"Problem?" Her devious smile is all faux innocence.

"No problem." I am impressed I can maintain a level voice and a steady exhale. "There will be though if you don't get your fucking jeans off and ride me till I come." Her pink cheeks flush a little redder, her eyes darken with pure passion, and her slim throat takes a deep, slow swallow.

Now I've changed my mind.

"Wait... No time, just finish what you started, beautiful." I thread my hand into what's left of her messy bun and pull her back into position. Her eyes meet mine and flash with mirrored desire before bending over millimeters from my aching erection.

"Yes, Sir." She exhales a breathy sigh with her words, scorching the wetness seeping from my tip. Her tongue is quick to take the moisture, and her lips quickly follow. She sinks quickly onto my length, and eager to please, she almost swallows me whole.

"Fuuuuuck!" Every muscle in my backside tenses, and I grip the steering wheel like it is my only anchor to Earth. One of her hands pumps the base of my cock, which makes my spine tingle from top to tip. She palms my balls with her other hand, and her magic tongue is driving me insane, tracing the pulsing vein from the very bottom of me to the sensitive top. She tilts her head to flash me a wicked grin and smiles wide, pulling her lips free and exposing her bright white, straight, and from memory, surprisingly sharp teeth. I suck in a sharp breath and brace myself. I fucking hate teeth.

But there are no teeth, and I don't know whether to sigh with relief or growl with irritation. I do neither, because her heavenly mouth takes me as far as her breathing will allow. She swallows repeatedly, and I explode down her eager throat. My stomach muscles spasm from the intensity of my release, and I take a few moments to draw in enough air to compose myself. She softly licks me clean, and even though I am not remotely soft, she expertly tucks my cock back into its cotton cage. Crawling back to her seat, she faces me. Her eyes never leave mine, even as she slowly wipes her wet lips with the back of her hand and proceeds to lick that clean like a kitty. Damn, that is the sexiest thing—next to what she has just done, that is.

I reach out and cup the back of her head, drawing her forcefully to my waiting kiss. I press hard, the taste of me fresh but faint on her lips. Her taste is intoxicating, and I can't get enough. I twist my body and try to drag her from her seat. The car fills with a sudden bright blue light, and a piercing siren screams a brief but effective interruption. We both freeze, Sam's eyes, wide at first, transform with her impossibly huge grin once the initial shock has faded.

"Uh-oh, someone's in trouble." She wiggles her brows playfully, and I fire a scowl with no anger intended at her. She starts to giggle.

"Oh, someone's in lots of trouble, but let's get out of this first, shall we?" My tone is lightly reprimanding.

"We? You're the one who pulled over into a police only wait zone." She bites her lips to stop full-blown hysterical laughter as a figure appears at my window.

"Because a ticket is better than death…although…" I muse and press the window to open. I greet the officer and catch a quick glance at Sam. Her mouth drops at my fluent French. I pulled the car over just south of Belgium's border with the Netherlands. This country is one of the few that are trilingual, speaking Dutch, German and, lucky for me, French. The officer is stern, and a series of explanations and questions later, he gives me a warning but not a ticket. I shut the window when he tries to take another peek inside at my flushed faced fiancée.

I pull smoothly back into the traffic but keep to a sensible speed as the police car has pulled out right behind and is currently tailing me.

"You speak French?" Her clipped tone makes her question sound more like an accusation.

"What can I say? I'm very good with my tongue." She scoffs out a loud laugh mixed with an uncontrolled snort that sends her into a fit of giggles. I adore that sound almost as much as the little moans and sighs.

Once she has calmed herself, she raises her brow with an unasked query and fixes me with her enquiring stare.

"I did French as an extracurricular at Uni, and you know the Italian I picked up when I lived there. I find languages very useful and easy." I shrug lightly, but her face lights with interest.

"I'm impressed. So, what did you say to the officer?"

"I told him I thought my fiancée was having an allergic reaction and, for safety, I pulled over." She frowns and looks dubious. "I explained that the swelling had gone down and was now really only visible in your lips." I answer, deadpan and serious.

"Oh, my God, you didn't?" she gasps, both her hands flying to her mouth.

"I did, and it worked…no ticket." He flashes a wicked grin.

"He didn't believe you, did he?" Mortification at my

revelation colours her cheeks, and they turn an adorable shade of red right before my eyes.

"Nope. Might be why he's still on my tail…hoping for a sequel," I quip.

"He'll have a long wait." She sniffs derisively.

"What?" My head snaps round.

"Relax, Jason." Her hand pats my thigh, giving a reassuring little squeeze. "I didn't mean a long wait for another blow job." She snickers. "I mean a long wait before I put on a show for an audience."

"You had me worried for a moment." I let out an exaggerated breath that makes her laugh.

"And you have me still hungry." She pats her flat tummy, this time for actual food.

"We can stop in Bruges for breakfast if you like, but not for long." I flick the indicator for the next exit on the motorway.

"Yes, please. And why the sudden time frame? I thought this was a spontaneous trip?"

"It is…but I've still made plans." I flash my knowing grin.

"When we get to Amsterdam, you mean?"

"I do." I offer flatly. She narrows her eyes at my evasive responses.

"What kind of plans?" The tone of her voice is filled with suspicion. She's very perceptive. This may be last minute, but I want this weekend to be about our *normal*. I want her to understand we set our own rules.

"Just the usual tourist things people do in a city—sightseeing, museums, galleries," I muse playfully but drop the tone of my voice to a deeper timbre for portent, adding, "Dinner and a *show*."

Sam pokes her head out of the roof top window. The view from the loft room reaches far over the entire city on a clear day like today, but it's January, and it's bitterly cold. She briskly rubs some warmth back into her arms after shutting the window. Turning my way, she flashes me the most excited smile imaginable. That look alone makes my chest clench. She rushes toward me and wraps her arms tight around my chest, and she delights in squeezing the breath from my lungs. For such a slight figure, she has some impressive upper body strength.

"Thank you! This place is stunning." She covers my lips with hers but breaks away before I can get my fill. She giggles at my audible frustration and walks across the room to explore the en suite. The room is spacious for a central city hotel, but then it is the best on the Grachtengordel or Canal ring. Most are converted town houses, which are compact at best and the loft rooms can be a challenge for someone of my height. This is perfect, though, white painted wood-panelled walls that slope to the ceiling, heavy beams span the room but are high enough that I won't knock myself out every time I stretch.

"Oh, wow, have you seen this bath, Jason?" Sam calls out as I finish unpacking. I laugh when I enter the adjoining room to see her fully clothed mock swimming in the very large claw footed bathtub. "You could fit a whole football team in here." She squeals and throws her arms around my neck when I stride over and scoop her into my arms.

"No football teams, beautiful…just me from now on." My gravelly tone is more forceful than jovial at her remark, and I am rewarded with a full body shiver.

"Perfect." She beams. "Only you." She purses her lips for a kiss that never happens.

"Damn right!" I dump her unceremoniously on the sumptuous bed, and she screams with surprise, but instantly relaxes in the luxurious comfort of an over-stuffed bed. She lets out a deep, satisfied sigh and pitches herself up on her elbows. Ever so slowly, she draws her bottom lip in between her teeth, and her eyes darken with wicked intention that transforms her innocent features into temptation personified.

"So what now?" Her voice is an overtly breathy whisper, and she wiggles her brows seductively. Only for a moment though, because she yelps when I throw her jacket for her to catch, her quick reflexes prevent a direct hit.

"Behave! We are going sightseeing. We have a personal guided tour booked." Her eyes light with excitement. Her salacious alternate plans forgotten, she instantly jumps and shuffles to the end of the bed ready to join me.

"It kills me to say this, but you will be much more comfortable in the walking boots I packed." I actually groan at the thought of her taking off those killer fuck-me heels and wearing the utility sturdy fur-lined footwear I bought her. She raises her perfect brow and purses her lips.

"Really, Jason, I could walk a marathon in these. I know they are high, but I've broken them in so they feel like slippers to me. I'm sure I'll manage walking a few city streets." She mocks my concern.

"On a bike?" I clarify and watch her jaw drop.

"Excuse me?"

"We're going to be riding bikes," I repeat. My smile stretches far and wide as I watch this information sink in. "It's a great way to cover a lot of the city. We've only got a few hours, but if you think you can manage in what you're wearing…" I teasingly wave the more practical boot in front of me at arm's length.

"I haven't ridden a bike in forever, Jason. I hope it's like they say it is…you know…just like riding a bike?" She sniffs out a nervous laugh and grabs the boots. The soft mattress and abundant covers envelop her tiny form when she perches on the end of the bed. Even doing something as ordinary as this, she looks too damn tempting. It takes all my restraint not to push her back flat, cover her body with kisses, and take what's mine.

"No need to worry yourself about that today, beautiful. I hired a tandem for us to share, and the personal guide will ensure we see the best bits. We don't have time to 'do' the museums, but I'd like you to get a feel for the city. You won't be in any danger." I pull her up and into my arms as soon as she stands. Her smile spreads wide across her flawless face, and all I can do is look. She is *everything*. Her hands snake around my waist, and she grabs my arse cheeks and pinches hard, pulling me flush against her.

"I think the danger will be that I get to stare at *this* all afternoon, and I won't be able to do a damn thing about it." Her breathy words make my cock twitch, and her brows shoot up in response. "Do we really have to go out?" She grinds her heat against my now very hard erection and gives a sassy little wiggle.

"Again with the killing me here, Sam." I groan but have to admit this feels like a much better option. After all, when in the sex capital of Europe… "Ladies' choice, beautiful, our guide is waiting downstairs with the bike." I nod over to the telephone on the bedside table. "If you want to call down and tell her you want to ride me instead, I am more than good to go right now." I grin because this is a win-win situation for me, and I'm enjoying every second.

"Hmm, damn it!" She huffs and a sexy little furrow creases her forehead. "After this morning in the car, and staring at your arse all afternoon, I am going to be so ready to blow by the time we get back. I swear you will only have to look my way." She squeezes her legs together as if to emphasise her plight, and I get just that little bit harder. This might just be hell for both of us. She clears her throat and places her hand on one cocked hip. "Just so you know, you will have a horny time bomb on your hands," she warns, playfully pushing me away and letting out some built up heat in a loudly exhaled puff of air.

"I'll bear that in mind." I snicker but also have to adjust myself. It's going to be a long afternoon. "You ready?" I grab my wallet while she puts on her puffy jacket. She pulls a black knit woolen hat with a large fluffy pompom down to just above her brow, framing her face perfectly. Her bright, glossy red lipstick is a vivid splash of colour that draws attention from more than my eyes.

We make our way down the stairs to meet our part-time tour guide, and full-time local artist, in the lobby. The elegant white marble entrance has a thin strip of royal blue carpet that leads from the double glass entrance doors to a circular antique table by the reception desk. A tatty brown leather satchel leans against the oversized vase and looks wholly out of place. Much like the lady currently leaning to get a closer look at a large, ornate oval mirror hanging low on the wall. She turns and smiles when she hears us approach, and she instantly offers her hand. Before we even get the chance to say one word, she has introduced herself as Elsa, our guide.

"How did you know it was us that you were meeting?" Sam asks what I was thinking.

"It's low season, and it is very cold. Not many tourists wanting a bike tour." She chuckles by way of an explanation. "I have your bike outside. Are you sure you want a tandem? They can be tricky?"

"We're sure," I confirm, and Sam is also nodding with a

huge grin. This is going to be fun.

There is a light frost on the ground but nothing danger-ous as we weave our tandem bicycle from the heart of the city where our hotel is to the outskirts of Amsterdam. Elsa steers us down narrow streets and over many of the bridges that cross some of the one hundred and sixty canals. The streets and wa-terways span out from the center of the city in the shape of a fan and make it easy to navigate. In all, ninety islands make up one of the most popular and picturesque cities in Europe. Throughout the ride, I can hear Sam gasp and coo at the sights Elsa is pointing out along with snippets of information that Sam seems eager to absorb. She tugs on my jacket if she thinks I've missed something. I regret that I can't see her face, but we stop occasionally and I get the feeling that she loves every minute.

The farthest point we reach is Vondel Park, acres of land-scaped parkland, which would, no doubt, be heaving with vis-itors in the summer months. Today it is sprinkled with a few hardy dog walkers and, of course, cyclists. We make a complete loop of the outer path, past the lakes, and head back toward the hotel. The ever present flow of cyclists becomes heavier as we join what must be a shortcut through the under pass of the Rijksmuseum. We stop for a well-earned beer, and Elsa happily answers all Sam's questions that she was unable to ask while we rode through the town.

"So you will be visiting De Wallen later?" Elsa gives us both an easy smile. She has long grey hair that it neatly plaited down her back. Her thick glasses magnify the many lines crin-kling at the corners of her eyes, and she is wrapped in several layers of shabby chic colourful clothing. However old she might be, after nearly two hours of constant cycling, she isn't remotely out of breath.

"De Wallen?" Sam frowns and looks at me.

"The Red Light district." I grin and watch as Sam's cheeks pink up more than they have all afternoon from the January chill.

"Oh, I don't know," Sam mutters shyly.

"You should definitely go. It is the oldest part of the city and very beautiful. Many interesting bars and museums. It comes alive at night. I think it is the best time to experience the atmosphere." She smooths out a map of the city and draws a big black circle around the rosse buurt, another name she called the famous area. "But take care, also." She laughs lightly. "You will be safe with this one I am sure." She leans over to pat my arm and smiles warmly at Sam. Her Dutch accent flavours her English, but her meaning is perfectly understood. Sam snorts out a laugh at the massive understatement. I have no problem that I am overt in my protectiveness of the woman I love. It is born out of the scariest time in my life. A time I never want to repeat, and if that means everyone knows Sam belongs to me, so be it.

"We have tickets for a show," Sam explains, her voice light with excitement.

"Oh really, which one?" Elsa turns to me when Sam shrugs and shakes her head.

"*Chez-moi.*" I reply with a flat, impassive tone. It's Elsa's turn to blush.

"Oh." Elsa laughs nervously and quickly smiles at Sam. "That will be…that is…I'm sure you'll…" She gathers her satchel and mumbles something about needing the ladies but won't look directly at me. Sam turns to me with a curious pout to her lips.

"Oh?" Sam questions. "Should I be worried?"

"Do you trust me?" I gently take her chin and tip it so she

meets my gaze. She always meets my gaze, and her eyes perfectly reflect the love I feel.

"Of course," she states without hesitation.

"Then no, you shouldn't be worried." My lips cover hers, and she returns my urgent kiss. It's been too long already.

THREE

Sam

JASON HAS LAID OUT ON THE BED WHAT HE WANTS ME TO wear for this evening, and the thrill of the unknown just kicks my heart rate into overdrive. I've been on edge since the cryptic conversation with Elsa this afternoon. I'm tingly, excited, and more than a little aroused, entirely due to Jason's sensual massage and our bath together. The abstinence thing is becoming an issue and not just for me. He has been rock-hard and taunting me with his nakedness while we have been preparing to get ready. But he has plans.

"There are no panties?" I finish clipping the opaque soft wool stockings and stand with one hand on my hip and one just lifting the center of my skirt for a full on peep show. The short skirt is pleated soft leather that flares wide and skims my thighs just below the tops of the stockings. My bra is a type of mini corset that hugs my rib cage and makes my breasts look perilously close to spilling out with every breath I take. Jason turns from the wardrobe adjusting the cuffs of his shirt to sit just right. His eyes darken, and he bites back a growl that I can still hear rumble from his immaculate suit-clad chest.

"Jesus, what was I thinking?" he mutters, striding toward me. I hold my hand up to halt him, and although it presses flat against his chest, it does nothing to stop the momentum. I am stepped back hard and fast into the wall. His mouth is on my neck, searing my skin like a branding iron, the heat runs like a wildfire through my veins. My hands fist his shirt beneath his jacket, my knuckles pressing hard into his firm, unyielding chest. He bites down, and my whole body quakes.

"Ah!" My breath catches, and I finish my cry in a silent gasp of air. He stands tall, every inch of his firm body presses against mine. The sexual tension is tangible, and I want to rip through it—right now. I tip my head forward so my mouth is just a sleek film of lip gloss from his, but he collects himself, straightening out of my reach on a steady exhale of held breath.

"I have plans." His deep voice is thick with lust that he struggles to swallow back down.

"Your plans do involve fucking me at some point though, right? I just want to clarify, because I can promise you one thing; I will not make it through this night without a little relief." I visibly sag when he moves back, letting out a low throaty chuckle, which just makes me squirm a little more. God, that is a sexy sound.

"You have my word, beautiful, before the night is out you will be more than sated—" He wiggles his dark brow as I interrupt.

"Enough with the cryptic. Are you going to tell me what we're doing tonight?" I huff like a petulant child. Patience is not one of my virtues.

"Dinner and a—"

I snap my interruption.

"Show. Yes, I know that much. Fine, don't tell me." I pout and step around him to finish getting dressed. The black silk wrap blouse is elegant, the criss-cross back is sexy and the very low front exposes glimpses of my corset bra. It is all perfectly Amsterdam scandalous. Jason holds up a full-length cream cashmere coat with a fur-lined hood and helps me in, turning me and tying up the belt with an overly firm tug and an obnoxiously smug wink.

"Just tell me this: Is the whole teasing, touching, not actually fucking, all part of the plan?"

"It's a surprise, Sam. Where would be the surprise if I told you?"

"God, you're infuriatingly smug about this." I narrow my eyes, but he remains ever impassive.

"I am. I really am. Shall we?" He offers his elbow, the guise of the perfect gentleman harbouring the wicked sadist beneath.

"I am yours but to command, Sir," I say with a heavy dose of sarcasm and a slight curtsey before sliding my arm into his. He pats my hand and leans in to whisper, his nearness drenching me in his unique and intoxicating scent: a mix of mountains, mint, and pure manliness.

"I was really hoping you were going to say that," he replies with lethal sincerity and a grin that wouldn't look out of place on the devil himself.

The club is in the basement of a five-story town house, no different than the other hundreds of houses stacked and wedged on the narrow streets of the Old Town. This building is just off the main thoroughfare and the heart of the popular Red Light district. The small gold nameplate bearing the name Chez Moi is the only item on the glossy black door. The reception area is small with barely space for the reservations desk. Low-level lighting from candles creates a warm and inviting ambience. The walls are covered with a bold velvet pattern, and a large crystal chandelier hangs from the vaulted ceiling. The space might be small, but it is richly furnished and exudes luxury and wealth. I didn't think Jason would take me to a seedy club, but he had said it was a surprise, and that would've definitely been a shock.

The hostess greets us with a friendly smile. Her hair is pinned up in a sleek bun, and she has the most striking eyes, which are framed with dramatically long lashes. Her eyes are the only thing to notice though, because half of her face is concealed with a plain black mask. She hands Jason a slim, shiny, gift-wrapped box and proceeds to take my coat. I am left curious for only a moment. Jason loosens the elegant ribbon and opens the lid to reveal two similar black masks. He shucks his coat, handing it over, and takes the smaller mask from the box. He motions with a slow twirl of his finger and a salacious grin for me to turn. The mask is the softest leather imaginable and molds perfectly to the contours of my face. He secures it tightly, and I get the feeling there might be a reason for that. I turn back and watch him cover his own face. His piercing dark eyes look almost black, and sparkle with mischief. I can't stop my thighs pinching together at the liquid pooling inside me, and I am really missing my panties right about now. Long silent seconds pass as he holds me captive with that look. His lips, full and soft, give just the hint of a smile, and there is too much sexual tension to feel anything other than pure unadulterated lust.

Damn! The last thing I want is dinner and a show.

"If you would follow me, please." The light voice of the

hostess interrupts our sexy silent standoff. Jason's lips curl into a heart-stopping smile, his hand slips to the base of my spine, and he guides me to follow through a darkened archway. The hostess holds open one side of a large double door, and we step into another darkened room. Ambient lighting is in the form of simulated flames from sconces on the walls above secluded booths. The center of the room is a large circular plinth encased in frosted glass. I try and glimpse inside what looks like an enormous empty display cabinet, but the glass merely reflects the darkness of the room. We are led around the narrow path that separates the center display cabinet and the booths. From the chatter and laughter it is obvious all the tables are occupied, but the clever curve of the high backed seating makes it impossible to see inside.

I slide into the cozy padded booth, and Jason slips in beside me.

The hostess leaves and is immediately replaced by a mask-wearing waitress. Jason orders the taster menu and some Champagne without bothering to look at the menu being offered. I don't think he has taken his eyes off me for a moment.

"Very good, Sir." The waitress clutches the superfluous menus. "The show will commence shortly. If you do not wish to view, you can simply press the privacy button here." She points to an indented panel with two buttons. "And if you require any assistance press the service button." I roll my eyes at the way she drawls the word assistance, and her mask does little to hide her desire for *my* man.

"We won't need any assistance." Jason's curt response makes her back stiffen and sends a warm tingle straight to my chest. She flashes a tight smile and disappears into the darkness.

"What's with the masks?" I lean over and whisper. I'm not sure why, but it feels a little underground and clandestine. He leans down to meet me.

"You'll find out," he whispers back conspiratorially. I huff out in frustration. Damn, that man can keep me on the edge like a pro...*and I should know.*

"Are you wet?" His deep voice is like a rough tongue along my sensitive core, and I am instantly sentient and alert, if a little taken by the blunt question.

"Excuse me?" I swallow, but my throat is too dry.

"Would you like me to repeat the question?" His tone I recognise and its deep commanding timbre sets my heart thumping hard in my corset restricted chest. Dominant Jason has come to play.

"No, Sir," I answer without hesitation but don't lower my gaze. When we play, he allows me to keep the eye contact unless he tells me otherwise, but that is rare. I need the connection. I need to see how much he wants me...needs me. "I'm very wet, Sir."

"Spread your legs wide." His hands are resting on the table, but his fingers twitch when my leg brushes his as I do exactly as he says. I suck in a breath when the waitress returns with the Champagne, but with effort, I keep my position. Jason's lips curl in an appreciative smile as he hands me my glass. We clink and both take a long sip. I like that his throat is obviously just as dry as mine. He dips his finger into his glass and wets it before dropping his hand below the table and between my legs. I jump at the contact, cool liquid on hot fingers. He drags his middle finger along the length of my intimate flesh, as much he can from the angle and my position. I shuffle to the edge of the seat to gain a little more.

God, I want more.

He chuckles a low throaty sound, and his scorching breath bursts across my collarbone when he turns his torso to face me.

He is, oh, so close. I am going to combust or suffocate; I can't draw a deep enough breath.

"Jason," I gasp, but my cry sounds more like a plea. He sinks two fingers inside and curls them around, slow firm pressure, but nowhere near enough. He pumps a few more times and withdraws, causing the saddest little whimper to escape my throat. His fingers glisten with my arousal even in this dim light. He slowly sucks one finger clean, briefly closing his eyes with pleasure, before holding the other one at my lips. I open and suck his finger dry, causing his eyes to widen and a groan to rumble from his chest and his jaw to twitch with tension. Good, we're both in erotic hell.

"An amuse-bouche," he offers, drawing his full bottom lip between his teeth, savouring my flavour in his mouth.

"My bouche is anything *but* amused," I grumble, and he barks out a dirty laugh.

"No, from that pout I think you're right. Something you need, beautiful?" His eyes flick down to my deep cleavage, an enhancement caused by the tight pinch of the corset bra. The thick material hides my hard and aching nipples, but even without that, he must know I am off the charts horny and desperate for more than a few strokes of his talented fingers. I want to beg. He loves it when I beg, because it's a very rare occurrence.

"Sir, please." I exhale slowly, a sexy mix of sigh and moan. "I really, *really* need to come."

"Soon." He shifts back in the seat, failing to disguise his own arousal, but that at least gives me some comfort, certainly more than his frustrating response. My whole body sags but still trembles with anticipation. "Soon," he repeats and rests his firm hand on my thigh, holding rather than teasing.

The first course arrives, and I decide that I can't sit like a sexual time bomb all evening. I will be exhausted or just explode.

"When do I get my part of the deal?" My voice is tight but is surprisingly level.

"The deal?" His fork hovers at his lips, and he flashes me a look with, I assume, a raised curious brow under the mask.

"Our deal…I wear your collar and submit, and you let me tie you up and torture you. What? You don't remember that? I'm shocked!" I hold up my hands in mock horror.

"I don't believe I struck *that* deal. It was more of a statement of two unlikely events." He eats the food on his fork then waves it lightly at me. "Well, *one* unlikely event."

"Wearing your collar was just as unlikely," I scoff.

"Think that if it gives you comfort, beautiful, but wearing my collar was inevitable." His hand cups my jaw and is so big it nearly covers half of my head. I rest into his hold. His words are softly possessive and make me melt. "If it's important to you, I have no issue with it. I trust you; I just won't derive any pleasure from it so I don't see the point." He shrugs lightly.

"You wouldn't get turned on?" I can feel my brow furrow, but he won't be able to see the confusion on my incredulous face.

"Fuck, yes! I'm a man, and you're the sexiest fucking woman on the planet. Of course, I'd get turned on, but it's not the same. I don't get off on that. I'm not a switch. I get off on the control and your submission. But I'm a man of my word, and if it would make *you* happy…I said I would do anything to make you happy." His eyes fix me with nothing but the truth.

"Ah, you've taken the fun out of it now. How am I supposed to enjoy tying you up and torturing you if I know you take no pleasure in it? Damn, that sucks." I pout playfully.

"My brother, on the other hand, he is more like Leon than me," he goads.

"Now you are definitely teasing because you said no more sharing."

"I wouldn't share. I would let you torture Will while I watched you in action, and then I'd—" The waitress returns to clear our dessert plates.

"You'll what?" I rush out in a not so quiet whisper. He chuckles at the eagerness in my breathless voice.

"I can't tell you now."

"What?"

"It would be like unwrapping your birthday presents early." He taps me lightly on my nose.

"Oh my god, Jason, you are a sadist! I am dying here. None of the eating, drinking, and especially not the conversation—none of that has quelled that fact that I really, really need to…" The lights flicker interrupting my truculent tirade. The center of the room illuminates and the frosting to the glass clears to reveal an extremely well equipped dungeon. A man and a woman enter. He leads her into the middle and places her awkwardly against the St. Andrew's Cross. He is wearing some ill-fitting leather pants, and she is in a lacy white bra and stockings, but she isn't wearing panties. I suppress a snicker thinking maybe that is the Amsterdam dress code of choice. She is skinny, and he is fit but not toned and is quite pale. He starts to tie her up, and I turn to Jason.

"Is this the show? You've brought me to a live sex show?" I keep my voice low, but I doubt we would be heard through the thick glass. The performers on the other hand can be heard, surround sound, in the booth.

"Of sorts." Jason turns a dial by the service button and the heavy breaths from the speakers quieten.

"Still with the cryptic…It's clearly a show, but they look like it's their first night."

"It most likely is." He flashes a glance at the performance but mostly keeps his eyes on me.

"Jason?"

"They are patrons. It is quite possible this is their first time performing to an audience." My jaw just drops. He holds my gaze but doesn't elaborate. I turn and watch the scene unfold in front of me, feeling for the first time in my life like a voyeur. The man is tenderly stroking the skin of his partner, her arms, her cheek. He tentatively grasps her breasts and she arches into his hold. The movement encourages him, and you can see the remnants of stage fright being replaced with confidence and desire.

"Does everyone have the same view we do...I mean is everyone watching this?"

"Yes."

"Can they see us?"

"No."

"Why would they do that?"

"Why do you think?" His knowing grin is wide and wicked, and I don't bother to reply to the question. I know why people would want to do something like this, perform for others, experiment with any form of kink really. *The thrill.*

"The masks. In the ladies earlier, I was about to take it off, and the attendant stopped me. Is that the reason?" I nod toward the man now kneeling between the woman's legs. His back is to us but, by her clenched fists and gaping mouth, I think she's having fun. "So no one gets recognised before, during, or after."

"Precisely."

"Hmm," I muse and let my gaze follow his back to the show. I have never seen a live show before, porn yes, but nothing up close and very personal. These are not actors or prostitutes; these are ordinary people exploring their sexual desires safely in a private-public way. The woman's skin flushes with excitement. I fight the need to pull my legs together, but Jason feels them twitch. His grip on my thigh stills my involuntary movement. The unbearable ache that has been bubbling under the surface all evening is driving me insane. I drop my hand onto his thigh.

"Nuh-uh, hands where I can see them." His light reprimand is accompanied by a nefarious smile.

"It's only fair. You're killing me here," I whine.

"You like the show? You like to watch?" His question isn't flip. His tone demands a considered answer.

"Voyeurism isn't my thing. Watching someone have sex is for masturbation as far as I'm concerned, but this is different. This is a mix of the two, watching and being watched, and that is very erotic…seductive. I can't imagine what she is feeling." I draw in a deep steadying breath as my pulse rate rockets.

"Can't you?" His question is leading and hangs heavy in the air. I swallow the thick lump choking my next needy breath. I can't believe how turned on I am. I hated when Richard fucked me in front of his friends. How could I be aroused by the thought of this? How could I want to be her, in that room, on display, being worshipped, adored, and fucked raw. How could I want that? I do because this, this is very, very different.

Jason hasn't taken his eyes off me. I can see him in my periphery. I can feel him in the blood burning through me like lava. The lights on the stage dim with perfect timing, capturing the climax but not the come faces. No one wants to see that.

"Did you enjoy that?" His hand threads to the back of my neck, and his fingers dig in to grab a fistful of hair. He moves in close as I gasp, millimetres from his lips.

"I think we could do better." His back straightens, and he pulls back to meet my serious stare.

"You want to repeat that for me."

"I didn't think you liked repetition, *Sir*."

"I don't. But, I think in this instance I need you to be *very* specific as to your meaning." I shift round to face him, my knees coming together for the first time in a long time.

"I said I think we *will* do better."

"Fuck!" He groans as if in agony.

"Yes, please." His lips crush mine and his hand slams over the "Call for Service" button.

All the years I considered myself putting on a show, dressing the part and acting my arse off as Mistress Selina, I never once felt this excited or turned on. Oh, and nervous, don't forget nervous. Jason disappeared for about ten minutes, and we waited in a 'green room' for the performers whilst the stage was prepped for a further fifteen long arduous minutes. Plenty of time for me to change my mind and back out, but every time Jason looked at me with undiluted fire and lust, my smile got just that little bit bigger. After his last and final check, he takes my hand, pulling me from my seat. He strides purposefully through the display room door. What little light there is bounces off the mirrored walls, casting a softly, sinister glow. But this is a stage I am more than familiar with. A dungeon, fantasy, or playroom, they all serve one purpose for Jason and me... *pleasure*.

"First position, beautiful. Let's show them how it's done." He circles me as I drop to my knees. His fingers sweep along my jaw line, and he tilts my head right back. I struggle to swallow when he flashes a wicked grin. He takes his sweet time drawing his lip between his teeth as he peruses the array of implements at his disposal.

He unhooks a sturdy leather swing hanging from an even sturdier looking chain and bolt through the ceiling. He loosens all the straps and then curls his finger for me to come to him. I hop to my feet and walk to face him.

"Take off your blouse and skirt." I lick my dry lips and do as he asks. He sucks in a breath, and his eyes widen as they draw slowly from my high heeled ankle boot, up my stocking clad legs, to my corset bra, and finally resting with untamed desire on my wanton gaze. "So beautiful." He breathes out, and I can't help but smile. He calls me that all the time, but sometimes when he says it like that I actually believe him, inside and out. "Undress me, but don't touch my skin." I fight back a smart remark and a groan. Damn, he *is* a sadist.

"Yes, Sir." My fingers are deft at removing his tie, but his buttons prove a little tricky…so damn close to that soft taut skin over cut muscle. It's all I can think about. I use my fingernails, light and nimble to remove the shirt from his shoulders and get to work on his belt. I tug the material away from his body with more strength than he was expecting, and he chuckles then braces himself with a wider stance for balance. His trousers drop to his knees, and I am grateful he is commando because there is no way I could remove skin-tight boxers without touching him. I drop once more to my knees and help him out of his shoes and pants. I look up when I get to his socks. He can't keep them on, and I can't remove them and obey his wish. He flashes an easy grin and quickly removes each sock. He is gloriously naked, and I am rightly worshiping the heavenly image before me. How did I get so lucky?

I don't think I have ever seen him so hard. His cock is straining to touch his belly button and looks angry and desperate. I certainly get the latter. *I am the definition of desperate.* His fist grabs the base of his cock, and I bounce up from sitting on my heels. I'm pretty sure I would be panting if I didn't think I would look ridiculous—not that I care what I look like with him, but it's not just him. He places the velvet tip to my lips, and I open with a satisfied sigh.

Finally.

He pushes in and my tongue darts to take the glistening arousal dripping from the crown before swirling along the length. He pushes slowly farther down my throat. His hand sweeps the fallen hair from my face back around my ear and comes to rest on my throat. His fingers gently massage with a rhythm matching his gentle thrust. He hits the back of my throat, and with a gentle stroke of his fingers, I swallow a little bit more and take him deeper. He rolls his head back and makes the sexiest groan that makes me melt. He slips from my mouth and, because he hasn't said I can touch him, I have to let him, but I sag. He grins at my swollen, pouting lips. He lifts me high, and I wrap my legs around his firm, narrow waist, gripping him with my thighs like my life depended on it. Relishing the feel of his scorching hot skin on my inner thighs, I sink my weight to try and gain a little extra contact where I need it most. My fingers finally find freedom in his hair and I tug, grip, and pull with wanton abandon. His lips crush mine, his tongue diving in, demanding entrance and taking what is his. I parry his attack with my own desire until he finally breaks us apart, and we both gasp for much needed oxygen.

One of his hands leaves me and grabs for something behind me. The next moment he carefully lowers me onto a wide sheet of soft leather; my bottom is on the edge, but the natural sway and instability of the swing has me falling onto my back. The leather supports my body perfectly, but my legs are dangling, and my hands grip the chains for balance.

Jason scoops one leg into a padded loop, also secured to the bolt in the ceiling, and slides it to just above my knee. He repeats this with my other leg and makes sure the padded part of the strap is comfortable against my skin. He takes a moment standing between my wide spread legs, my body hoisted. His hand rests flat on my tummy, and he pushes me away with a slight sway of the swing. Swinging back I bump back against his thighs, his cock still straining at full attention.

"My turn to worship you, beautiful." His voice is a deep rumble that I feel like wave of electricity, a charge that prickles my skin, as every single tiny hair on my body jumps to stand. He drops to his knees and blows a blast of cool air on my molten center. I must be dripping; I know I am, and the sexy sucking sounds he makes are evidence of the fact. I buck and grip the chains trying to ease the intensity of this amazing feeling building. His tongue is firm and relentless, and when he circles my clit, I cry out. I really wasn't lying when I said I was ready to explode.

"Please, please may I come, Sir?" My voice is strained through gritted teeth. Every muscle in my tummy clenches hard with anxiety that he might deny me. I'm getting better at orgasm denial but I will die if he doesn't let me come.

"My tongue will be very disappointed if you don't." He takes the respite to wipe his glossy mouth on my thigh. I relax with obvious relief.

"Oh, I wouldn't want to disappoint your tongue, not when it's been so *very* good." My voice is a mix of excited anticipation and breathless relief. He grins, and I drop my head back with a heavenly sigh at the long firm sweep of his tongue. He slides two fingers as deep as he can and curls and twirls a blissful rhythm that sends me cresting so damn high I am blinded by the stars dancing behind my lids.

"Oh God…please…Oh…ahhhhh!" I scream and cry out when he sucks down on my clit, and I free-fall, weightless and drifting on wave after wave of absolute pleasure. His glorious mouth buffets the waves, and his tender lips kiss and rock me back to earth. My eyelids flutter open to see Jason towering dark and dominant, pressed at the apex of my thighs, his cock heavy in his hand. He sweeps the thick head along my slick folds, gently teasing until I am fully sentient once more. "Mmm," I moan and arch into the erotic movement that instantly has a deep ache building in the base of my spine. The anticipation is killing me, but it's obviously too much for him too, because with one hard thrust, he pushes deep inside me. The momentum instantly has the swing lifting me from his cock, but he grabs my thighs and pulls me roughly back.

Oh my fucking God!

I would cry out, but I have no breath to speak. He has pushed every bit from my body and filled it with his massive cock. He has *never* been so deep. I didn't know it was possible to go that deep. Unbelievable pleasure paired with pain that dances on the edge of just too much, but is divine nonetheless, a tantalising tortuous paradox. He pauses on his down stroke, and I lift my head to see concern and heat in his eyes.

"Are you okay?" I can feel his thighs tremble against me as he fights to restrain himself. If this feels half as good for him as it does for me, it is Herculean effort he is utilising, holding back like that.

"We have *got* to get one of these." I bite my shit-eating grin back but laugh when he drops his head and lets out an equally happy sound.

When he raises his head all humour has dissipated from his eyes, and his face is a picture of fiery feral passion. I clench and brace, suck in and hold a baited breath, waiting for him to unleash euphoric heights and erotic hell. He bucks his hips and pulls out, thrusts hard again and again and again. Each time he plunges deep, I swing away, and he grabs me, pulling me back, hard, back to where I belong, thoroughly impaled and loving every single inch.

One of his hands gripping the top of my thigh moves to a breast bursting out of the confines of the corset. The rough jerking movements is too much for the soft flesh. He squeezes, a rough, desperate grasp and pinches the nipple. He bends over to take it in his eager mouth. He never breaks his relentless pace. My hands rest on his sweat-covered shoulders, and I sweep them to his waist, holding firmly for some illusive stability. He moves his hand to my throat and starts to apply pressure. My body reacts like an instant detonation, no countdown, no steady build, just fucking nuclear explosion. I gasp for air and come, hard.

I don't remember much after that. His hand may have threaded around my neck. I think he might have told me he loved me, but he could've said *Kangaroos make him horny* for all I know. Because I am aware of nothing except him, deep inside me. Him holding me like I am his anchor to the earth, when the truth is he is mine.

FOUR

Jason

SHE'S GLOWING UNDER MY FINGERTIPS AS I HELP HER DRESS. Giggling in fits when her fingers fumble with the tiny buttons on her skirt. Her arms flop listlessly to her side when I take over the simple, but seemingly impossible task. Her smile is soft, sleepy, and her eyes hold so much love, I know with a profound ache in my chest she would destroy me if she ever chose to take that away. She leans heavily into me when I put my arm around her tiny waist, making our way out of the club and on to the still busy street. She sways when we are hit with the late night winter breeze, and she snuggles deeper into my protective frame.

"Think you can manage the walk back, beautiful?" I hold her close and relish the full body shiver that makes her tight little body ripple against mine.

"My legs are like jelly; I think you broke me." She grins with a satisfied little laugh.

"Well, I can't have that." I scoop her into my arms and wince at her high pitched squeal that shatters the quiet of the street. Her subsequent deep throaty laugh, however, fits perfectly with the ever-present atmosphere of darkness and sin in the De Wallen. She wraps her arms around my neck, lets out a deep sigh that morphs into a yawn. Her head rests against my chest, and she is asleep before I even reach the short distance to the corner of the street.

She surprised me tonight. No, that's not right; she completely blew me away. The show I thought would be fun, something a little different, but knowing her history, I didn't dream she would want to perform like we did. I should've known better. My girl is strong and brave and fearless. She may be scarred by her past and the hell that Richard put her through, but she doesn't let that constrain her. It doesn't define her, and she will not let it stop her from doing exactly what she wants, what gives her pleasure. *Lucky me.*

I wake up with a muscle-aching stretch, not because the hazy winter morning sun is peeking through the heavy curtains, but because I am alone. I woke several times in the night and each time I am exactly where I want, my arms wrapped around my prize, entwined and perfect. I rise up on my elbows and listen for telltale sounds in the room and from the en suite. Nothing. I drag my hand roughly down my face, trying to rouse properly when the handle on the door to the room rattles. I leap from the bed, and in two long strides, I pull the handle and swing the door wide. Sam jumps back on a gasp, her eyes wide with surprise, quickly dropping from my face. Shit!

"And good morning to you," she drawls, biting her bottom lip to stop a full-on smirk.

"Oh, my goodness!" A shocked gasp and blur of elderly

woman behind Sam in the corridor is confirmation that my naked state has not gone unnoticed. Since the corridor is now empty, I don't bother to retreat, but I do grab Sam's arm, dragging her into the room and my waiting arms.

"And where have you been?" I draw in a deep breath, my nose buried in her thick messy bun. She's intoxicating, and I'm now hard. I stretch my other arm out to slam the door, but Sam wiggles from my hold.

"Wait, wait." She steps into the corridor. "I'll show you." Her voice is a little muffled by the chinking and rattling of flatware and glasses. She pushes a trolley into the center of the room. The large serving tray is set with two ornate silver domes, Champagne chills in an ice bucket, and that smell... steaming hot, freshly-ground coffee.

I take an exaggerated sniff and pat my tummy when she lifts the domes to reveal a feast fit for an army.

"I so want to fucking marry you." I step up to her and lift her so she wraps her legs around my waist. She throws her head back and laughter bursts from her lips, filling the room with utter joy.

"That's lucky." Her smile is shy at first but blossoms and steals my heart with its purity. "Because you've got me. Ball. And. Chain." She punctuates each word with kisses on my waiting lips.

"Speaking of chains—" I wiggle my brows suggestively and drop her so she is just above the tip of my attention-seeking erection. She might not feel my heat through her jeans, but she understands my intention perfectly. She tenses her thighs to prevent the drop and lifts herself free, pushing me playfully out of the danger zone.

"Hold it right there, Mister! I hunted and gathered this morning." She waves her hand at the full Continental breakfast:

pastries, meats, cheese, and fresh fruit on one plate. The other plate is definitely off menu, a full English breakfast. She grins sheepishly.

"I didn't see this on the menu." I take a crisp strip of bacon and bite down. My stomach aches with anticipation of more bacon, juicy fat sausages, glossy scrambled eggs, tomatoes, mushrooms, fried bread no less, and baked beans.

"It wasn't. I said I hunted and gathered remember? After last night, I thought you might need the sustenance." She lifts the tray and places it on the bed. I crawl over and sit behind her, wrapping my legs on either side. I am starving but I am not interested in the food much anymore. She shuffles back into my hold and pours some coffee. Then she takes a pull of a croissant, the sweet flaky pastry crumples under the pressure, flattens and disintegrates. She offers me a bite over her shoulder, but I shake my head. She may want to eat, but I still want what I want…her.

"You're not hungry?" She shifts in my hold, and her face is crinkled with concern. She doesn't understand that she would make a starving man forget to eat. Her eyes flash with unexpected worry.

"I am, and this looks amazing. On point with the gathering, beautiful, but you are more appetising than any food and much, much more satisfying." I pepper kisses on her neck and along her t-shirt covered shoulder.

"Okay, but you're going to have to sit there watching me eat all this, because I am starving." She shrugs, dismissing my amorous little speech and pops the remaining pastry into her mouth, chewing down with a grin.

"You'd eat all that?" I chuckle.

"You know it." Her words are muffled as they fight with her half-eaten food.

"I do." I grab the full plate of steaming cooked food and

slide back to lean against the headboard. I pull the sheet to cover my morning erection and lay the plate down.

"Hey, you said you weren't hungry. I was going to eat that." She pouts playfully but hands me a knife and fork, shuffling to sit beside me.

"I can't have you too full." I bite a piece of the fried bread, which is crisp, golden, and a heart attack away from nutritional food. God, it tastes good.

"Too full...why, what's on your to-do list today?"

"Just one thing on my *to-do* list, beautiful." My voice drops a sensual octave.

"Oh." Her skins dances with a slew of prickles, and she shivers. Her eyes fix on my lips; it is she who now struggles to swallow.

"Oh."

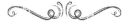

We spend the morning wandering the streets. Unlike the UK, many of the shops and boutiques close on Sundays so the city is relatively quiet. We take a canal boat tour that meanders through the waterways at a leisurely pace so you can really see the beauty of the buildings and see why this city is called Venice of the North. The tour stops several times at key tourist hot spots, but we are happy to sit back and lazily absorb audio feed culture from the comfort of the arse-numbing plastic bucket seats. Several couples leave the tour at the stop near the Anne Frank house, and Sam lets out a heavy breath and relaxes against my side.

"Are you okay?" She tilts her head up to meet my gaze, her face a light blush of colour.

"I just keep looking at every couple wondering if they were

there last night, watching."

"That bothers you?"

"No, not bothers, it's just very different from anything I have ever felt before. When I'm Mistress Selena with a cli—" She hesitates when my whole body tenses. I fucking hate her talking about being with anyone else. "When I'm Mistress Selena, I know it is a performance, and I play my part. Last night was very different. It was very, very personal. I was your sub, but I was very much me." Her smile is tentative, and the rosy hue on her cheeks deepens. She lets out a light laugh trying to cover her misplaced embarrassment. "I totally get the masks, but looking at other couples, I can't help wonder."

"Your concerns are misplaced, but your blush is adorable." I tickle her cheek with the back of my fingertips. "I doubt there is anyone here who was there last night."

"You can't know that," she scoffs. "We don't exactly have 'Kinky as Fuck' tattooed on our foreheads, but we are. You can't make a sweeping statement like that, and if I've learnt anything in my time as a Domme, you definitely can't judge a book by its cover."

"I would agree, but in this instance I can." She shifts to face me, her flawless face a picture-perfect mix of confusion and suspicion. "You don't honestly think I would let a bunch of strangers watch you?"

"Hmm?"

"I may choose to share some of you…*may*…but those little sounds and your face when you fall are too precious to share with strangers. I cleared the restaurant. That's why it took a little longer for me to arrange our time slot."

"But I wanted to…I mean, I was happy to…perform."

"I know, beautiful, and that in itself is fucking amazing. You are amazing. I honestly wasn't expecting that reaction, but you asked, and there was no way I would deny you, when I know how brave you were to ask." I cup her delicate face with my large hands; she looks so small in my hold. Her dark chocolate eyes glisten with unshed tears at my words. "Before you, I wouldn't have dreamt of giving it a second thought, but you are just too precious to share with strangers. You are mine. My heart and my soul…Understand?"

"Wow." Her lips crush mine, and I can't help the smile that splits my face—making it difficult to maintain the delicious dance of demanding tongues. She climbs awkwardly onto my lap, her knees bent on either side of my thighs, and her long coat draping over us, creating a blanket of cover. She bounces perilously close to my now rock-hard cock. I groan at the instant unbearable ache in my balls. Jesus, this woman is going to kill me with pent-up lust. I hold her hips firmly to stop what she's about to do, which is drive me insane. She fights against my hold, but I am unyielding, and she pulls back with a resigned and playful pout.

"Spoilsport."

"This may be a liberal city, but we would still get arrested for fucking in a glass topped boat. But you keep wiggling that delectable arse and screw what I just said, the whole damn city can watch you come apart. I will spend the next ten years trying to erase all YouTube evidence when I change my mind because this—" I slip my hands to her tight round arse and grip harder than necessary, but it seems I need to clarify. "—this is mine."

"Yours." Her eyes, her smile, and her body soften, and she folds herself into my arms. *Perfect.*

After almost an hour, the boat glides to a stop next to the Bloemenmarkt, Amsterdam's famous floating flower market.

"Can we?" Sam first stretches to get a better look out of the window, but from this angle there is nothing to see except the backs of the numerous white tarp, framed, tented stalls.

"There aren't any flowers; it's more a bulb market."

"I know. I'd like to have a look all the same." She jumps from her seat and holds out her hand, which I take, eager to keep that smile exactly where it is, spread wide and glorious on her face. The market is a series of stalls knitted together and floating on large permanent barges on the Singel canal. It is home to thousands, maybe hundreds of thousands of tulip bulbs, and Sam is actually quite engrossed searching through the different varieties.

"Searching for The Black Tulip?" I call after her as she disappears into the interconnecting stalls. I find her bent over a large display. I wrap both arms around her as she leans over to read the descriptions of the flowers. There are over three thousand recognised varieties in the Netherlands, according to the tourist information leaflet. I wonder which one she is searching so intently for.

"Hmm?" She turns to kiss my cheek before turning away to carry on her quest.

"Dumas's *The Black Tulip*." I recall the abbreviated story I just finished reading in the tour guide. "In the story a reward of a hundred thousand florins is offered to the person that can produce a truly black tulip. It was a huge reward at the time but remained unclaimed. To quote, 'Black tulip became a symbol for tolerance and justice but also divine love between two people'. So I'm cool with you looking, just know that you are looking for something that doesn't exist."

"I did know that actually…but not from the story. My mother grew tulips, prize winning flowers in every colour imaginable except my favourite: blue."

"Blue doesn't exist either, beautiful, unless it's been dyed. I think what you are looking for is also unattainable." She lets out a sharp bitter laugh.

"Oh, I know but that perfectly represents how I felt growing up. She demanded the impossible," she muses sadly, shaking her head, but there is only a trace of hurt in her deep brown eyes. Even that trace is too much. "Here, this is pretty close." She points to a picture of a vibrant blue purple flower above a bucket filled with small dry, flaky bulbs, waiting dormant for their moment to shine. "I know they aren't natural; these are a hybrid. They are a product of our environment, just like me." Her eyes shine bright, all sadness quashed with the strength of her smile, spreading wide across her adorable face and lifting her spirits. Happy with her purchase, we make our way back to the hotel and begin the journey home.

We hit the outskirts of London when Sam turns to me. She has drifted in and out of sleep for most of the journey.

"I had a wonderful time, Jason, thank you." Her soft smile spreads warm and wide, lighting her eyes, illuminating her face.

"My pleasure, really, my pleasure." I drop my hand to her knee and slide it firmly up her thigh. The sleepy noises and dream-filled sighs she has emitted over the last five hours have kept me in a painful state of semi-arousal the entire time. We are nearly home, and I am more than ready to finish what she started all those hours ago on the boat. "You never need to worry that marriage will change a single thing about who we are. The kink runs deep with our kind." I tap my fingers in a light rhythm, the tips teasing the apex of her legs. She scoots down, lifting her feet to the dashboard and pushing her core into my hand.

"It does. It really does." She giggles, and I join in her infectious joy. My laughter abruptly stops though when I pull my car around the end of my street and see two things: The lights blazing from almost every window in my townhouse and a badly parked motorcycle in my resident's space. Leon. I double park next to the bike and turn an accusatory glare at the sheepish looking figure beside me.

"Mind telling me how Leon gained access to my home." I arch an eyebrow.

"Our home," she rightly corrects, and her tone has an edge.

"*Our* home yes—yours and mine—not Leon's," I clarify, and my tone is less clipped but more plain irritated.

"I left a spare key at the flat just in case."

"Hmm," I mutter, but it comes out as a disgruntled sound.

"Don't be mad. He was lonely last time I went round. He misses me, and I said if he was ever lonely to just come on over." Her face is soft with concern.

"I'm not mad. I'm…" I continue to air my frustration, but she interrupts.

"Horny…I can see." She snickers but slaps her hand wisely over her mouth to stop a full explosion of laughter. "I'm sure he won't stay long."

"I'm sure he won't," I retort.

"Don't be like that. He's my best friend, and he is always welcome." Her brows knit together, and her eyes flash with sadness. I don't want that, but she's oblivious to my real concern.

"He's your best friend who now looks at you like you're next on the menu," I clarify.

"Ah." She sucks in a slow thoughtful breath, her lips pursed at this revelation.

"Ah," I repeat. The thoughtful silence only lasts a moment before she breaks it.

"But that is hardly his fault. Look, he is probably trying really hard to act like he was before Christmas, but the man thinks with his dick. He'll get over it. He just needs another toy." She pauses, her eyes taking in every inch of my face for tells that I am buying this explanation. I have my doubts, but he is her best friend. Her smile creeps tentatively across her face, and her tone is more a plea, which hits me hard. "He misses me, Jason. We lived together on and off for nearly ten years, and that is longer than most marriages."

"Not ours," I state as a matter of fact.

"No, not ours" She leans over to plant her soft full lips on the tight thin line of my mouth. "He's adjusting, and it would really help if you two got on."

"We get on," I scoff.

"Each other's nerves, maybe." She pats my thigh and opens the car door. "Come on, the sooner he gets his Sam fix, the sooner you can have yours." She bites down on her bottom lip and winks. She turns and bounds up the steps to the front door, swiping her finger before disappearing inside, leaving me with the bags and a tight, painful, jealous pinch of pain in my chest. Stupid, but it's still there, nonetheless. Her friendship with Leon is something I struggle with, one minute loving that she has someone else who clearly adores her to hating that she has someone else who does so.

I dump the bags by the front door and follow the delicious smell and laughter into the kitchen. Leon is stirring a pan on the cooker, his back to me but half facing the room. Sam is pouring chilled white wine into the third of three glasses. She walks over to hand me one, kissing me lightly on the cheek and tipping up to whisper in my ear.

"Play nice."

"He doesn't look like he will be leaving any time soon," I growl under my breath, and she rolls her eyes at my stubborn refusal to see past my own selfish needs.

"Play nice," she repeats with a sterner tone, which has lost a good deal of its playfulness.

"Fine." I kiss her forehead and do my best to shuck off my dour mood. I know he is important to her and that makes him important. Period. I drag my hand roughly down my face, acknowledging that my extreme tiredness and the long drive is probably a large contributing factor to my lack of empathy. I am certainly behaving more like a sex-starved petulant teenager than a mature adult and future husband.

"This is a nice surprise, Leon. You shouldn't have." Despite the undercurrent and glare from Sam, my words are level, and Leon grins, unfazed by my taunt.

"I bet." He shakes my offered hand. "Stupid to cook all this for one, and I thought you'd appreciate some home cooking. After all, you've been living together for a while. You must be sick of take out," he jokes, and I laugh at Sam's expense.

"Hey, no ganging up with the insults. I'm right here." She screws up a dishcloth and hurls it at Leon. He ducks, missing the missile, and blows her a kiss in return. I have a large table that fills the center of the kitchen, and I take a seat next to Sam. Places have been set, and Leon looks like he has everything under control. Despite my initial irritation, this is actually really nice. Sam is relaxed and smiling; Leon is certainly at ease in our house, and for the first time in forever, this place feels like a home.

Leon dishes up three large bowls of beef stew and creamy mashed potatoes. My tummy makes an audible approval that I don't try to hide. This looks so good, light fluffy mash drenched in rich gravy. If it tastes half as good as it looks, I might just ask him to move in, too.

"Tell me what you got up to, and don't spare the blushes." He grins and pointedly winks at my girl. Yeah, maybe I *won't* be asking him to move in.

"We took a boat tour and I bought some bulbs. Oh, and a chocolate vagina for you, but it's packed, so you'll have to wait."

"A chocolate vagina? Really? Not weed or a hooker? You suck as a best friend," he quips.

"I thought at least it would mean you'd get some—" Sam's cheeks pink right up when Leon blurts.

"Pussy." Leon grins and Sam cringes.

"Thank you, Leon. Yes, that," she snaps.

"What was that?" I ask around a mouthful of really good food.

"Sam doesn't like pussy," Leon teases.

"Oh, that's a shame," I offer with a knowing smile and a cheeky wink.

"I don't like the word," Sam states flatly, and my interest is piqued at her evasive answer.

"So you do like pussy, just not the word pussy?" I push, feeling the swell in my pants at the mere thought of my girl with another girl.

"Is there any chance we could stop using—actually, can we change the subject?" She takes a long slow sip of her wine, hoping the time delay is enough to have moved the topic along. Fat chance.

"After you answer the question." Leon and I state in unison.

"I don't know. There, answered. Now, move on boys." She takes another large gulp of her wine, and as much as I want to pursue this line of questioning, I don't want to make her uncomfortable, which she clearly is. I also don't want to encourage Leon, or to aggravate my raging hard-on any further; it's fucking painful enough as it is.

"Fine, what else did you do? Did you both get high and eat your body weight in waffles?" He wiggles his brow playfully at

Sam, but her eyes flash nervously at me. My jaw is tense. I can't help it. I hate drugs. Even though I am aware of the pros and cons of Marijuana, and I'm all for choice, my own personal experience with Will has left me with a zero tolerance. No matter how legal or innocent the intention. Sam didn't express a desire to visit any of the Hash bars, but I wonder from the shy shared looks whether that was because of me. "Did you actually manage to get Missy here to smoke a joint? I mean it's legal there, Sam, you had no excuse," Leon taunts with a playful smirk.

"Had better things to do." Sam shakes her head at Leon, and a brief frown furrows his brow. Sam looks at me, and Leon follows her gaze with confusion.

"Sam's being sensitive, but it's fine." I draw in a deep breath. Part of me is thankful Sam has kept my past as secret as I'd hoped, and a much bigger part is warmed to my core that she didn't share this with her best friend. "My brother was a drug addict, and my view of 'harmless drugs' is a little tainted because of it."

"Ah, sorry man, I didn't know. I mean there is no way he is now, right?" Leon's genuine shock is confirmation that this is completely new information.

"No, he's been clean for years, but—"

"We're a product of our environment." Sam reaches across the table and takes my hand, squeezing comfort and love from her tiny fingers directly into my soul.

"This is code, isn't it?" Leon throws his fork down in a huff and a clatter. "This is what I hate about couples. They start to have these fucking shortcut codes and a secret language. All lovey dovey and deep meaningful stares, which pisses me off." He roughly crosses his arms over his chest, and a dark scowl shades is face.

"Jeez, you're sensitive or possibly stupid…maybe both."

Sam snickers, retrieving her hand and reaching for her drink. "It's not code. Jason's view on drugs was shaped by what happened to his brother. Environmental, duh!" She pulls a cute dumb face that makes us both laugh. "Isn't that right, honey bunny?" She pushes her tongue into her cheek and fights back giggles with pursed lips. Leon slaps his hand to his mouth and pretends to hold back vomit while making muffled retching noises.

I stop drinking after my second glass, but Leon continues. Sam tries to keep him company, but her sips are getting more infrequent. He bought a lemon tart because he confessed he couldn't be arsed to cook a dessert too, but he knew very well Sam's preference for all things sweet. I clear everything but the coffee while they catch up. Sam includes me as best she can, but Leon monopolises her for most of the evening. When she yawns, I take that as my opportunity to reclaim what's mine.

"Thank you for the meal, Leon. It was really good, but it's been a long day, and as you can see…" Sam's face pinks up with embarrassment when she fails to hide another huge yawn.

"So when are you two getting married?" Sam's sleepy eyes snap open wide. Shit! I am never going to get her to bed.

"We're in no rush," she offers, but her eyes meet mine. Her voice is tentative, and her statement inflects like a question, for me. I walk over and crouch down on my haunches so we are eye to eye.

"True, but I would like you to start getting some ideas together. I want you as my wife, and I want you to have the perfect day, the latter I understand can take time. Sometimes, when people say there is no rush, it is because there is actually no real intention, and I want to make it very clear that that is not the case here. For me, the sooner the better, but for us there is no rush." Her hands cup my face, warm, soft, and possessive.

"Urgh," Leon grumbles, and that is also enough for tonight. I stand and scoop Sam into my arms.

"It's been a pleasure, Leon, but I'm taking my girl to bed. Feel free to stay, but don't expect a quiet night. Is that code enough for you?"

FIVE

Sam

JASON STEPS INTO THE KITCHEN, AND I NEARLY MISS MY mouth completely, my spoonful of cereal bumps my lips, dribbling milk down my chin. He winks at me and walks over to the coffee machine to fix his morning espresso. I have yet to see him in any garb in which he doesn't look drop dead gorgeous, but in a sharp three-piece suit, he is absolutely lethal. Crisp white cuffs peep from a midnight navy, Italian, hand-cut cloth; his tie is a burnt ochre with flecks of gold that match the specks in his eyes. His hair is still damp from the recent shower, and he looks fresh from his early morning jog. He must have Red Bull running through his veins after the tedious drive yesterday and his Olympic gold medal performance in the bedroom last night. Which left me shattered and limp, very much like I am this morning, hunched over my breakfast but greedily taking in the morning glory that is Jason.

"Keep looking at me like that, beautiful, and you won't be

going in to work at all today." I shake my head to break my gaze, feeling heat in my cheeks at being caught drooling. I really had been staring *that* hard.

"How do you do that? I'm a wreck and you…you look like you you've stepped off the cover of GQ, and I bet you've just run a marathon." I wave my hand up and down his immaculate self as exhibit A.

"A half marathon, don't exaggerate and that wasn't the exercise I was thinking about." He grins and stalks over to me.

"I'm seriously thinking of joining a gym just to keep up. I thought I was fit, but you're like the frickin' Energizer Bunny." He perches on the edge of the table in lieu of taking a seat. He doesn't often eat breakfast, maybe a bite of toast from my plate, but I have nothing to share today. Besides, his preference is to start to the day with something hot, liquid, and highly caffeinated.

"I love your curves. Don't change a damn thing." His hand slides up my thigh and squeezes the flesh and muscle.

"Oh, you did not just say that." I drop my spoon to a dramatic crescendo that halts his hand mid-massage.

"What?" His face flashes with genuine surprise, his concern evident by the deep crease of his frown.

"Call me fat." I slap his hand away from my silky pj-covered leg.

"Obviously, I did." He sits back and meets my glare with a fixed expression, impassive. His tone is flat and without inflection or a hint of humour. "I find you repulsive, which is why I have a permanent hard-on. Jeez." He blows out a puff of frustrated air. "You hear what you want to hear, but for the record and the love of all that is holy…You. Are. Gorgeous." He leans down and punctuates each word with a soppy wet kiss. "I love the soft swell of your tits and the curve of your hips and your tight round arse, and I am not going to apologise for that ever." He kisses my lips once more, next my nose, my forehead, then my brows, cheeks, and continues to pepper my face with a million butterfly kisses, whispering as he does. "I love every single inch of you, beautiful. Inside and out." I squirm a little and, laughing, I playfully push him away.

"I just think since I've stopped whip-welding, there might be a few more inches." I rub my belly, which has a small round bump from breakfast, but I know is normally flat. I'm not over weight, just under-toned. "And I will need to start some sort of fitness thing to keep up with you," I challenge.

"Don't on my account. If you're ever too tired, I'll just roll you over and fuck you in your sleep." He shrugs, his wide wicked smile is a mix of pride and smug.

"Oh, my god, you would, wouldn't you?"

"No, beautiful." He chuckles, sipping the last drops of his coffee. "I want you sentient…sleepy sex is fine, but necrophilia is a kink too far." He rightly wrinkles his nose at that hard limit.

"Ya' think?" I mirror his distaste. I know we are both advocates of the 'no judgement' rule, but we are also proponents of Safe, Sane, and Consensual.

"Has our guest risen, or did he not stay after all?" Jason nods his head up toward to the guest room above us.

"Risen and retreated while you were pounding the streets. He told me to thank you for the hospitality." I smile sweetly.

"Was he being ironic?" He sniffs derisively.

"Jason," I warn.

"I'm not remotely sorry. I am selfish when it comes to you, but he is your friend, and for that, he is always welcome. Take it or leave it," he states flatly as a matter of non-negotiable fact.

I jump up, skidding my chair noisily back across the hardwood floor, and throw my arms around his neck, squishing my body with some force against his granite hard frame. He lifts me with ease as if the extra inches I've mumbled about haven't in the least affected my weight.

"I'll take it, thank you." His hands fist the silk of my pj bottoms and slide possessively over my arse. I mash my lips to his; his tongue is a luscious mix of bitter coffee and him. A heated sensual duel of lips and tongues and desperate breaths ensues before he regains control. Pulling back with a pained groan, he lets me slide slowly down his body, but he doesn't relinquish his hold when my feet hit the ground. Instead, he simply envelops me in his strong arms, a firm possessive embrace filled with lust and love.

"What's with the magazines?" My eyes follow his gaze to the table where I had been picking through a selection of the numerous publications spread all over the table.

"Oh, Sofs sent some over the other week. Thought I might like to start having a look." I shrug and step out of his hold. I scoop the magazines into a not so messy pile. Dropping them on an edge to align and straighten, I place them neatly on the table.

"Good idea." He squeezes my butt and slaps it when I bend to clear my breakfast bowl from the table. I give a playful scowl but shrug off the topic.

"Hmm, I guess," I mutter on my way to the dishwasher.

"Don't sound so excited." He forces a laugh, but his tone is tinged with hurt. I spin to catch the same feeling reflected in his eyes. Damn it, I'm an idiot.

"No, no, I didn't mean it like that, honestly, but…" I scurry back across the room to him and take both his hands in mine. I wait until his eyes are completely fixed on me. "I *am* excited, Jason, but I don't have a family or many friends so the whole idea of a big day is daunting. Not to mention shopping for a dress on my own." I shake our hands lightly, my words hold sincere concern, but I try to keep my tone light.

"Why the fuck would you be on your own? I will be with you." I chuckle at his indignant tone.

"You can't! It's tradition," I add and fight the desire to roll my eyes at his good intentions. "And I am guessing you don't want me to take Leon?" I raise a brow high with my query. He stiffens to his full and considerable height, making me shake my head on a light inevitable laugh. "No, I didn't think so. So, I'm going solo, and that is just not something to get excited about. Traditionally, this is a mother-daughter rite of passage with the odd best friend from nursery thrown in. I have neither, although I am not complaining about the former, but I am dreading all the sympathy remarks when I explain why my mother isn't sharing this moment. I'll get that pity look when all I'll want to do is shout 'ding-dong, the witch is dead.'" I let out a deep breath and flash a sad smile.

"I don't want you going on your own." He pulls one hand from mine and strokes the hair from my face. His hand is comforting and warm as it cups my cheek. "What about Sofia?"

"She's probably busy. I'm a friend but not a *best* friend." I worry my bottom lip, feeling the pressure of forcing myself on an unwitting friend. This is a big deal.

"You won't know until you ask, and I bet she'd love to help. She sent the magazines, didn't she?"

"I guess," I repeat and move to turn away.

"Where's my lioness? I don't recognise this tentative cub," he teases, threading his arms around my waist from behind, pulling me close once more.

"You're right." I draw in a deep breath. I may not have the loving mother or the childhood friends, but I do have friends, and I do have a voice. "I'll call Sofia later, and if she's not free maybe Bets or Charlie."

"Charlie?"

"Leon's new Domme," I clarify the new name.

"Perfect, any or all of the above, just don't go on your own. Fuck tradition. If it comes to that, *I'll t*ake you." He kisses the side of my neck, and I shiver from tip to toe. "Or I'm sure my mum would help."

"No, no, it's fine. I'm not so pathetic I can't find a single female friend to go shopping with." I rush to halt his kind but terrifying offer. "It's no big deal."

"I think it's supposed to be a big deal." I turn in his arms to see his brow furrowed and a tight line where his soft lips are hiding.

"I didn't mean it like that. There's just no need to call in your mum, a woman I haven't even met." I shuffle nervously from one foot to the other, my voice drops to an uncharacteristic but understandable whisper. "She might hate me and my wicked ways for leading you astray." He barks out a dirty laugh.

"Oh, beautiful, that ship sailed long before you, and trust me, she knows it." He barely contains his laughter enough to speak. "She will be beside herself that I have been tamed. Believe me, she is going to adore you." He scoops me up his body, and I wrap my legs tight around his waist, giving a teasing little wiggle when I settle just below his belt.

"Tamed hmm? I'd like to see that." I roll my hips, my heat against his hardness.

"Oh, you would, would you?" His gravelly voice is a deep sensual rumble, but his grip stops my teasing maneuver.

"I know it would be a trial for you, but I'm sure I could make it fun. You do still owe me." I try to grind, but I am going nowhere unless he wants me to. He doesn't. He fixes his dark eyes on me, holding me in his arms, and my heart in his hands. Long intense seconds root us to each other, and I barely breathe. I don't want to be the one to break this moment where I feel bare, raw…owned. His slow, sexy smile splits his lips and transforms his face into the picture of sin and salvation.

"And I am a man of my word. Consider it your Valentine gift." His kiss is light, his tongue darts out to trace the seam of my lips, and I moan at its frustrating brevity. "Book a room at the club on Friday and I'm yours. One fucking night so make the most of it." I push out of his hold and, once on my feet, jump up and down, clapping my hands like a demented seal.

"Oh, my god! Really?" I can't contain my excitement. Not so much because I will be his Domme, but that he is willing to sub for me. I'm giddy.

"Don't get too excited, because I guarantee, it won't happen again," he grumbles playfully.

"I am excited. I can't help it. Ooooh, the possibilities." I bite my lip to stop my shit-eating grin.

"I'm regretting this already." He groans but pulls me into a tight hug, kissing my hair and breathing me in.

"One night, baby, and I promise you'll enjoy every single second." My breathy words have an instant effect. He adjusts himself, but his face remains impassive.

"We'll see, beautiful. Just bear in mind, we have an early start and a long drive to my parents on Saturday so—"

My wickedness interrupts him. "Take care where I stick—"

"Sam," he bites out his own interruption. His tone is gruff and holds no humour. I hold my hands up in surrender; enough teasing.

"Joke. It was a joke. I'm guessing pegging is a hard limit then?" I pull my lips into my mouth to hide my mirth, but I step back just in case I am taking the teasing a little too far.

"Damn fucking right! Jeez, what did I just agree to?" He

lets out a heavy sigh that is all show and no substance. "I'm outta here while I still have a pair of balls. I have three days to get you to retract your request or for me to back out," he muses.

"Man of your word," I sing-song my response.

"Man of my word," he mutters begrudgingly. He grabs the back of my neck and plants a tender kiss on my lips, his face tight with tension and angst. I cup his smooth cheek.

"Thank you," I whisper, and his face softens, his eyes crinkling with a familiar smile. I wasn't going to pursue this deal, but in the back of my mind, I felt an imbalance. I trusted him with everything in me, and although I know he loves me, I couldn't help wondering if he really felt the same. I have my answer.

"Anything for you, beautiful, anything."

"Sam, your four o'clock appointment is here." Amanda, my co-worker, grins as she peeks around the corner of the resource room where I am nose-deep in journals.

"I don't have a four o'clock." I check my phone for scheduled meetings just in case I'm wrong, but I shake my head at Amanda as confirmation of the mistake. I do, however, take to opportune interruption as a chance to stretch my back out with a satisfying crunch over the back of my chair.

"I'll take it if you're too busy," she says with far too much enthusiasm for a Friday afternoon.

"They asked for me?" I pull my neck to each side too until I get that pop from my aching bones.

"He did. Oh wait, that's him." She points to the screen saver on my phone and every muscle in my body relaxes and then ignites. "Is that your fiancé?" She swallows thickly, and it's sweet the way her mouth just gapes open on an exhaled gasp. *He gets that a lot.*

"Yes, that's Jason, my fiancé." That word still feels so strange on my tongue. No, not the word, just the whole 'holy shit, I'm getting married' part of the situation. I shake myself and lightly shrug. Amanda lets out a heavy sigh when I add, "And my four o'clock, apparently." I don't bother to pack my stuff away because even if it is for a moment, I don't want to keep him waiting. He has never been to my office, and I'm excited to show him around. I briskly round the corner and stride down the long corridor. I can see him standing there, dominating the small reception area. My heart hammers excitedly in my chest then drops; it's not Jason. The recognition is almost instantaneous, and it's not the fact that he is no longer wearing the suit he had on this morning or that his tan is more South Florida than Southbank. It's the whole package. Will has same tall muscular build and strong stance, similar eyes with a piercing stare, and that smile—damn, I melt every time that is leveled in my direction. But the difference I know in my heart is what makes *all* the difference.

"Hey, darling." Will walks to meet me, and although there is clearly affection in his eyes and love too perhaps, it is a fraction of what I witness every single time Jason looks at me. *I haven't seen Will since Christmas day.*

"Will, what are you doing here?" I let him pull me into a big bear hug, even lifting me off my feet before he eventually sets me back down.

"Jason said he's been really busy, so he asked me to come and help out." His eyes dance with mischief, and I am thankful that I now know him a little better, since he calls all the time to chat with his brother, so I know he is yanking my chain.

"Of course he did," I reply with a dubious quirk of my lips

and hand on my hip.

"Yeah, maybe not, hmm? He can be so selfish." His eyes darken at the same rate I feel my cheeks heat. It doesn't take much for me to have an instant high-definition flashback of our foursome at the best of times, but having Will in glorious Technicolor before me, it's difficult to picture anything other than my very own fantasy made reality. Not good. "I'm in between contracts at work and had to get some Visa stuff sorted." Will interrupts my very wayward thoughts, which I am also thankful for.

"Oh, right, good. That's good." *Smooth Sam, real smooth.* Will chuckles and I let out a puff of air and try to clear my throat.

"I've been at the American Embassy all morning, but they won't have my documents until Monday. So I thought I would visit my favourite soon to be sister-in-law." His easy grin instantly diffuses any awkwardness, and, yes, I am hugely grateful for that, too.

"Cool, does Jason know you're here?"

"I sent him a text and left a message with Sandy. I would've popped into his office, but they won't let me in the building." He bites back a wicked grin.

"I can't think why?" I mock. "Jason has told me of the havoc you create, so don't go trying the innocent act with me."

"Oh, I know you know I'm not innocent." He glances over my shoulder as he says this, and I hear a girlish gasp and giggle from whoever he is flashing that cocky grin at.

"Just came to create havoc here, I see," I quip and he barks out a dirty laugh but fixes his eyes back on me.

"Came to see what time you get off work, actually, and grab a key if it's going to be a while."

"Can't you get in? It's finger print. I would think Jason has you programmed in as an approved print."

"You would think wrong."

"And there was me thinking he trusted you."

"Only when he's there to keep guard." His voice drops to a low, sexy rumble filled with ominous intent. "I can't blame him for that."

"Afraid you'll have a house party or something?" I snicker.

"Or something." His tone makes me look up, but he closes his lids before I can see what devilishness danced there.

"I have a bit of work to finish up, but I won't be too long. Do you want to wait?"

"Could I have a tour?" His eager tone catches me off guard. "Really?"

"Sure." He nods with genuine enthusiasm, and I get a thrill that I get to do this with at least one of the men in my life.

"Oh, I'd like that, not even Jason's had a look around where I work. He keeps meaning to, but he's been completely snowed at work. The big boss is out on paternity leave, so it's all fallen on him." I don't know why this needs an explanation, but I give it all the same.

"That's the price for the big bucks."

"Even so, he's worked every weekend since Christmas. Other than our weekend away, I've seen more of Leon these past few weeks, and I don't count the odd hour he's awake at home. Anyway, I miss him, that's all." I don't attempt to hide my tone, not so much frustrated as solemn.

"Then he's very lucky, but he knows this. We all know this," he grumbles, and his back stiffens so I have to tilt my head to keep eye contact now he is at his full height.

"Do I detect a touchy subject?"

"Not in the least. I'm happy for him. That he has you, I mean. He deserves to be happy. If you detect anything, it's a longing for the same that's all."

"Ah, Will, you're a sweetie. Who'd have thought there would be two sensitive souls in one family?" I place my hand over his heart and watch his eyes take in my every move. His hand covers mine, and his fingers interlock. A sweet smile flits across his face, but is quickly replaced with a wicked gleam in his eyes and a wolfish grin.

"Sensitive, kinky, with massive cocks, if you don't mind." He lifts my hand to his mouth, and his lips smile against the skin on the back of my hand.

"I don't mind, not one bit." I chuckle and wait for him to release my hand, which seems to take a little longer than normal.

I give Will the grand tour of my workplace, and to be fair, he tries to look interested. It's just an open plan office in a refurbished warehouse with bare brick walls and minimal furniture. Nothing remotely glamorous, but I love it. Everyone is friendly and my boss is the kindest man on the planet to be so accommodating and give me a second chance at the job when I failed to show up for the interview. At least *I* think he is. They also have very flexible office hours so I can work late, leave early, or even from home as long as I get the work done. I am still the lowest of the low in terms of the legal team, but I'm learning. I always feel that my work is valued and appreciated. Like I said, I love it.

"It's quite like my new place," Will says, when we finally stop back at my desk for me to finish up.

"Really?"

"The conservation charity spends all its money on the projects, not the buildings, so they tend to be a little run-down." I smile, but then I take a moment to look at my workspace through his eyes. I suppose the building does look a little tired; the furniture is dated but functional, so I never gave that a second thought. The decor is more artsy than neglected, the carpets are a little threadbare, but when it comes to this place, I will happily wear my rose tinted glasses. "But you seem happy here."

"I am." I beam.

"Doesn't your friend work in a legal firm, too? Why not work for his company. I bet the money is better."

"You mean Leon? He's a partner in his firm, so yeah, the money is better for him. Actually it would be for me too, but that's not what I was interested in. I don't need the money. I wanted to do something good. The Mission does really good work and holds a special place in my heart and Jason's," I add quietly. There are still people around even if they are getting ready to leave.

"And mine." Will captures my gaze; his eyes hold so much, swirling with turmoil and hurt, love and loss. If I didn't know his story from Jason, I would be begging to hear it from him now, just to ease his pain. "I like that you work here, Sam. It means a lot. I mean, I know you didn't do it for me, but I still love that you do." He shuffles, and I take his hands and give them a gentle, reassuring squeeze.

"Thank you, Will, that means a lot. " I smile at his sentiment and then shrug it off with a cheeky grin. "Besides, I loved my old job so much. It was important to find something that held just as much interest because I knew it was unlikely it would be quite as much fun."

"Your other job?" he asks. From his blank expression, he does this without thinking. My knowing silence draws a slow expression of understanding across his handsome face. "At the club," he says, and I nod, smiling my appreciation that he kept his voice soft, choosing not to announce to the whole office floor my stage name and previous occupation.

"You know what? I can call it a night now. I'm ahead with what I wanted to get done, so how about we grab a drink in one of the bars by the river and see if we can't tempt your brother to play hooky, too."

"Christ, if you can't tempt him, I'm not sure what throwing me into the mix will achieve."

"I'm not throwing you into the mix." I raise a brow, my tone pointed and serious. "That is not my call to make, just so you know." I hold his gaze, then my own wicked smile creeps across my face. "But I don't see the harm in a little light teasing."

"Bait, you mean I'm bait?" He fails to sound affronted, and his grin just widens when a voice blurts out.

"I'll happily take a bite." Amanda pokes her head up from behind her computer screen, and I jump. I didn't see her hiding, but I hear her now, that dirty laugh and lustful glare is burning a hole in Will's backside. "Sorry, I know he's your fiancé and all that, but I'm an old lady, so I'm allowed to be inappropriate."

"Oh, this isn't my fiancé, this is his brother. They're twins." Her jaw snaps shut, and I can see the strain in her cheek muscles as she fights back whatever she is too fearful to unleash. I grab Will's hand, because I fear for him, too.

"Something more inappropriate?" I ask her, suppressing my own laughter. She nods energetically but keeps her lips sealed tight and almost soundproof, just a sad squeak escapes as we wave our goodbyes. We reach the lift, and I let out my laugh.

"What was that about?"

"Be thankful you have no idea." I pat his cheek and press the button for the lift.

SIX

Sam

"You can go to the club. I'm fine staying in. It's been a long week, and Jason won't be too late… probably." We had a few drinks at the bar around the corner from Jason's home, but when it became clear he wasn't going to be joining us, I just wanted to come home. I dump my bag on the kitchen counter and open the drawer to look through the stack of take-out menus.

"Will you come with me?" Will peers over my shoulder at the selection I am flicking through.

"Let me think… go to the best sex club in London with my fiancé's sexy twin brother? Um, not if I want you to be sleeping in the spare room instead of intensive care." I nudge him in the side since he is standing very close.

"We don't have to play. It is possible to go there and just chat, have a few drinks."

"Possible, yes. Likely, hmm, not so much."

"Can't keep your hands off me, is that it?"

"Cute." I waggle a warning finger in his direction and ignore his loaded question. "I don't go to the club without Jason… ever. Besides I'm knackered and just want to order pizza in my PJs and fall into a carbohydrate coma on the sofa."

"Is this a preview of married bliss? Because you are not doing the campaign any favours." I flick the pen I had poised over my food selection at his head, but he ducks. I laugh, but it feels a little hollow, and I get a strange unsettling feeling that turns my insides, and it's an effort to swallow the thickness in my dry throat. "Did I touch a nerve?" He did, but I shake it off. Jason and he are tight but if I have doubts, or whatever this feeling is, it is Jason who needs to hear about them first hand, not via his brother.

"Are you staying in or not?" I snap with overt hostility.

"Hey, I didn't mean anything by it. I'm just jealous, that's all. Jason is a lucky son of a bitch, and I'm being an arsehole." He steps up to me, his hands offered up in surrender, and now I feel like the arsehole for overreacting. I let him wrap his arms around me, and it feels so good, that familiar strength and protective embrace. I look up as he looks down. "Forgive me," he asks, his eyes soft with a trace of uncertainty. The fleeting look is strange though. He is so filled with confidence and swagger, a borderline extrovert if he weren't so British, but maybe it isn't so strange that he tries to hide his vulnerabilities just as much as the rest of us.

"Nothing to forgive, Will. I'm sorry I snapped. It's been a long week, and I miss Jason like crazy, which makes me crazy." He squeezes me tighter before letting me breathe again and releasing his hold.

"Pizza and ice cream then?"

"PJs, pizza, and ice cream."

"Perfect."

We started to watch a movie but couldn't stop talking, so gave up and retreated back to the kitchen for experimental cocktail making. Even that didn't fare too well, and the kitchen now looks like a TGI's training bar. I have every single bottle of liquor on the side, various mixers, fruits, syrups, and an eclectic selection of glasses. The fancier the cocktail, the more disgusting it seemed to taste, and we both agreed that maybe less is more. I now have a line of six shot glasses with vodka and a dollop of ice cream on top, vodka floats, three each.

"This is like a drinking game for preschoolers. Where's the tequila?" Will grumbles, and I snicker then burst out laughing, because this is hysterical. I am shit-faced drunk and about to get a little drunker.

"No, no! No tequila. I get really drunk on tequila." I think I actually hiccup with that, but I am giggling too much to distinguish between the two sounds, neither of which I have control over.

"And this is you *not* really drunk?" he challenges, his face cracking a wide smile.

"I may be a little drunk." I press my finger to my lips to shush myself and make sure he understands he needs to keep this secret.

"Okay then, vodka floats…last one to finish has to clean up the kitchen," Will states, and I snatch up the first glass, slamming it down empty before he finishes his sentence. The race is on. I slam the last glass down and jump from my seat to do my victory dance. My arms stretch high in a whoop whoop, and my stomach rolls. Shit. I race to the hall and the downstairs toilet, crash through the door, and dive for the toilet bowl. Oh, my god, I'm going to die. The door softly closes behind me, and since I didn't put the light on, I am in darkness, which is nice. My arms are braced around the rim of the toilet to stop me from falling off the face of the earth and spinning out of control—much like the room is currently doing. Even in the darkness, I can feel it tumbling in on itself.

That was impressive, to go from happy drunk to stinking, 'this might be alcohol poisoning' drunk in one shot…*a one shot too many*.

My stomach retches, and I groan as, once more, the contents of the last few hours make their way back up my throat, burning acidic liquid and a vile aftertaste that ensures I keep heaving until I am raw and empty.

Several hours or maybe seconds later, a bright light splits my head in two, and I cry out, burying my face into the crook of my arm.

"Leave me in the dark. No, just leave me to die, please." I cough and spit the water pooling in my mouth. I must be empty; for the love of god, please let me be empty. I feel a firm heavy hand on my back, cool against my sweaty skin.

"Okay, beautiful, drink this." I can't see what he wants me to drink, but Jason's voice is so filled with love, I want to cry, and that would be ridiculous.

"I'm not beautiful," I sob, rolling back on to my heels and slouch to the side of the toilet. My hair is slick to my face, and my whole body has that nasty sticky film you get from relentlessly throwing up. My stomach is so tender I bet it's been hours.

"Okay, beautiful, if you say so." He chuckles and lifts me into his arms.

"Look at me, how can you think I'm beautiful? I look disgusting and I'm a whore. Grace, the whore." Fat ugly tears stream down my face, and I cling to him like he is the only good thing, and I am not worthy. I keep my eyes scrunched tight as he carries me through the house. The brightness of the lights is pure agony to my senses. He lays me gently in our bed and pulls the covers to tuck around my now chilled and trembling body.

"If you weren't drunk, I'd tan your backside for that last comment. Grace was never a whore—you were never a whore, and you are so very beautiful."

"Grace was so innocent." I fail to hold back the tiny tears that trickle down my cheeks at the unwanted memory.

"I didn't ask Grace to be my wife. I want you, Sam. Only you." His large hand feels hot against my cheek, both soft and strong. I lean heavily into his hold, his dark eyes searching mine. Concern etched on his face, his expression stern and serious, but his tender smile just makes him look all the more stunning to me. He breathes out slowly. "We make the perfect pair of non-innocents." He kisses the tip of my nose, and I let out a boozy laugh.

"Imperfect, I think you mean," I joke, but I definitely don't mean him, he is absolutely flawless.

"Perfectly imperfect." His soft lips touch mine, and he whispers the most perfect words to my ears as I sink into drunken oblivion. "I love you, Sam."

"What the fuck were you thinking, Will?" I wince and freeze at the kitchen door. The bellow of Jason's voice is like a frickin' foghorn to my delicate state.

"No, no, no! Shhh, no shouting. Fragile flower right here, no loud or sudden noises, please." I drag my sorry self across the wooden floor in my bare feet and crawl onto Jason's lap. I need the comfort, the warmth, and I need him to calm down. "Urgh, that was not my smartest idea, but it was *my* idea." My head rolls back so I can look up to try and catch Jason's eyes. He is scowling a death glare behind me, and I have to tap his chest to get his attention. "Hey, it was *my* idea. Will wanted to go to the club, but he decided to keep me company instead. He gave up a night of debauchery, Jason. He shouldn't be shouted at for that."

"It wasn't a hardship, Sam. It was fun."

"For you, maybe," Jason grumbles, but the fierceness has left his tone, and his arms just wrap a little tighter around me. I think he is taking as much comfort as he is giving.

"I had fun. Right up to that last bad shot, I was having a great time."

"Bad shot?"

"Yeah, all the others were fine, that last one was a wrong'un." I laugh but stop myself at the sound, which is like a jackhammer in my skull. "Ow," I simper and groan.

"Ah, poor baby. Do you want some breakfast or hair of the dog?" Jason chuckles, his mouth pressed to my head.

"No hairs ever again, and I'm not sure food is such a great idea." I brushed my teeth so my mouth doesn't feel quite like the floor of a taxi cab, but even so, the idea of anything solid makes my stomach roll, like that would just be a dare too far.

"What about a walk?" Will offers brightly.

"Hmm, maybe, yeah, some fresh air might work."

We walk along the Southbank, not really heading anywhere in particular. It's cold but dry, and after about an hour, I feel revived enough to stop for coffee. Looking at the boys, they are just about ready to devour anything that stands still long enough.

"Two mega full English breakfasts, coffee, juice, and…?" Jason pauses, looking at me for my selection, but I am going to play it safe.

"Poached egg, please." I hand my menu to the waiter. We stopped at a restaurant just off Piccadilly, which is richly decorated with gilt mirrors and swaths of velvet drapes, dark red carpets, and plush leather booths. I imagine it is quite a romantic place in the evening, although it feels a little over the top at this time of the day, I happen to know it also serves a kick-ass breakfast. The waiter returns with our drinks just as Jason's phone pings. I can't help my shoulders' slump when his face darkens as he reads the message.

"I'm sorry, beautiful. I have to go and deal with this." Jason slides out of the booth, but leans back to kiss me.

"No worries." I try to smile because I know he doesn't want to go any more than I don't want him to, and I don't need to add guilt to an already shitty situation. He strides off, his shoulders set, and he reaches the door before he makes a sharp U-turn and storms back to the table. He kneels on the curved bench and drags me up his body. It's awkward because of the table, but it's fantastic too. The irrepressible need and desire courses through him and straight into me. His hands secure me and caress my body. His touch is urgent; his kiss is the best, sweetly sensual and desperately possessive all in one glorious package. His tongue explores my mouth like it's the very first kiss on earth, reverent and glorious. I whimper and crumple against him, his strong arms holding me where my frame has lost all substance. He breaks the kiss, and I feel the loss like a vacuum in my soul.

"Just so you know, I fucking hate leaving you, and this situation is temporary. It will not always be like this, understand?" He growls out the words like it physically hurts him to go. *I feel exactly the same.* "I'll have my breakfast later."

"You want me to get them to put it in a doggy bag?" I wrinkle my nose at the thoughts of sloppy eggs and beans in a baggy.

"No, beautiful, that's not what I want." His tone drops, and I get that euphoric tingle in my sweet spot that makes me clench everywhere: my jaw, my thighs, and all the muscles inside.

"Oh," I sigh. His thumb traces a delicate line along my jaw, and then he backs away.

"And you take care of *my* girl." His words might be playful, but the tone of the delivery is anything but, and Will shifts beside me.

"Always," he replies, and Jason gives him a curt nod. Will turns to me. "Does he not know you at all? There was no fucking way I could've stopped you from drinking last night if that's what you wanted to do." He rolls his eyes, shaking his head with frustration.

"He knows me, and he knows that would be true for him, too. He's just cross he wasn't there, and you're an easy target—an *easier* target."

"Ha!" he huffs out a disgruntled puff of air. "It's not like he hasn't ever fucked up."

"Oh," I elongate that word, as I slowly lean toward him with intrigue in my tone. "Do tell?"

"I am almost pissed off enough to do just that, but since he's mad at me right now, I better not."

"Ah, you're no fun," I tease, nudging him in the side.

"That's not what you said at Christmas."

"Will." My drawn out use of his name is thick with warning.

"Sam," he mocks me and winks away the sexual tension with enough charm and a dash of blatant cheek.

The rest of the day is actually lots of fun. We take a couple of the street bicycles and ride around Hyde Park, the lake, and out across the road and into Green Park, up the Mall, and to Buckingham Palace. We make our way to the back of Knightsbridge and return the bicycles. I have decided to treat Will to lunch at Sofia's family restaurant, if we can get a table.

"This place must be good to have ridden over the whole damn city for." Will drapes his arm over my shoulder and ruffles my windswept hair.

"It is good. Well, I'm sure it's good. The new manager at the club and a friend of mine, Sofia, it's their family's restaurant." I try to tame my mane, but the bike ride, blustery weather, and Will's meaty hands means I am fighting a losing battle. I settle for scraping it back into a low messy ponytail.

"Marco? This is his family's place?"

"Yep, he's Sofia's twin, he worked here for years and was offered one of their other restaurants to manage but wanted to try something different."

"He certainly got different." Will chuckles and holds the door to the restaurant open for me, but as I step inside I can see this wasn't such a great idea. The place is heaving and there is a queue of customers at the bar. "You know I can cook," Will offers as he too clocks the fat chance of us getting a table.

"But you're a guest, shouldn't I be cooking?" My nose wrinkles involuntarily at the thought of me being in charge of an entire meal. *Carnage comes to mind.*

"I'm family, not a guest, and I don't know, should you? I don't think that's written anywhere in stone, and it certainly isn't written on that screwed-up face. Besides, I like cooking. I mean I would like to cook as a way of thanking you for letting me crash with you guys."

"You're family, you said that yourself. Do you always do that when you stay, then?" I narrow my eyes when he averts his.

"Um, no, not so much, but only because we're both usual-ly out—" He snaps his mouth shut as his brain to mouth filter kicks in.

"Out trolling?" I place my hand on his chest and smile. "It's all right, Will." He is rigid under my palm. "You two are hardly the poster boys for abstinence."

"We didn't troll." He seems to stiffen a little more at my perceived character assassination.

"I don't suppose you ever needed to. The ladies would've flocked to your feet, I'm sure. I'm not judging, Will, seriously. I'm the last person to judge. I'm sorry. I didn't mean to upset you."

"I just don't like you thinking I'm some sort of manwhore. I like sex, but I'm—"

"I don't think that, Will," I state with absolute certainty, holding his gaze as I do. He gives me a slight nod, and I wrap my arms around his waist. "I'm sorry. I didn't mean anything by it, Will. Really I didn't." I am a little shocked by his reaction, but then I spent so many years not caring that people called me a whore because I knew different that I guess I have a thicker skin. He kisses my head, and I pull back. His wide bright smile is a picture of forgiveness.

"So I'm cooking then?"

"That would be great," I say, just as the headwaiter ap-proaches us with some menus. I shake my head, and we turn to leave, bumping straight into Sofia.

"Sam!" She throws herself into my surprised embrace. I was holding the door open, and my arms were an open invita-tion, apparently. She holds me until I feel like if I don't hug her back, she is just going to remain stuck to me like a limpet. I pat her back and try to relax. Not that I am antiaffection, I am just not used to this from girl friends. *I don't really have friends who are girls.* "Did you get my magazines? I hope you didn't mind me sending them. I have stacks because I can't bring myself to cancel the subscriptions." She laughs, because her own wedding must have been easily two years ago.

"I did, thank you. It's all a bit daunting, if I'm being honest. I don't really know where to start." I shrug like the weight of the 'big day' is physically resting on my shoulders; they barely move at all.

"The dress. Start with the dress." She clasps her hands excitedly and does this little bounce on the balls of her feet. Her dark brown eyes sparkle, and her smile just lights her face. I am a little in awe of her reaction and not in a good way. I am definitely missing something—some wedding gene.

"Right, okay." I try to smile, but it catches, and I'm sure I actually bare my teeth in a strained grimace.

"I know some great places to shop for the perfect dress. If you want, I'd happily come with you. I mean only if you'd want. If you have someone else to—"

"I'd like that." My rushed acceptance interrupts her and takes us both by surprise. I let out a breath, and she seems to hold hers as if waiting for me to change my mind. I don't, and I let my own smile mirror hers. "Thank you." I can feel my cheeks heat, and my voice catches with a surge of emotion, which I swallow down, quickly adding. "We have to rush, but that is really kind of you, Sofia." I grab Will's arm and pull him away from the door, waving over my shoulder as we make our way down the street.

"I'll call you!" Sofia shouts after us, and I turn to see her enthusiastic wave and beaming smile, and now I feel like crap for bolting.

"What was that about?" Will asks after an uncomfortable silence deepens like a dark cloud, cloaking me.

"Um, nothing. Sofia was just being polite. I didn't want to hang around in case she felt obligated to offer all sorts of help she probably doesn't really want to give," I mumble.

"What?" He barks out an incredulous laugh. "Are you shitting me? That's what you got from that conversation? Wow!" He shakes his head, but I'm just staring at him with confusion plastered all over my face. "You know you are quite adorable when you're delusional."

"I'm not delusional," I challenge, letting go of his arm and stepping away as if the distance will help my rebuttal.

"Yeah, you are. That girl there was itching to help. So much so I think she had confetti in her veins. You didn't see that?" he scoffs.

"No, I didn't see that. Perhaps it's you that's delusional." My fake laugh falls flat, and his amused expression and knowing eyes just bore right through me. I shake my head at his misguided observation. "Look, she's an event planner, so, maybe she just likes weddings." He taps me hard on my forehead, and my instant reflex is to jab him in his stomach with a tight curled fist. He grunts but continues to laugh.

"No, darling, she wants to help you with yours. I doubt she does this for random strangers or people she doesn't really like. People aren't that nice, Sam. So when she offers something out of the blue like that, it's probably because she wants to. I mean *genuinely* wants to help."

"You think?"

"I know." He pulls me into a rough hug, and we continue to walk. "I wouldn't have believed that if I hadn't seen it with my own eyes." His tone is lightly mocking, but his reassuring squeeze helps to soften the judgement. I take a moment before letting out a heavy sigh.

"I've never had girl friends, Will, so I don't really know

how it all works. I don't know the rules. If there is a sisterhood code of behaviour, I never got the memo."

"No school friends?"

"Nope. I wasn't allowed any friends. No, that's not strictly true. I just was never allowed outside of school. Friendships only grow with shared experiences and parties, after school clubs, even going round to a friends' place to study, and I wasn't permitted to do that. It didn't take long before I stopped getting invited, and then I just stopped being a part of a group." I let out a bitter laugh. "It actually got worse when Richard became my boyfriend, if you can believe that. Before him, I was invisible and after...Well, after, I was just outright hated." Will slips his hand into mine as we walk. His fingers thread and grip. "When I left home it got better because I had Leon, and that's all I ever needed: just one person who had my back."

"You have Jason and me." Will looks over at me; his warm eyes and tentative smile make my chest ache. I squeeze his hand and return his heart-warming smile.

"I do, and I mean I have work colleagues but no one close. Not close enough to ask about this sort of stuff. I just figured I'd be doing it on my own."

"Well, don't," he states and rolls his eyes with obvious frustration. "When Sofia calls you, bite her arm off okay?"

"If she calls." I hate that I sound so reticent, but this is uncharted territory for me.

"Jeez, I'm never going to get another erection if you keep this pussy act up. Where's the badass that blew three men's mind a few weeks back." I snuggle into his side and laugh out a dirty sound that matches the images playing in my head now that he's mentioned his last visit.

"She's getting wet just thinking about that night, thank you very much." He lets out a strained groan. "How's the erection now?" I challenge with a wide and wicked grin, pushing my hip out and into his side as we walk, knocking him off balance. He grabs my hand and pulls me back to his side.

"Hard and painful, so thank you very much."

SEVEN

Sam

"CAN I DO ANYTHING TO HELP?" I ASK LOUDLY, WITH MY best attempt at sincerity, but in my head I am secretly chanting, 'Please don't say yes. Please don't say yes'.

"I've got it all covered, darling, but thanks." Will flashes a cocky killer smile my way. "This is one of my mum's dishes. It's a one pot thing, so it's pretty easy to put together, but so damn good." He slams the oven door shut and dusts his hands off in a briskly dramatic clap. "It's just a waiting game now, a couple of hours and that lamb will just fall apart." He beams and rubs his flat taut tummy in anticipation. "So what shall we do in the meantime?" He wiggles his thick brows and I blurt out a predictable laugh, shaking my head with exasperation.

"How about you tell me what Jason was like as a tearaway teen?" I steer his relentless innuendoes down a safer path.

"I was the tearaway, remember? Jason was the good guy—*is* the good guy." He pinches out a tight smile, but the muscle in his jaw is set solid. It wasn't my intention to make him uncomfortable, and I rush my words to rectify this.

"Hey, you're a good guy." I reach across the kitchen table where he is now sitting opposite me and take his hand in mine. "You just lost your way, and I struggle to believe Jason was ever a Saint." He lets out a small laugh, and his eyes wrinkle with a genuine smile.

"He really wasn't. Did he tell you about the girl we shared in Sixth Form College?" He grins, and I sit up straight and lean forward, because this sounds more than a little interesting.

"Um, he might've. I don't remember." I try to shrug off the truth of my ignorance and add some disinterest to counter my overly eager tone when I am so obviously desperate for Will to tell all.

"Liar, there is no way he would've told you." He laughs and then purses his lips, biting back the juicy tale. "Actually, he'll probably kill me if I spill…Forget it." He waves his hand in a slicing motion across his neck, but I grab his hand and turn his wrist back in a light, effective, and extremely painful twist. "Ahhh!" he grunts but doesn't fight it. If he did, I am just as likely to break his wrist at this angle and neither of us wants that. I just want him to carry on.

"Oh, no, no, *no*. No fucking way you can drop *that* and walk away. Spill the story, Will, or you'll get to see my nasty side." I put the smallest amount of pressure on his hand to make my point, but his groan is more erotic than pained.

"You know that's not a threat, right?" His wicked smile and heated gaze makes me remember Jason's comment about Will being more like Leon than himself when it comes to administered punishment and pain. I release my hold, and he lets out a deep and dirty belly laugh. I roll my eyes. *Relentless.*

"Tell me. You have to tell me. I promise I probably won't

tell Jason that I know." It's not much of a plea, but I won't promise something if I'm not one hundred percent I can deliver.

"Oh, that's all right, then," he mocks in a heavily sarcastic tone.

"And I'll protect you if he does try and kill you. How about that?" I bat my lashes and clasp my hands together to add a little begging to my plea.

"It wasn't that bad, but, ah, fuck it. Okay, I sort of had a girlfriend, but we were never really exclusive, or I was a douche. Whatever. Jason and I would share her, but we never *actually* told her." He has the decency to grimace at this confession, but I let it slide even if I happen to agree that it was a douche move. "Anyway, she told me that she fantasised about having us both together and arranged to meet us after our classes in the gym store. The lock on the door was pretty loose, and it was common knowledge it was a good place to get some."

"And you both went?"

"Um, horny seventeen year olds? Hell, yes, we went." He rolls his eyes at my naïveté. "Anyway, she was all shy and asked us to strip first. Honestly, you didn't need to tell us twice, then she asked us to turn around while she took her clothes off."

"Hmm," I encourage, but my mind is racing ahead with this tale. He pauses, and this adorable pink hue flushes his stubble sprinkled cheek.

"We waited and didn't even peek, but after a few minutes of silence, Jason turned, cursed, and sprinted to where our clothes should've been. They were gone, the girl was gone, and the only things left on the floor was a pair of her frilly panties and a gym skirt. We searched that whole damn store room for something else, but she must've cleared it out because there was nothing in lost property, no other gym bags, no banners or random sheets we could use to wrap around ourselves. There was nothing but the skirt and panties she had left for us. You have to remember no one had phones back then, so we couldn't call for help. But I think that was a blessing because no cameras either. We had to walk—well, sneak our way across town dressed in girls' under-wear, and no one has any evidence, thankfully."

"Jason wore panties?" I snort a loud incredulous laugh, and my eyes water, as I can't stop laughing. "Oh, my god, I can't believe he did that!"

"He didn't." Will laughs, too, holding his hand over his face and shaking his head with embarrassment. "He ripped up the gym skirt and just wrapped the material, trying to cover as much as possible. He left me with the panties that didn't fit and were tiny enough to offer no fucking coverage at all. Christ, our mum was mortified."

"You told your mum about sharing a girl?" I drop my mouth wide with shock.

"Fuck, no, she'd have had a heart attack, after she killed us, that is. No, we told her it was a prank, but still, she was horrified that her boys had walked through town, nearly five miles home, damn near butt naked."

"Brilliant! I love this girl. If I had been allowed friends, I would've snapped her up."

"It taught us to be up front, that's for sure, and it turned out she was more than up for sharing. She just didn't want to be played. Lesson learnt: cards on the table from the get go."

"So girlfriends are told at the beginning what might be in store?"

"They would be, but I guess that's unlikely now, isn't it?" He raises a brow, and I just smile. I'm going to take the fifth. I would like to say, "Never say never", given that Jason is happy to share my fantasy. But I am not so sure I would be quite so happy to share him.

Will's eyes flash with a knowing spark, and his smile widens. "I like that you feel that possessive. It's sexy as fuck, by the way."

"It's the Domme in me, what can I say?" I lift and drop my shoulders. I'm not sure that's it, because Jason is the epitome of a Dom, but maybe it doesn't make me sound so crazy needy.

"But not with Jason? You're not Domme with him?"

"I have my moments, but no." I tip the remaining wine from the bottle into his glass and tap the bottom. "Oh, no, it's broken?" I stick my bottom lip out in an exaggerated pout.

"Is this wise? I got into trouble the last time you got drunk." He takes a large sip.

"But I'm not actually drinking this time," I point out, and he frowns, looking at his empty glass and my can of Coke.

"How did I not notice this?" He slaps his hand to his head like he is the world's biggest sucker. He's quite adorable.

"More wine?" I push back from the table and make my way to Jason's impressive wine fridge.

"No, I'll have a beer. This stuff seems to make me talk too much."

"I like you talking." I return with a chilled Corona, but we have no limes, so I slice a lemon and cram a wedge in the bottle before I place it in front of him. "So you have a girl back home who knows 'upfront'?" I slide into the seat next to him.

"I don't."

"Good." I shake my head when his eyes widen at my comment. "Sorry, that came out wrong. What I meant was I didn't picture you as a cheater, so I'm glad you don't have a girl back home. But then I guess if she was clued in, then that would be good, too, if she was cool with it, I mean." I let out a heavy awkward breath. "And to think I'm this articulate when I'm not drinking."

"It's okay, I understand. I'd never cheat. That's the fucking worst." He spits the words with shocking venom that makes us both sit up straight and look at each other in surprise. "Sorry," he mumbles and takes a long pull of his beer.

"It's okay."

"What's he done now?" Jason strides into the room cloaked with unwitting tension, breezes through it, and heads straight to me. His hand slides around the back of my neck, and he bends down to give me the sweetest kiss. His eyes would be filled with apology, if they weren't so damn tired.

"Will has cooked lamb hot pot." I lick my lips, and he would normally hone in on that movement like a shark does the scent of blood, but his head snaps to his brother.

"Mum's lamb hot pot?" Will nods, and the smuggest grin creeps across his face. All trace of whatever the hell that was is gone. Jason groans. "Fuck, yes!"

EIGHT

Jason

T HE AMAZING SMELL WAS WAFTING AS I CAME IN THE front door, but Will confirming he has cooked my favourite meal has almost rescued this day from being a complete fucking nightmare…almost. We have good people at Stone, but when we have a delicate acquisition that Daniel would normally handle personally, and he is a little distracted, I have to go where I'm needed. I hate leaving Sam on a weekend; no, scrap that, I hate leaving Sam. Period. I steal another kiss because her head is just tipped ready and waiting. My lips are a little more forceful, and she rises to meet my mix of lust and needy aggression currently devouring her.

"Ahem, would you like a moment?" Will coughs his interruption, but it's Sam who pulls back. I couldn't give a fuck if he's here or not.

"Don't be silly. A moment is never going to be enough." She grins against my lips, but pushes me away playfully, stands, and moves to stand farther back. "Sit and I'll get you a beer. You look like you could use one." She sashays over to the refrigerator, and I slump into her vacant chair.

"I really could, although I would still prefer that 'moment'. I'm sure Will can manage on his own."

"You're incorrigible. Will has cooked for us," she states flatly, handing me the open bottle of iced beer. "I think you can keep it in your pants until after dinner, at least."

"Think again," I grumble, but she steps out of my reach and scurries around the kitchen table, using the large expanse of weathered oak as a successful barrier. *As if that would stop me.* She snickers, and her eyes dance with mischief and knowledge. I hold her gaze and delight in the flush of pink on her smooth, flawless cheeks. *She knows I will have my moment.* I take a long pull of my drink and turn to Will.

"So what have you two been up to?"

"Tourist shit. We took bikes for a ride around the parks, ran into Sam's friend, and then stopped at the market down the road to pick up supplies. Thought it's the least I could do as a thank you for all your hospitality." Will's brief summary is relayed with a warm smile, but his last comment is thick with sarcasm and pitched directly at me.

"When have I not been hospitable? When I let you crash here, or when I let you spend the day with my fiancée?" I counter.

"What do you mean let?" Sam butts in with an indignant tone.

"I could've taken you with me today." I stare her down.

"You could've tried." She holds my gaze, unblinking and hot as hell.

"You did verbally rip my bollocks off," Will adds and breaks my hold over Sam as we both look at him.

"You let Sam get completely smashed," I growl, and I can feel my temper rise.

"Again with the let—you get a brain transplant at work or something? Since when do you 'let' me do anything?" she snaps, and the anger dissolves, replaced with a wave of utter exhaustion. She's right; he's right. I drag a heavy hand through my hair and let out a heartfelt sigh.

"Fuck, I'm sorry. I'm just a bit on edge. I'm not sorry I laid into you for watching her get wasted, but I do know you would've been up against it trying to stop her." He narrows his eyes at me, then his face softens, and he twist his lips into a wide winning smile. I turn to face Sam. "The only thing I have or want control over with you, beautiful, is your safety, your heart, and when you come." My salacious grin and the fire in my eyes counter my stern tone.

"Forgiven." Sam leans over the table and places her hands on my face, staring with so much heat and love, it makes my chest pound with the strength of each heartbeat. "But you need to take some time off or you're going to give yourself a heart attack. No work tomorrow, understand?"

"You know it's not like that, Sam. This is just an exceptional situation that I have to handle."

"You're not going in, so think about ways you can 'handle' it over the phone, because that's all you're allowed, and that's only a maybe. It will all depend on if I'm in a giving mood," she states flatly, and I get the impression she is completely serious. *God, I love this woman.*

"Yes, ma'am." I purse my lips in a wry smile and lift my hand to my forehead in a Boy Scout salute.

"I'm going to hold you to that," she warns with a wicked wink.

"Don't tell Mum, but I think that was better than hers." Jason wipes his plate clean with the end of the crusty baguette before pushing the dish away. He leans back and pats his tummy, which despite the mammoth quantity of food, is disgustingly perfect and ripped.

"Oh, I am definitely telling her that!" Will puffs his chest out with pride, blows on his knuckles, and then polishes a pretend badge on his chest. I chuckle at his boastful stance, but it is completely justified. The lamb was melt in the mouth and the gravy was rich and to die for. "I'm going to get the train up tomorrow, just to show myself. Do you wanna' come? I know she's anxious to meet you." He holds Sam's startled bunny-in-the-headlights gaze, but then laughs. "Maybe not, then."

"Sorry." Sam lets out a shocked and nervous laugh. "I didn't mean to look so—"

"Horrified," Will offers as Sam struggles for the most appropriate word.

"I was going to say surprised," she corrects, but her expression is still this side of terrified. "Maybe just a bit more notice." She flashes a worried smile at me, but she doesn't need to be worried. The last thing I want to do is spend the day on a train.

"Mum doesn't like surprises, Will. Besides, I'm sorting out a proper visit."

"You are?" Sam's neck muscles strain to swallow that lump in her throat.

"I am. Don't panic. She doesn't bite, and my Dad is great." I wave off her concern.

"How could he not be? I'm sure the apples didn't fall far," she teases, but tension still edges her features.

"Who's Grace?" Will drastically changes the subject, but whereas I stiffen, Sam's brows furrow into intense lines of worry.

"The other night you said Grace's name, and Will must've

heard you." I stand and walk around the table, pulling her up, and then sitting back with her curled up on my lap.

"Oh." She relaxes a little, but I think that is because of my embrace, not so much my clarification.

"Sorry, Sam, I didn't mean to pry. Jason's right, I heard you talking in between bouts of hurling, and you sounded upset. I just wondered if Grace was a friend or someone important. You don't tend to mention many people so…Look, I'm sorry." He shrugs and grimaces at my scowl, but it's too late to retract it; it's out there now and up to Sam what she is comfortable telling my fucking nosy brother.

"No, it's okay. I guess she just comes out to play when I'm completely shit-faced because I don't think about her at all." She lets out a heavy sigh, and my arms constrict like a snake, holding her just that little bit tighter. My lips press against her silky hair, and she leans into my hold, absorbing the comfort I know she needs when she thinks about her childhood.

"Grace is my birth name, but I changed it when I left home at eighteen. I have not so great memories associated with being Grace. I know she's part of me, but not a good part. I think she was strong in her own way to endure what she did, but I'm more than happy with being Sam."

"Sam fucking rocks!" Will states emphatically, and she lets out a tiny laugh.

"Sam rocks my world, that's for sure." She tilts her head back so she can look up as I gaze down. Her dark eyes swim with emotion, and her lashes are laden with moisture.

"Thank you." She closes her lids but when she opens them, all traces of sadness are gone. Just. Like. That. She absolutely floors me. She is so fucking strong. "Anyway, I chose the name Sam in the bar when I met Leon, the day I left home."

"Really, how so?"

"Well, like I said, I didn't want to be Grace, and I had to think quick. I saw the rows and rows of liquor bottles and just picked the first that could pass as a girl's name."

"Sam?"

"Sambuca,"

"It could've been worse, you could've been called Gordon, Tia, or Jack."

"Oh, so many, many much worse options." She giggles. "I like the name Sam, but more importantly, I *love* being Sam." Her tone is filled with justified pride.

"I love having Sam." My voice is low and husky against her skin, and she giggles.

"Because Sam is a kinky fucker who obeys your every command." Her perfect brow is arched high at the rhetorical question.

"Damn right she does, and speaking of commands. Bedroom, first position...now!" She shivers in my arms, and my cock strains to impossible proportions in my pants, beneath her cute little arse.

"Riiight," Will groans. "Maybe I will head off to the club, after all."

I stand with Sam in my arms, her attention is fixed on me, and I can see her eyes burn with pent-up lust. I set her on her feet, but before I can repeat my 'now' comment, she has skipped from the room only pausing to place a quick good-bye kiss on Will's cheek. I reach in my pocket and throw my keys high over the table to Will. He snatches them from the air.

"Take my car if you go and don't bring anyone home," I clip, my request not a request at all.

"Not an option." His expression is implacable, but his eyes flash with something I can't quite place, but it's gone, and so am I. "I'll see you later," he calls after me.

"Don't count on it."

Shit. I have this shooting pain across my shoulders, and the instant I try to move my arm, I realise I can't. I can't move either of my arms. The reason my shoulder is cramping like a motherfucker is because I am handcuffed to my headboard. I stretch my neck hard to the left then right to ease some of the muscle tension, but it is set like concrete. The fact that I am aching like this means I have been asleep in this position for some considerable time.

"Sam!" I yell out and wait. Nothing. Several more full-volume shouts and I get a twinge of unease that she has perhaps left me here and fucked off or worse. "Sam, get your fucking arse back here right now and uncuff me, or so help me, I swear—" I stop mid shout when the bedroom door opens, and Sam enters with a tray of sweet smelling food. Barefoot, she silently shuffles across the floor and places the tray on my bedside table. Her smile is timid, and my eyes bore into her, watching her every move. She steps back, slightly out of my reach, not that I could reach her but she's rightly cautious.

"Care to explain?" I rattle the cuffs roughly, and she sheepishly bites her lips together.

"They are pretty self-explanatory, wouldn't you say?" She looks sheepish because she knows leaving someone cuffed is a big fat no-no. "They've only been on for a bit and I watched the whole time, well, except to go and get breakfast. You were perfectly safe." She lifts the cover on the tray, and a warm waft of fresh baked pancakes hits me harder than the fresh cafetière of coffee beside the plate.

"Not the point." I reprimand. "Okay, beautiful, what's

going on? You only ever get the pancakes out when you're worried." I pull hard against the cuffs and growl with frustration. I need her in my arms. This is unbearable and she will know that. "Talk to me, beautiful."

"I worry you work too hard. You looked so tired last night, and I needed to make sure you weren't going to take off in the middle of the night to go back to work."

"Why would I take off in the middle of the night?"

"Well, recently, every time your damn phone rings, you seem to have to go into the office." Her words are clipped with frustration, but I can see the genuine concern in her eyes. I breathe out a gentle puff and keep my voice calm. I know she has my best interests at heart, but tying me up was never going to be a great idea.

"This is exceptional. You know it's not always like this. Wait, my phone rang? I didn't hear it. Where is it?" I look toward the nightstand where I left my phone charging, but it's not there. "Sam?" I growl, fighting my rising anger.

"See, you were so tired, you didn't even hear it ring." Her hand drifts behind her, and I can only assume my phone is currently perched in the back pocket of her pyjama shorts.

"But I'm awake now, so how about you uncuff me and let me see who called." I grit out the words slowly through my clenched jaw.

"It was the office, someone named Greg. He didn't leave a message." Her hand is still tucked behind her back.

"Cuffs." I smile tightly, but my jaw is ticking nicely, and her eyes hone in on that little muscle as her head shakes slowly.

"How about you let me keep you cuffed and I make it worth your while to stay there all day." Her sensual tone does unfathomable things to my insides and my painfully hard cock, but…

"Tempting, but I still have to make that call to Greg. He won't have called me to shoot the breeze, Sam. It will be important."

"Hmm, a compromise then. I will let you make the call if you let me keep the cuffs on you."

"That's not a compromise, Sam. That is you getting your way."

"And that's bad because?" She fails at her attempt to look sheepish because her eyes shine with utter wickedness.

"It's not bad, baby, but it's definitely not a compromise." She holds my phone out and waves it in a teasing manner.

"Your call, Jason." She says my name in a singsong carefree tone that makes me flip.

"No." And there is no misunderstanding my resolute tone.

"No?"

"I'll happily play tie up, but I won't be manipulated. Even if it is done with the best intentions, beautiful." I add her nickname to try and soften the curtness and rage that is peeking through my veiled attempt at remaining calm and controlled.

"Shame." She places the phone next to the breakfast tray and sits beside me, the bed dips only slightly. Her fingers slide beneath the covers, and she pulls them down and off the side. I am naked, secured to the bedpost, and have the most enormous hard-on that springs to attention as soon as the sheet is dropped. Her hand wraps around the base, and she grips me tight. I hiss through my teeth because that pressure is fucking perfect. I can feel the blood surge under her hand, and I swell against her hold. She climbs onto the bed, her soft thighs encase mine, and her hair forms a curtain of loose hair partially covering her face when she dips to swipe her tongue over my sensitive tip. Her eyes never leave mine, predatory and scorching. Her tongue takes another swipe, and it's all I can do not to come right then. I suck in a sharp breath and let out an agonising groan when her lips cover the head of my cock and slide down as much as she can in one smooth beautiful move.

"Oh, fuck!" I would close my eyes, it feels so damn good when she does that, but her dark eyes are fixed on me as she works her way up and down my thick cock. And if that isn't the hottest thing, I don't know what is. Her hand moves over me in unison with her delicious mouth, and her tongue traces lines up my length and then sweeps and swirls over my tip, driving me fucking insane. My hips roll to encourage the rhythm she is setting, but I am under no illusion she is running this show. Her other hand cups my balls and tugs, her fingertips press the pressure point just behind my sack, and I feel the first surge of my climax. I choke out a gasp because her thumb presses firmly on my crown. It's like a fucking emergency stop. Shit! Before I can voice my objection, her hot wet lips are again taking me deep into her mouth and swallowing me down. The climax that had been denied starts to swell immediately in my balls and burns from the base of my spine through every single nerve ending.

My wrists burn with the strain I am putting on the cuffs. I so want to run my hands through her hair and just hold her right there, mostly to stop her from doing that again. I bite back a curse when she does exactly that. *Damn it*. Her smile is nefarious at best, but I think there might be a sadist lurking beneath the surface when she takes her sweet time dragging her tongue up the length of my throbbing erection after the third denied climax. Her breath is hot and feels like a flame on my raw, sensitive skin when she sighs and rolls back onto her heels.

"About that compromise." She smiles sweetly, and I know from the look in her eyes, she could do this for hours. I also know she won't top me, however delectable her bottom may be.

"Sorry, beautiful, what was that you said? I am a little out of it waiting for my next non-orgasm." Her eyes narrow, and she searches my face for any sign of the lie, but I am impassive, and I have never been so grateful she can't read the fucking torture that is on my face. She huffs and jumps from the bed. I let out a raucous laugh that sends her face into a furious reddening rage. She snatches up a pancake and forces into my laughing mouth. I continue to laugh while chewing down the food.

"Impossible." She turns and storms from the room.

I swallow the pancake, smiling to myself. It only takes a moment before I frown because I may have won that battle, but this victory hasn't actually improved my situation.

I shift and pull myself round to a kneeling position. The cuffs are sturdy, none of those hen party shit types you can get, unfortunately. The bedpost is also pretty heavy duty, solid steel frame. I rattle the bars, and it barely moves. Standing up, I try to pull up in a sharp jerking motion, which only cuts the cuff into my wrist. The pain is nothing, but the blood flows all the same. Shit.

"What the hell are you doing?" Sam gasps from the door and is instantly at my side, the edge of her cami-top pulled and screwed up against my wrist to stop the blood tricking onto the pillows.

"What does it look like?"

"Jesus, Jason, I was only gone a minute. I went to get the key."

"I didn't know that. For all I knew you had gone out for the day." My tone is flip and a little hostile.

"That doesn't even make sense. I want to spend the day with you, you idiot. That's why I cuffed you in the first place. You just don't play fair."

"I play very fair." I arch my brow and level a hard glare her way filled with as much irony as is possible. She has the decency to look a little sheepish.

"Okay, *I* don't play fair but I just—" She pulls in a deep breath, struggling for the right words. I help her out.

"I know, beautiful." I lean forward in lieu of being able to cup her face. She meets me half way and kisses my waiting lips. "How about we lose the cuffs and start again?" She fishes the key from her pocket and frees me. My wrists are raw, but I don't give them a second thought. I am instantly on her, pinning her to the bed and pressing my full weight on top of her body. "You are everything to me, beautiful. You know that? I will make this time up to you, but if I have to work, I have to work, and if I decide to let you tie me up, it's because I have made that choice. Understand?"

"I do now."

"Good." I cover her mouth and push my tongue roughly between her lips, sweeping in, and she fights me, fights my every push and pull. It's fantastic duelling for the next gasp and sigh. "By rights, I should make you pay for that little stunt, but I know you thought you were doing a good thing, so I will let it slide, just this once."

"You can punish me. I don't mind." She wiggles her sexy little body beneath me.

"Then it wouldn't be a punishment, would it?" I shake my head and sit back against the headboard, pulling her into my lap. "How about you feed me, and we work out what we are going to do in bed all day."

"Really?" Her smile is utterly breathtaking.

"Really." God, that smile just breaks my heart. She fucking glows with that simple concession. She leans over and puts the plate of pancakes on my stomach between us.

"They're a bit cold." She takes a nibble and offers me a bite.

"Hmm, they are, but still taste good. Besides, I don't mind, because the only thing I want on my tongue that's hot is you."

"Hot?" She wiggles her brows, sexy and suggestive, with eyes that dance with fire in them.

"And dripping." My voice drops to a low growl that rumbles from my chest.

"Always." She swallows back a whimper and sucks in her bottom lip. I can feel her heat and dampness against my skin. I groan when I hear my phone vibrate. Her shoulders drop, but she reaches over and hands me the mobile. I flick the screen and take the call.

"Guy, what do you need?" I keep my tone level, despite Sam arching back and pulling her camisole top clean off her body. She cups her perfect breasts and rolls the hard peaked nipples languidly between her fingers. *Oh, shit.* "You can handle that yourself." I choke back a cough when she pushes her middle fingers in her mouth, sucking them loudly and drops that hand into her shorts, hitching up a little so I know exactly where her fingers are heading. I have no idea what Guy is telling me, and there is no way I can contribute anything remotely constructive with this little show playing out in front of me in high definition "You need to handle this, Guy." I repeat a little more strained this time. "I won't be in today. If you can't sort it yourself, email me what you want me to check along with your notice." Sam raises a brow at my clipped tone, but dammit, there is a reason The Stone Corporation pays well. *Although it isn't necessarily so the Chief Operating Officer can eat his fiancée for breakfast.* I end the call and drop my phone on the floor with a thud and focus my glare on a startled looking Sam.

"Scoot up here, beautiful." I cup my fingers, encouraging her to climb farther up my body. She jumps to her feet, wobbling on the mattress as she pulls her pyjama shorts down and balances to get them completely off, kicking them across the room. She carefully steps on either side of my torso and lowers herself so her thighs slide on each side of my head. Now, that's what I call a breakfast of champions. My hands, thankfully free, grab her arse cheeks and pull her core flush to my eager mouth. God, she smells amazing. My balls ache like a motherfucker, and my cock strains against my stomach, *utterly intoxicating*. I drag my tongue along the soaking wet folds, lapping and sucking, my lips pulling her most intimate parts into my mouth. The tip of my tongue searches and dips inside. She is so damn wet I drink her down as she greedily rocks her hips against my face.

My fingertips grip harder, not to control her pleasure, but because I can't get enough, and the need to mark is so primal, I feel it in my soul. She cries out, and her hands fly to my hair, fingers pulling and gripping, as if I am her only anchor to Earth. My tongue sweeps long strokes and flicks lightly over her clit several times before I draw that needy nub of nerves into my mouth and suck down hard. It's an almighty detonation that I would have heard fall from her lips if her thighs hadn't clamped so hard around my ears, effectively cutting off any sound. Her legs tremble, and she shudders under my fingertips. Her essence pools onto my tongue, and I drink her down, every last drop.

After a few more full body shudders, she crawls back down my body and falls—no, collapses onto my chest.

Only after a few excruciating minutes of my hard-on brushing the curve of her backside every time I take a deep breath does she tip her head to look at me, a wry, cheeky smile curling her gorgeous mouth. *Oh God, that mouth.*

"Need a little help there, buddy?" Her eyes flash to between us.

"If you wouldn't mind, that would be perfect," I reply deadpan. She barks out a dirty laugh, and lifts up onto her knees and shuffles back to hover over my very angry-looking erection. She shivers as she slides down to the hilt, and her whole body grips and shudders as she holds me like a vice, sweet, hot, and sexy as fuck. Her head rolls back on a sigh, and when she looks at me through heavy long lashes, it is with the most heat outside of a supernova and just as spellbinding. She starts to rock, and with little encouragement, she is setting a perfect, punishing pace, and judging by the rapid breaths, flushes of colour on her cheeks, and the subtle sheen to her skin, she is just as close to a climax as I am.

"Jason…I'm close…sorry. I…I can't hold—" She moans out with a sexy catch of breath.

"Come for me, beautiful, I'm right with you," I groan.

"Oh God, thank you, thank you." Her head drops to her chest, and she pumps her little arse faster, chasing that release for both of us. I get the fire and shooting spike of pleasure at the base of my cock. My hands fist the flesh of her curves, and I grind her down onto me as I thrust hard and fast once, twice, and roar out a cry from deep in my belly, when every single muscle inside her grips my cock and squeezes me dry. She flops onto me, and I sweep my arms around her heaving frame. Her desperate breaths match mine, but we quickly fall in sync and calm to a less frantic breathing pattern.

"I think I'll need the day in bed to recover." I can feel her lips smile against my chest at my words.

"Me, too." She slides to my side, one sexy leg wrapped around my body, locking me to her.

"I said I wasn't going anywhere, there's no need for the vice grip, beautiful." I chuckle when she just flexes a tighter grip.

"I know, but I am happy with the vice grip. I feel safe with my legs coiled around you." I roll her on to her back and drop my weight heavily on to her.

"And I am happy when I have you like this, with me on

top."

"Hmm, is that so?" Her eyelids are already closed, and she follows those words with an adorable stifled yawn.

"Damn right, but mostly, I am happy when you are with me because then I know without a doubt that you are safe."

"Are you coming back here tonight?" I ask Will, as he is packing his rucksack in the kitchen. Sam fell asleep, and I took the opportunity to make some fresh coffee and get supplies to last the day. If she wants a day in bed, she's going to get a whole day in bed.

"No, probably not. I'll stay over at Mum's and catch the early train in the morning. The embassy should have my documents ready by lunch time, and my flight is tomorrow night." He pulls the straps tight and clips all the loose buckles and zips shut.

"It really was a flying visit?"

"Yep." He rakes his hand through his hair and looks nervous. "I thought maybe you two could come and stay with me for a bit before I start my new job. I still have some time off and thought it might be nice to hang out."

"Yeah, sure, that sounds great." It really does, with the hours I've been working, but I have no idea why he'd be nervous about that. "You look like you were going to ask for my first born there, what gives?"

"Sorry, I just wanted to ask something else." There goes his hand again, and I know that's not good, because I do exactly the same when I'm on edge.

"Go on."

"Sam...is she...I mean, she seems okay after what

happened, and I just wondered if she's just really good at hiding?" He looks strangely uncomfortable, which is even weirder because we have talked about this. He is pretty much the only one I can talk to about this, outside of Sam, so why he is having trouble bringing it up is just odd.

"She is really good at that, but I'm better at making sure she doesn't. So, yeah, she's good, really good actually. I've never known anyone so strong."

"Me, either, and she's really okay with the sharing?"

"That's two questions. It's me you should be asking, because I'm the one sharing, and no. But also yes, because that was for her. Her fantasy, and she needed that more than my jealousy. Besides, I can control the jealousy because I know for her, it is just that…fantasy."

"So it was just a one-time thing?"

"That's three questions, and that's between us, but you'll be the first or second to know. Do you mind telling me why you're acting so fucking weird all of a sudden? It's not like we haven't talked about this before. This is not new information, Will."

"Sorry, man. You're right, we have. It's just I guess the more I get to know her, it feels different, and I didn't mean to pry."

"Yes, you did. I know you care about her, and it means a lot that you do." I punch him on the shoulder. "I trust you, Will."

"Well, that just makes you an idiot." He laughs and punches me back on the top of my arm.

"Arsehole." My arm throbs because he hit it just right, fucker. He swings his bag over his shoulder, and I follow him to the front door. He stops on the threshold and pulls me in for a hug.

"When she got all bossy yesterday, man, that is seriously fucking sexy. I can't believe you've never let that side out to play." He lets out a low breath and a deep chuckle, pulling his collar wide at the neck of his t-shirt to supposedly let out some steam.

"It's sexy as fuck when she gets all possessive and caring, I agree, but I don't have a submissive bone in my body, so I just don't see the point." He nods in understanding, and I ponder for a second before feeling the need to clarify, since he hasn't walked away. "The only point would be if it was important to her, but she knows how I feel, so I don't think it would be *that* important." I absently rub the welt on my wrist. His eyes flick to my hand, and he grins when I add. "Well, if she didn't know how I feel, she does now."

Sam

CHARING CROSS TRAIN STATION IS HEAVING, AND I AM A minnow swimming against the tsunami of commuters trying to get to work. I live in a city that boasts top designers and world famous shops, but Sofia insisted on taking me out into the sticks to hunt down my wedding dress. She dismissed my suggestion of Harvey Nichols, Browns, or even Harrods in favour of what, she promised, was unique and perfect for me. I edge my way along the perimeter of the station to the spot we had arranged to meet. It's after nine, but the throngs of people keep coming in relentless waves as each train pulls in busting at the doors with crumpled and disgruntled passengers. I can't see what the lure of the countryside is that would induce me to endure that daily hell, no matter how green the grass or fresh the air.

I spot Sofia, hard not to, in her bright red three-quarter length wool coat, nipped at the waist with a thick buckle belt and a matching woolen hat with a huge fluffy pompom. She waves like a crazy person when she sees me, pushing through the crowd to close the distance. She squeals and wraps her arms around me, hugging with the strength of a bear, not the petite and immaculate Italian princess she resembles. She doesn't act like a Princess; at least I have never witnessed any behaviour that is remotely precocious. Although Marco, her twin and manager of the club, has informed me she is more than capable of tossing a tantrum or two, but she is hardworking and has only ever been kind, genuine, and sweet to me. Today is a perfect example. She jumps us both up and down, excitedly displaying hidden strengths in those tiny arms.

"I'm so excited. I can't believe you asked me!" She beams at me, dark eyes sparkling with sincerity and joy. "I'm so honoured, Sam. I won't let you down." Her breathless excitement is replaced with a seriousness that takes me by surprise. It's just a dress.

"Um, I think it's me that is honoured, Sofs. You taking time off work just to buy a dress." She steps back, her hands flying to hold her gasp in. She shakes her head dramatically, her eyes wide with horror.

"Just a dress—you sound just like Bets. What is wrong with you two? It's not *a* dress. It's *the* dress." She threads her arms through mine and leads me head-on into the opposing wall of walking commuters. "It's like we're not even the same species," she mutters, tutting and shaking her head.

"Just a little out of my comfort zone, Sofs." I shrug and offer an apologetic smile.

"Well, you are slap-bang in the center of mine, and if you'll let me, I'll happily lend a hand." The pitch and tone of Sofia's declaration is filled with hope, and her eyes sparkle with anticipation, which honestly takes me by surprise. Something I fail to hide in my voice.

"Really?"

"Are you kidding me? I'm an event planner, Sam, I live for this shit. Although at work I don't get to do weddings. I have done one wedding, and even if I do say so myself, it wasn't too dusty." She puffs out her coat-clad chest with justified pride

"Sofia, it was perfect." She lets me go so we can file through the ticket turnstile. "Did you really do all that yourself?" I raise a sceptical brow.

"Pretty much." She nods and holds my gaze. "I know that's difficult to believe. You've met my family, after-all, but I had to take charge or my mum and aunts would've taken over, and there wouldn't have been a venue outside of Buckingham Palace that would've been big enough or grand enough." She smiles but rolls her eyes with humour. "Mums and their daughters." She snaps her mouth at her mistake, and before I can shake off her error, she has pulled me into another bear hug. "Oh, God, Sam, I'm sorry. I didn't mean anything." She squeezes harder, and I swear I feel a rib crack. "You're going to sack me before we even start, aren't you? Sorry, so, so sorry." She pulls back and holds my gaze, her face a picture of remorse.

"Sofs, stop. It's fine." I laugh, and I would be speechless but her face is still etched with heartfelt concern, so I continue. "I happen to agree." The soft edge to my response and sincere smile has a visible impact on her frame: her shoulders relax, she lets out a breath in a puff, but her eyes are still fixed on me. "Your mum dotes on you, Sofs, adores you, is your biggest cheerleader, and that is a beautiful thing. It is how it should be between parents and their children. Unconditional and unre-served, but just because I didn't have that type of relationship with my mother doesn't mean you can't talk freely about yours. That's just crazy." I pause to let my words sink in, and as they are quickly absorbed, Sofia is, once more, bright eyed and beaming at me. "And there is no way you're getting the sack. You're the only candidate, so you can pretty much say what you like, you're going nowhere." We walk the length of the platform to the middle of the train.

"Even so, I am sorry."

"Enough with the apologies," I clip but keep my tone light, holding my hand up to halt any further discussion.

"Okay." Sofia flashes a quick smile, finally accepting that topic is dead. "And I doubt I'm the only one, though, but I am super glad I am."

"How about the only permissible candidate?" Sofia's brows pinch with confusion, and she waits for enlightenment. "Jason wasn't a fan of me asking Leon, and he said he would come if you couldn't. He wasn't going to let me come on my own. Which is sweet, but—"

"Um, no, to both," Sofia snaps an interruption, wildly shaking her head in horror. "No way you would come on your own, and no way Jason could go with you."

"Sam, I would've understood if you'd told me to go to hell after what happened with Peitra." Sofia has been nothing but a brilliant friend, but still, Peitra is part of her family. "She's lucky she didn't get life, Sam, and she would've for kidnapping. It's only your statement that meant she got away with—"

"She's still your cousin, Sofs, and family is—"

"Family is everything, Sam, but it can also be fucked up and not who we would choose to have in our lives. What she did… You could've died… So, no, Sam, you are not the one I will be telling to go to hell."

"Families." I shrug off the heavy turn of the conversation with a puff of frosty air and an exhale of held breath. Since her arm is still threaded through mine, she squeezes it in the crook of hers, securing me to her side. The brief silence is broken when she turns to me,

"I can't imagine what you went through, but one thing you don't ever have to worry about is where my loyalty lies. You're a dear friend, Sam, and this is your day so, let's not dwell on events we can't change, and focus on making magical the events we can." Her bright smile and pure, kind words make my eyes tingle and my nose pinch. For fuck sake, when did I get so damn emotional? I swallow back the surge of raw feelings threatening to hijack this day before it even begins.

"Sounds good to me." I blink a few times, dispersing any residual liquid before it pools into big fat tears.

"Good." Sofia holds both my hands in hers and does a little excited bunny hop, unable to contain the pent-up joy in her body a moment longer. "And Jason is not allowed to see the dress you pick. That means no describing either. You have to promise," she warns with a sudden seriousness in her tone that is at odds with the bundle of bubbling excitement that is the woman before me.

"Lips are sealed." I motion to zip and lock my lips but leave a tiny gap to ask. "Although, since he's paying for it, shouldn't he have some say?"

"Absolutely not." She waves her hand, dismissing my silly notion with a flick of her wrist. The train doors open, and we step into the now-empty carriage and take seats next to the window, which has a table and four places to sit, two each facing each other. Sofia slides in next to me, still shaking her head. "Not a peek, it's tradition. Some traditions are flexible, but that one is set in stone," she warns, and I nod in agreement, failing miserably to hide my amusement.

"If you say so." I chuckle at her indignation.

"I do." The train pulls out, and we fall silent as the city vista slips away, replaced by frosted furrowed fields and winter-worn skeletal trees and hedgerows. "How much help do you want? I don't want to step on toes, so it's probably best if you lay out what you want me to do. Or is it just today?" Her dark brown eyes are so similar to Marco's, it's unnerving when her features otherwise are so delicately feminine. She holds my gaze, but I notice her gloved hands are clasped tightly together.

"Seriously, you don't mind helping?" Her eyes light up wide and incredulous. She beams at me, shaking her head.

"Was I not clear? Because I'm pretty sure I was over the bloody moon when you called." Her genuine pleasure about today is infectious, and I find I am enjoying the first flushes of excitement too.

"Not just being polite, then?" I tease.

"God, no, I don't have time for that shit. You're one of my best friends, Sam, and seeing you and Jason finally get it on, I'm really happy for you. So just take it I will do whatever you want me to. I don't need a title or anything." Her words may say one thing, her intonation and pleading eyes say something entirely different.

"You want a title?"

"I really do." She puts her hands together in a glove-muffled clap.

"What like Queen or something?" She snorts out a laugh.

"Maybe just Maid of Honour, although I quite like Queen." Her bright smile dances playfully across her face, but I am struck hard by the sentiment.

"Would you?" I hate that my voice has even a hint of insecurity, because that is not me, but this whole rite of passage, girl-bonding thing, is something I have never done. I have friends, but whenever I needed a little more, there was always Leon. I have never asked for anything; I have pretty much fended for myself for ten years. More than ten years when I consider the non-existent nurturing I received from my mother. But as foreign as this feels to me, Sofia makes it surprisingly easy.

"Abso-fucking-lutely, I thought you'd never ask." She grins a smile that would shame Alice's Cheshire cat.

She had arranged three appointments and saved the best until last. At the far end of the town is a long Victorian parade of shops with a paved pedestrian courtyard. One side has a canopied overhang that is supported by thin white columns stretching the length of the parade. We pass several boutiques, a teashop, and an Italian cafe where we stopped for lunch in-between fittings. Third from the end, Sofia stops and pulls the shop door open for me to enter. The ornate metal curled around a small bell above the door announces our arrival, and we step into a room so light it rivals the mid-morning sun in high summer. Sparkles and masses of cream, ivory, and white silks bounce and reflect the light off the many mirrored surfaces and are almost as bright as the smile of the young woman that greets us.

"Hello, hello, welcome, come in." She waves us in with both hands and bounces a little on the balls of her feet with obvious excitement. She steps up to me before hesitating; her hands twitch, and I wonder for a moment whether she is going to give me a hug. There is clearly an internal struggle with desire and propriety waging. Instead, she pulls one of my hands into both of hers and pumps them up and down vigorously. "I'm Katie. This is my shop, and all these dresses I designed and made myself—the veils too." There is that megawatt smile again, bursting with pride this time. I can't see all the dresses in detail because they are covered with a protective sleeve but the one in the window is stunning. Lace over silk, full skirt nips at the waist, and a high collar, not my personal taste, but I can appreciate the skill and detail.

"The dress in the window is very beautiful," I remark and she lets go of her hold and walks over to the dress in question.

"It was my first, so it's a little dated now. I keep if for show, but it wouldn't do for you." She shakes her head dismissively. She motions for us both to take a seat. "Would you like some champagne?"

"Do bears sh—" Sofia coughs out an embarrassed interruption, but I can see Katie is stifling a snicker or two.

"We'd love some, thank you." Sofia answers and rolls her eyes at my smirk. I can't help myself. The last two fittings were tortuous, enduring pompous snooty ladies with zero sales skills and even less manners. One visibly turned her nose up at my kitten panties, the photo image neatly covering my own *kitten*. The other, I swear, picked out the ugliest dresses for me to try, and when I asked if there was anything remotely sexy, she was horrified. When she said, 'A bride isn't supposed to be sexy, she is supposed to be virginal', it took all my effort not to retort, 'That ship sailed when we had a four-way with his brother and my best friend', but for Sofia, I held my tongue. If this fitting is the same, I am ordering my dress from eBay.

Katie returns with a chilled bottle in a silver iced bucket and three glasses. I like her already.

"Now, would you like to have a look through or would you like me to select some of my designs that I think will work best?" I take a large gulp of my drink.

"At this point, it doesn't seem to matter what I *would* like." Katie's brows pinch together above her pale blue eyes.

"Come on, Sam, don't be like that." Sofia nudges me, knocking my drink but not spilling it.

"I'm not ungrateful, Sofs, but you have to admit those last two places were awful."

"They really were. They weren't like that when I went, but then I had Mama, and you don't get away with that sort of attitude with her."

I scoff lightly. "No, nor me on a normal day, but this is not a normal day."

"It certainly isn't a normal day," Katie interrupts, picking up her glass and raising it toward us both. "This is a precursor to the best day of your life, so let's start it right. You get exactly what *you* want. So tell me what you asked for that was so impossible?"

"Sexy. I want a sexy wedding dress. Jason is hot and I want to make him groan when he sees me at the other end of the aisle because he knows he can't have me for a few hours." I clink my glass at her, waiting for the judgemental brow, but it doesn't come, not even when I add shamelessly. "I know Jason, it won't be hours. I'll be lucky if I make it to the vows."

"Oh my, that *is* hot." She sighs, downing her own drink and fanning herself. "I have the perfect dress." She puts her glass down and turns away, but instantly she turns back. "Look, I am happy to pull out several other dresses, but I know the perfect one. Do you want to go through the motions or do you trust a complete stranger?" Her face is light with excitement and for the first time today, I share that feeling.

I glance at Sofia who lifts her shoulders in a noncommittal shrug. My decision then. "In your hands, Katie, do your worst."

"I only ever do my best." She grins, and while I am expecting her to pick through the mysterious hanging gowns, she again disappears into the back of the shop. She is tiny, maybe five foot four and petite; her blonde bob is tied neatly in a ponytail. She is wearing a fitted black pencil skirt and tight back t-shirt with Katie T embroidered on the back. None of this I can see when she returns, as her hands are held high above her head and she walks the covered dress in like a gothic headless bride. She reaches high on her tiptoes and hangs the dress on a hook next to a massive gilt mirror opposite where Sofia and I are seated. There is a cubicle, but she pulls the curtain closed and proceeds to move three oriental partitions to cover the main window to the street. She glances around the room with a finger tapping lightly on her lips like something isn't quite right. I take the time to pour another drink. Sofia starts to shake her head when I offer to refill her glass, her resistance half-hearted at best. Katie pulls out a large sheet from a drawer and throws it over the huge mirror and smiles, having prepped the room to her internal specifications.

"Right, Sam, up, up." She motions for me to stand while she starts to unzip the long protective sleeve.

"Kit off to undies?" I ask but I have already taken off my sweater and am undoing my jeans.

"Bra, too." She gives a playful smile at my wide eyes and panicked glance at the glass fronted shop window. "They won't be able to see in, I promise. Just make sure you stand in the center of the shop." She smiles mischievously, but my momentary disquiet is instantly replaced by wonder.

"Oh, wow!" I whisper, my fingers reaching to touch the delicate lace. Even though the hanger fails to do the gown justice, I can see it is a stunning dress. "Is that lace sheer?"

"Kind of. Let's get it on and you can see for yourself."

"But won't people be able to see…everything?"

"You said sexy, not slutty." She sounds mortified and places her hand on her heart like I have wounded her.

"Sorry, it's just…"

"Here." She ignores my concern and scoops the dress into

her arms. "Can you drop so I can lift it over your head? You damn Amazonian goddesses and your height!" She snickers as I easily drop to my haunches in my bare feet and panties. "I'm just jealous. This dress really only works on someone of your height, build, gorgeousness, and confidence." She steps back, letting the surprisingly weighty material glide down my body, kissing my curves, and holding to me like a delicate second skin. Thin straps hold the unbelievably soft lace bodice and full-length mermaid tail dress up, but the scooped backless cut means they are the only things holding the dress up. The edging barely covers the curve of my backside, the material hugging me perfectly so there are no immodest gaps displaying more than is decent. This dress is decadently sinful. It's a paradox, and it is fucking perfect. Katie fusses and straightens, pulling and primping. I stand silent, just gazing down at my body. I have no idea what is looks like on with no reflection, but from Sofia's glazed expression and silence, I think it looks as good as it feels. Katie steps back and pulls the sheet from the mirror in a dramatic flourish, which isn't nearly as dramatic as my gasp. My hands fly to my mouth, and my damn eyes prickle. What. The. Fuck? I am not this emotional…ever. It's a dress, for fuck's sake. I draw in a deep, steadying breath. But it is a beautiful dress. No, it's more than that; it's my beautiful dress, and it's perfect.

"I know I am going to sound all sales womany, but this was made for you, sweetie." Katie crosses her arms, again fighting her desire to hug me, I think, but her face is beaming with pride. Rightly so—she created a masterpiece.

"You don't need to be a sales woman with this, Katie. I'd be crazy not to take this dress." My eyes flit to Sofia, who stands and positions herself beside me, slipping her hand into mine.

"I don't know about Jason, but I'm thinking of switching

sides." She nudges me, and I snicker.

"God, Sofs, you're so disgusting, always making everything about sex," I tease and laugh when her cheeks flash bright red with instant mortification.

Katie helps me change, and we discuss cost and other fittings because apparently it's not that dress I'm buying; that was a sample, and granted, no one else had tried it on, still she wanted me to have something custom-made, and she wanted to tweak this design specifically for me. I wasn't going to argue. She was on-point with that selection, and I have absolute faith that she will make me feel like a Princess; a sexy-ass Princess, but still a Princess.

By the time we finish, I am starving and can't face the train journey home on an empty stomach.

"I need to eat." I pat my grumbling stomach, having only had a very light lunch, and with nearly a whole bottle of champagne between us, I am also a little light-headed. We huddle together, walking against the biting wind. Sofia nods, but her affirmation is muffled by the thick woolen scarf trying to strangle her. "What about here?" She nods, and we enter the first half decent looking bar that serves food. It turns out it serves very good food, but also wickedly good cocktails.

We flop into the seat on the train in a fit of giggles that started over what, I don't remember, and just continued throughout the meal, the many…far too many cocktails and the walk to the train station. I try to hush Sofia as I pick my vibrating phone from my purse. My fingers are gloved and my ability to focus is somewhat impaired: I miss the call. Turns out I missed several calls. I press the call return button and Jason picks up on the first ring.

"Hey, beautiful, are you okay?" His voice is deep and thick with concern. I need to not sound drunk.

"I am perfectly fine, thank you, Jason." Nailed it.

"Are you drunk?" His tone has switched from concerned to pissed. *Dammit.* I know he will have been worried, and if I had returned any of his calls this wouldn't be a problem. It needs to not be a problem.

"I bought a dress." I try for deflection.

"Are you drunk?" he repeats, his tone less impassive, more tempered fury, and it's got my back right up.

"I'm an adult, Jason, and if I want to get shit-faced, I can. You know exactly where I am and who I am with, so back off. You wanted me to do this, and after a shitty start, I managed to find the perfect dress and have some fun too. And, yes, I may well regret the two for one cocktails in the morning, but not now. You have no right to be pissed."

"I have every right. You didn't answer my calls, and I was fucking worried, so, yes, I have every right to be pissed, but I'm not pissed. I was just fucking worried." His tone is stern, but the undercurrent of concern far outweighs his irritation.

"I was perfectly safe, Jason." My voice softens because I can feel the tension in his voice. I know why he feels this way, and we both hate that any reminder of that dark time hurts us both. But him more so I think, because he felt so impotent. "I'm sorry I didn't call. I called as soon as I saw the missed calls, but I am sorry you were worrying. You have my tracker, Jason. You knew where I was. I am perfectly safe."

"Drunk on a train with Sofia isn't perfectly safe," he grumbles, but the fire has left his voice.

"A little drunk and the next stop is Charing Cross in thirty minutes. I'll be home before you know it. I will probably be home before you with the hours you're clocking." I risk a tentative laugh to try and lighten his mood.

"I just want you safe," he repeats almost to himself, and my heart aches that he hurts like this.

"I know."

"Call me if someone so much as looks at you, okay?" I bite my lip to stop from snickering at his ridiculously over-protective demand.

"See you at home, Jason. I love you, but I can still take care of myself."

"I know you can, beautiful, but that doesn't mean I will let you." He hangs up before I can retort, my drunken self a little slow with the witty comeback.

TEN

Jason

"DAMN IT!" I CURSE IN THE QUIET OF MY OFFICE. I SLIP the phone into my jacket pocket and scoop my unfinished report into my briefcase. I know she's capable of taking care of herself, and I am stoked she's bought a wedding dress. But I am less than fucking pleased my beautiful girl is about to hit a central London train station this late at night, armed with little more than her sexy arse, her smart mouth, and Sofia. I check my watch. I have time if there is no traffic, but this is London, there is always fucking traffic.

I manage to park around the back of the station in a narrow dead-end street. I slam the car door and set off at a fast pace, clicking the lock behind me as I race to the main street and the side entrance of the station. Checking the arrivals board, I catch my breath when the train information indicates a delay. I open my phone and see I have a missed call from Sam. It rings again just as I am about to press the call return button.

"Hey beautiful." My tone has less urgency now I know she's near, but my heart is only going to stop the jack-hammering in my chest when I actually have her in my arms, safe.

"Hi, I called to let you know the train is delayed, but actually, it's pulling in now so that's good. I should be home soon. Are you still at work? Have you eaten?" She's rushing her words, and I don't know if it's the alcohol or whether she thinks I'm still pissed.

"I'm not at work and I have eaten, although I am still *hungry.*" I deliberately drop my tone and lay a thick layer of salacious intent on that last word. I hear her breath catch. Oh good, it didn't go unnoticed.

"Um, I could probably help with that." Her voice is a breathy whisper.

"Oh, I know you could. Just so you know as soon as I see you, I am going to *devour you*" My tongue wets my bottom lip as I watch her train pull slowly to a complete stop, having reached the end if its line.

"Promise." She sighs, and that slow exhale makes my balls ache and my cock twitch to life.

"Promise," I state. My voice is softly hoarse, but my gravelly tone is more of a threat. I can hear the smile in her voice, but more importantly, I can see it too. Sofia has her arm threaded through my girl's, and they are hurrying to the ticket turnstiles.

"I will hold you to th—" She freezes when her eyes meet mine. Sofia turns to check her friend and slowly follows her line of sight to me. Sam bites her smile as her eyes search my face for some tell, and I keep my expression neutral. Now I can see her and know she is fine, I can relax and have some fun. I watch her slender throat contract and swallow; her chest rises under her warm winter jacket as she draws in a deep and steadying breath. She tips her chin and strides purposely toward me. Before she reaches me, I can't help myself; I close the distance and sweep her into my arms, across my body, and dip her low, swallowing her gasp with my kiss. Deep and urgent, breathless and sexy as fuck, she returns each swirl of my tongue, each moan and more, as if we are the only two people in this station. But we're not. Sofia coughs after an awkwardly long time, clearly gauging that we have no intention of stopping. I promised I would devour, and I keep my promises.

"Um, I'm going to grab a taxi," she mumbles. "So, thanks for today, and I'll see you around." I stand, pulling a dazed and pliant Sam with me. My arm is tight around her waist when she sways, not from the alcohol she has consumed, but from the desire evident in her heavy hooded lids.

"No need for a taxi, Sofia. We will drop you home," I inform her.

"No, don't worry; it's no bother. It's a ten minute taxi ride, and you look…" Her face turns bright red, and her eyes widen with embarrassment as she struggles to finish that sentence. Sam helps her out.

"Don't be silly. We practically drive past your place, and after all you've done, it's the very least. Really, Sofs, the very least. I am so happy you came today."

"It was my pleasure. If you're sure…" Sofia's eyes flit over to the long queue of people freezing in the wind whipping around the taxi rank and puts up no further polite objection.

"We're sure," I state and take Sam's hand and lead her to the exit. Sam stretches her other hand and makes sure Sofia is also in tow.

Sam slips into the back seat with Sofia, and now I feel like a fucking chauffeur as they continue to giggle about nothing. I feel Sam's hand at my neck and her fingers try to twist the hair at my nape. I like that, even as she is engrossed in conversation, she needs to touch me. No, I fucking love that, but she was right to sit in the back. My hands grip the steering wheel, knowing exactly where one of them would be if she had sat in the front, regardless of who was in the back. Sam's voice is at my ear as she breaks the train of thought that is causing a painful pressure in the base of my cock as it endeavours to expand in very cramped conditions.

"Jason, it's the most beautiful dress. You'll love it." She sighs and my heart swells more than my cock for once at the utter joy in her tone.

"I don't doubt that for a moment, beautiful. I'm glad you found something you liked."

"Oh, I loved it. It's made of—" Her words are muffled, and a struggle ensues as Sofia manhandles Sam into silence.

"Noooo!" I flinch at the volume of the screech that bounces in the confined space of my R8. "Sam, you can't...not a word," Sofia scolds.

"I just wanted to share a bit. I wasn't going to describe the low—" Her words are silenced once more with a light slap of a palm over her mouth, and her sentence is finished with in incoherent string of muffled nonsense.

"Nah-ah! Not. A. Single. Word. Understand?" Sofia's tone brooks no argument, and I chuckle when Sam muffles her acceptance and adds a promise to reveal nothing more. Not that she actually revealed anything other than she thought it was perfect. That in itself is not breaking news—anything on her would be perfect—but preferably nothing is better. Perfection needs no adornments.

I park the car and switch the engine off. Sam had switched to the front seat once we dropped Sofia home, but promptly fell asleep as soon as I started the short drive to our home. She is still sleeping even as the engine dies. I get out and walk around to her side, open the door, and still, she is dead to the world. Unfortunately, the car is too low to lift her straight into my arms without knocking her unconscious on the doorframe.

"Hey, you sleepy drunk, I can carry you to bed, but you need to get yourself out of the car." I tap her nose, which twitches under my fingertip. Her eyelashes flutter and open, her sleepy sexy smile spreads wide across her face before a cute frown forms, and she turns on her side away from the cold night breeze circling around the open door.

"It's cold, leave me be," she grumbles.

"It'll be much colder in about an hour when the heat has left the car. Come on, beautiful, let's get you to bed." I lean over and unclip her belt. She continues to grumble, but lets me ease her out of the car and puts up no fight at all when I lift her into my arms. I kick the car door shut and walk up the front steps with my arms blissfully full. I swipe the finger print entry and decide to take her straight up the stairs. I can finish my work later; she is going to need me.

I lay her on the bed where she wakes enough to help me undress her.

"I'm really sleepy." She crawls under the covers, all soft and gloriously naked, but she looks exhausted. So as much as I want to jump right in after her, jump on her, I tuck her in and go to fetch her some water. I kiss her forehead before I turn to leave; she is unconscious the moment her head hits that pillow. I still have work to do.

I didn't hear the footsteps on the stairs, but I hear the light padding across the kitchen floor. I rub the tiredness from my eyes, but before I can stretch the ache from my spine and tension in my muscles, her fingers are pressing a heavenly massage on my shoulders from behind. I groan when her knuckles dig into a tight knot of muscle.

"Have you been working this whole time?" Her voice is soft but filled with concern. It's almost three in the morning, and I tucked her into bed just after twelve.

"I have a lot on at work, and I wanted to clear my workload." I stretch out my neck to one side and feel the pop of pressure release. Her soft warm lips brand my skin, and I close my eyes and feel the burn. Her tender kisses trace a path to my ear when her warm breath whispers.

"Clear it for what? You have plans you're not telling me?" Her lips pull my lobe into her mouth, and her teeth bite gently to hold me captive. I feel the bite in the base of my spine and the pinch in my balls. I suck in a breath and hold back a groan.

"Keep teasing, beautiful, and I will bend you over this table," I grumble low and serious. I can feel her lips smile around my caught skin.

"Now who's teasing?" She sucks my lobe in and lets it go with a long drawn out release. "You *have* to be too tired—" She squeals as I swiftly take her across my body whilst standing up. I flip her mid-cry and push my palm flat and hard between her shoulder blades.

"Never too tired, beautiful," I interrupt, my lips against her ear, my voice hoarse with instant feral lust. I roll my hips against the flimsy silk shorts that offer absolutely no protection against my now raging hard-on. "Never too tired," I repeat. It's more like a possessive growl as I stand up but keep her pressed flat with one hand. My other hand deftly releases my cock and tugs her shorts down the curve of her perfect arse. I fist the base of my cock and slide it between her cheeks. She wriggles but tries to open wider for me. Her shorts though are trapped around her thighs when I kicked her legs wide as I pushed her flat; this is as wide as she can get. Not a problem. I push into her heat slowly, but she's so damn wet, and I am on the edge of exhaustion, so the gentleman part of me is taking a nap right now. I lunge, full force, slamming my cock balls deep and more. She grunts out a puff of air that I feel I have pushed from deep inside, filling her as I am. I pull back and do the same. This time her back arches, and she tilts her hips to take me deeper. God, I love this woman. I grab her hip and pull her back as I thrust forward, and I know from that particular pitch of cry, it hurt. I also know from that little moan that escapes the back of her throat that she fucking loves it. I thread my other hand into a fistful of her long mane and pull her back into a perfect bend, all stretched and taut.

"Harder," she gasps, her throat struggling to swallow at the angle I'm forcing. She turns her head to meet my gaze. Damn, she's on fire. Her eyes shine with such passion, liquid with wanton need and deep with desire for me.

"Fuck!" I growl out at as pure fucking ecstasy shoots through my body at her demand. I obey. I obey her because she fucking owns me. I thrust deeper, harder, and she holds her breath, eyes pinched tight, absorbing everything I'm giving her. I pump, relentlessly chasing the release that is crawling from the ache in my balls, poised on the edge, and I growl. "Come with me, Sam."

"Oh, God…I…I can't…You're so deep…feels so good…Ah, hmm…but…" She pants out the words, struggling to speak, but I know she can…she just needs a little help. My fingers on her clit would work or, in this instance, my thumb slipped into her tight arse. She drops her head, making me release her hair, her forehead thumps on the table as her whole body trembles and she takes me with her. Wave after wave of blissful, erotic, and sexy as hell contractions pulse around my impossibly hard cock. My fists grip her hips, anchoring me to her body as one. She sucks in long, deep breaths, as do I. But her body continues to shudder, ripple and ebb as her climax dissolves under my fingertips. I slip out of her and pull her into my embrace, sitting back into my chair. She snuggles into my hold, nestling into my chest and breathing me in as much as I do the same with her. My nose is in her hair, inhaling all her exotic scent: jasmine, ginger, and Sam. She is utterly intoxicating, addictive and lethal, my only drug.

"What plans?" she asks after our heartbeats have quietened and our breaths are not so frantic.

"This weekend, we're visiting my folks, but I thought at the end of the month, we could take a week out and visit Will, count some turtles or some shit." She sits up and swivels so her legs are draped over mine, her now dripping heat over my still-interested cock. Dammit, I need to sleep; she's gonna kill me with this insatiable desire. Her hands cup around my neck, and she looks up with sleepy eyes and the widest smile.

"I would love that." Her sweet lips cover mine, her tongue darting inside and dancing with mine. I pull her close and hold her there, still...immobile. She giggles into my mouth. "No need for that, you nearly killed me with that last orgasm. I need to sleep, too. I have no idea how you are still conscious." I stand, and she coils her long legs around my waist. I kick my trousers free so we don't fall when I start to walk and take us both back to bed.

"It helps I have the sexiest fucking woman in the world... whenever I want her...I'll sleep when I'm dead, beautiful." I thought she would giggle, but she holds me a little tighter and is quiet. "Hey, you okay?"

"I'm good," she says quietly, but I stop and wait for her to look up.

"Sam?" I prompt when she doesn't

"You work too hard." Her face tilts, and her eyes are deep, dark pools brimming with liquid. My chest feels tight and burns with the love I see reflected in her gaze. It's scary as hell, when you realise just how much another soul means to you. How vulnerable that makes you, weak, but it is also the *very* best thing in the world. It is the very reason to take that next breath because you get to share it with the one person that makes every day worth living.

"Hey, I'm not going anywhere." I brush my lips with hers and draw a smile at the slightest touch, instantly easing her troubles. "We just have a lot on, and Daniel is prepping for paternity leave, so it's unusually crazy. These last few weeks are not my typical, I promise." I tip my chin for her to kiss me, and she does, her hands moving from my neck to my face, cherishing me with her touch and the softness in her dark chocolate eyes.

"I'm not moaning. I just worry." She holds my gaze and my heart with her tender love and concern. "How about we skip tomorrow evening and have a night in just us?"

"Fuck, no, I made a promise. It's Valentine's Day, and I gave you my word. I may work hard, but I play hard too, and I am a man of my word. The Reaper himself is the only damn thing that will keep me from you tomorrow night, beautiful."

"Wow, I have never had anyone *that* eager to submit." Her grin is pure wickedness. I kick the bedroom door open and stride in, throwing her high onto the bed. Her shrill scream is drowned by hearty laughter.

"Eager to get it over and back to normal." I crawl up the bed as she edges away, slipping on the silky covers so I easily catch her beneath me.

"Normal?" She is breathless and biting that damn lip.

"Me on top of you," I state as a matter of fact.

"I like our normal." Her face beams and, just before I devour more of what is mine, I concur.

"Good."

There's a tentative knock on my office door, and my fingers pinch the pressure at the bridge of my nose, but my eyes are still closed. I asked Sandy, my PA, to field any interruptions so I could crash for an hour. I may have the sex drive of an eighteen-year-old, but after pulling a near all-nighter with my girl, I am painfully aware I don't have the reserves to keep me fully awake the next day. I draw in a deep breath that turns into a yawn and full-body stretch. I open my eyes and glance at my watch, four twenty. I've been asleep for over an hour, but I don't feel remotely refreshed. If anything, I feel groggier, but that is because I didn't wake up…I was woken.

"Come in," I call out, not hiding the irritation in my clipped tone. Sandy peeks her head around the door, and where I am expecting a half apologetic grimace, her face is pale. "What's wrong?" I am instantly on my feet and striding to the door. "Sam…is Sam all right?" I know it's been months since the kidnapping, but I can't help my first reaction is always her and her safety. I doubt that will ever change.

"Oh, I don't know. I hope so." Her face softens, and she averts her eyes. Her brow is knitted with concern, and she is now wringing her hands. "I'm sorry to disturb you, but…but." Her voice breaks, and her pale blue eyes pool with water. I wrap my arm around her shoulder and try to pull her into the privacy of my office, but she stiffens and shakes her head. "You need to see this." She dabs her eyes with a folded handkerchief and walks back around her desk and looks at me to follow, I do. I stand at her shoulder while she opens up an email from her spam folder and clicks on the attachment.

The grainy, pixelated video recording starts to play; the camera is hand held and moves wildly before settling on an image I never, never wanted to see. The video freezes before I can shut it off, the distorted image frozen on the screen is nowhere near distorted enough. A beautiful girl, arms held over her head by someone laughing, I can see the tension in her muscles as she fights against his hold. She is so small, the man holding her down and the many men circling the show, she doesn't stand a chance. Her legs are spread wide, again held that way by more than one man, two on each leg are still fighting to keep her still.

From what Sam has told me, I know about her past. I know it is Richard standing in between her legs with his back to the camera. But all I can focus on are the tears, so many fucking tears. I place my hand flat on the desk to steady myself. Must still be dreaming. This has to be a nightmare. Who the fuck is behind that camera?

"What…who sent this?" I click to close the screen and look at the email address I don't recognise.

"I don't know, Jason. I pressed reply but whatever I send just bounces back." She shrinks back in her chair. "I'm sorry, Jason, but I didn't realise what these were."

"These?"

"Yes, they started about a month ago. I just assumed they were spam and adjusted the filter to send them straight to the trash folder. I never opened them, but I know company policy is to delete all emails from unrecognised senders."

"So you deleted them all?"

"Yes." Sandy nods.

"But not this one?" I query.

"It came through with a false email address from our

research department. I didn't spot it at first and clicked to open it, it linked straight to this email. I only noticed the difference in the sender email once it had taken me here. I didn't know. I'm so sorry." She sniffs and dabs eyes that are watery with tears.

"Sandy, it's not your fault." I place my hand on her shoulder for comfort, and she pats my hand to offer me the same. I can feel the tension radiating off me in waves, but she is obviously upset, too. "It is apparently very important to *someone* that I see this. I just need to know who that someone is and what they want," I mutter, still staring at the email address and icon for the attached document like it's a missing jigsaw piece.

"What they want?" Sandy looks up at me for answers I don't have yet.

"I don't think this is for my family album." I grit my teeth and close the screen down. "Someone wants something from me or Sam. I need to make sure they get whatever that is from me and don't go anywhere near Sam with this." I turn to face Sandy. "Forward all the files to me. Nobody is to know about this…no one and especially not Sam." My tone is firm and resolute.

"Of course, Jason." Sandy nods but looks shocked that I would suggest any different.

"Call James in IT and tell him I need a secure and private meeting set up."

"When?"

"Five minutes ago," I retort and walk off toward our IT department.

I don't fully understand the technical ins and outs of what our genius head of IT is telling me, but the nub is I can't trace the email, and the best chance of ever getting a lock is to 'catch' the email as it's hitting our mail system. He reliably informs me that with a bounce back, we might be able to attach a hidden code and blah-blah-blah.

"I need to know who is sending this, James," I snap, biting back the urge to hurl insults about not needing a fucking tutorial on the *how*, but I'm not an arsehole. I am just strung out, tired, and worried about my girl. I haven't shared the contents of the email, just expressed it as a matter of top priority. We've been at this for hours.

"This is strange," James mumbles but turns the screen to me. It's just a bouncing light hitting spots on the screen over a flattened map of the world. I raise a brow for him to enlighten me. "One of the emails had an IP address, and it's in the UK. It might not mean anything; other messages bounced all over the place when I tried to track them, but this one was the first and actually had a location, of sorts."

"Of sorts?" I raise a brow for him to elaborate.

"It's the arse end of London, mostly swamps and estuaries. There are no residential or commercial buildings there. Oh, wait, there might be a power station, but no homes, definitely no homes." He is scrolling on a split screen with a Google map of the location, zooming into a mass of green swamp and blue water.

"Grab that laptop, you're coming with me." I swipe my jacket from the back of my chair and stand to leave.

"Jason, I doubt there is anything there, and it's after nine." James taps his watch like that would make me reconsider.

"And?" I growl and fix my impatient and most deadly glare his way.

"I'll get my coat," he mutters as he quickly closes his laptop, packs away the cables, and grabs his phone.

"Good." I don't bother to wait but hear him run the length of the corridor to catch up to me at the main lifts.

"Fuck!" I slap the steering wheel in frustration as we hit slow moving traffic, but really I was hoping for a little luck on the roads. I reach for my jacket to try and dig my phone out but come up empty. "Fuck!"

"Problem?" James ventures, but his tone is rightly cautious. I am more than a little on edge. It's not his fault, and I take a calming breath before I reply.

"Possibly, but if I don't make this call *definitely*. May I borrow yours?"

"Sure." He hands me his phone and my face must register something strange because he just stares at me.

"I don't know her number. I don't know any of the numbers." I did know her number, but she got a new phone for work and couldn't see the point in having two devices. I never learned the new number.

"Oh." He retracts the phone with an apologetic curl of his lips. "Sorry."

"Shit," I mumble. This is not good. She'll be expecting me at the club any moment. Damn, she is going to be pissed. I shake my head. I can't think of that now—not when I have the chance to catch the utter scum who thinks it's okay to spread filth and hurt and devastate an innocent soul. "Talk to me," I snap, dragging my thoughts and focusing on the right now. "Where am I going?" James is sitting beside me with his small, state of the art laptop and tracker. He has pinpointed the static IP address, and we are currently forty miles away but the traffic has thinned and we are now speeding along toward the end of the motorway.

"Wait, give me your phone again. I do know the number of the club. I can get a message to her, at least." I mutter more to myself as James has already handed his phone back. I punch the numbers and wait for concierge to pick up.

"Stephanie," I interrupt her greeting. "It's Jason Sinclair. I need you to get a message to Sam."

"Of course, Mr. Sinclair. What is the message?" Her tone is polite and professional, and I can picture her pen hovering as I try to figure how best to tell Sam I might not make it tonight after all.

"Can you tell her I'm sorry, but something came up. Tell her, no wait, ask her to go home, and I'll make it up to her. Can you emphasise the sorry part," I add because that lame-ass message is going to land my bollocks in a vice, I just know it.

"Of course, Mr. Sinclair, I'm sure she'll understand. I'll go and find her right away."

"Thank you." I cut the call, feeling slightly better than the complete shit I felt moments ago for standing her up. I gave my word but this couldn't wait. I shake my wayward thoughts and focus on the dark road ahead.

We exit the last junction, but the motorway has already dwindled into a minor road. The junction feeds us onto an even smaller road still, and we speed along in darkness and near silence. The road is deserted, and there are no streetlights or houses to be seen. No light other than the one I cast with my full beams. The flashes of landscape reveal nothing but darkness, barren, bereft of bushes or trees, just emptiness, and I get a twist in my gut that this is a huge waste of time. But I have to try. If there is the slightest possibility that I can end this now, I am taking it.

"Next right is a dead end but leads almost to the coast. That's where the signal is." James points up ahead, and I see the sign for the turn but barely ease off the acceleration to take the tight corner. The tarmac gives way to an unmade road ending abruptly at a gate that looks like it hasn't been opened in decades. We exit the car, but I leave the beams on to give us some light. There is a small shed just the other side of the gate and

I turn to James, who is squinting in the direction I am now pointing.

"Is that where it's coming from?"

James purses his lips and shrugs an apology. "The signal's accurate, Jason, to within fifty meters, but since there's fuck-all else around, I think it's that shed, yeah."

"Right, okay. Stay here and have the police on speed dial. If I'm not back in ten minutes, call them. Don't come after me, understand?" I state emphatically, my tone brooking no argument. He gives me a tight nod of acknowledgment and fishes his phone out of his pocket, holding it like a loaded gun carefully in his palm. I turn, and with one hand high on the top bar of the gate, I swing both legs over with ease and determination. The headlights behind me cast an eerie elongated shadow of my frame that stretches right to the shed. The abandoned building isn't a shed but a disused sub power station, obsolete with the new power plant, but probably still wired to the grid. The padlock to the door is missing, but my toe hits the chunk of metal as I push the door slowly open, bending to pick up the lock as I do. The loop metal of the lock has been cut with something heavy duty to slice the thickness so cleanly. I drop the useless lock and peer inside, confident it is empty. The red and green flashing light draw my attention to the corner where a small laptop is perched on an empty crate. I start to lift it up, but my heart stops and then beats so fast I feel like my chest is going to explode. I fall back at the flutter of what feels like a million wings in this tiny space. I nearly fucking shit myself at the ear piercing squeaks. I cover my head with one hand and reach down to grab the laptop before turning and getting the fuck out of there.

Once free from the flying rodents, I shake myself. I fucking hate bats. I continue to shiver and run my hand through my hair several times just to make sure. I jog back, hop over the gate, and go back to the car. The bats are now circling, not as many as I thought now that they are in the open, but enough. They flit across the beams of light like tiny birds, but I know better.

"You okay?" James asks still with his finger hovering over his screen. I nod and hold up the laptop.

"That was in there?" he asks.

"Yep. This and bats, lots of bats." I open the car door and slide inside, letting out a deep steady breath, even as my heart is firing on all cylinders.

"I don't like bats." James slams his car door and peers through the front window at the aerial display of night creatures.

"Me, either, but this I do like. This might help, no?" I drop the laptop onto his lap.

"Yes, it might. I will have a look on Monday." He slips the laptop onto the floor.

"You'll have a look tonight, tomorrow, and every waking hour there is, James," I correct. "This is my girl's safety at stake." His mouth drops for a moment at this information.

"Of course. Sorry, I didn't know this was about Sam." He picks the laptop back up and levels it in his lap.

"Well, you do now, but no one else needs to. The fewer people, the safer she'll be." Inside, the car is lit only from the soft glow on the cockpit display, but James can see the seriousness in my glare when I turn to face him.

"But you'll tell Sam?" he asks, but the question is moot.

"No, she doesn't need to live in fear when I'm taking care of it."

"You think that's wise? She'll be safer if she's prepared," he challenges but keeps his voice level and void of judgement.

"You're right, but after everything she went through last

year, she doesn't need to know this shit," I state, and the car falls silent. I draw in a deep breath and let it out, slowly feeling the tension in the car creep into my bloodstream. "I'll make sure she is aware of a temporary security issue." I notice James nod his approval at my obvious compromise. In an attempt to lighten the mood, I offer up my next concern. "If she ever talks to me again, that is." It is only a half joke as I reverse up the single dirt track to the main road.

ELEVEN

Sam

I TURN BACK FROM THE CURTAINED DOORWAY FOR THE umpteenth time. I take a long sip of my iced coffee. I never drink when I'm in charge of the playroom. My attention is diverted to Stephanie, one of the administration staff from the back office, hurriedly fumbling to thread her arms into her coat, her face is wet and she is rushing for the exit. Marco appears at the end of the bar where I am perched, waiting.

"Is everything okay?" He follows my gaze to where Stephanie has now left in the dramatic swish of the heavy velvet curtain.

"I hope so. Her husband just called. Her little boy has been rushed to hospital with a burst appendix." Marco's voice is filled with concern. His empathy for all his staff has quickly secured his place as the best manager this club has had in the five years I have been a member.

"Oh shit!" I get a flash of sickness in my stomach. That

feeling of helplessness for a loved one, ill or in danger, has to be the worst. I shake the darkness from my thoughts and add quietly. "He's in the best place, at least."

Marco gives a brief nod but doesn't say anything; there really isn't anything to say, and it's obvious our thoughts are for the best possible outcome for Stephanie's little boy. Marco pours himself a finger of whiskey. He skips my glass but proceeds to top up that of the gentleman seated beside me. A former client, Harry has been keeping me company while I wait… and continue to wait.

Jason is late, and he hasn't called. I absently swirl my glass, the cubes clink and spin in the milky liquid. I'm not really listening to the conversation between Marco and Harry. I chance another furtive glance toward the door but the unchanged sight has my volatile mood dipping into darkly depraved thoughts of punishment for breaking his promise. One moment, I am clutching my chest at the tight pinch of anxiety where I fear the worst, and the next I'm wondering if I missed my true calling as a sadist. A deep voice with an American accent booms close to my ear and makes me jump.

"I thought it was about time I called your companion a cab." He places his arm on the bar, effectively separating me from Harry and completely oblivious to my precious personal space. My posture is perfectly straight, but the unwelcome intrusion makes me want to lean away. I don't, I tip forward, forcing him to take a step back. There, that's a little better.

"Excuse me?" I raise a curious brow and hear Marco cough whisper 'newb'. A not too subtle code for a new club member.

"Don't be shy, sugar. You've been trying to hide all those looks you're been firing my way all damn night. I just thought it was about time I let your guy here know you're gonna be playing with me tonight." He winks at Harry, who bites his lips tight.

I can only assume from the crinkle in the corner of his eyes, the bite is to stop him from laughing.

"His name is Harry. Why would you call him Cab?" I respond with my best innocent and deadpan intonation.

"What? No, sugar, I want him to leave so...oh cute." He waggles his finger at me. "You're yanking my chain, aren't ya', darling?" He tilts his head like he is actually thinking about whether he is on the right track with his assessment.

"Little bit." I hold up my thumb and forefinger with an accurate measure of how little I am referring to, but he misses that reference and steamrollers on regardless.

"Can I buy you a drink? He waves the bar man over, but I interrupt before he can place an order.

"Got one. Got company, and I'm waiting on my date. Thanks, but no thanks." I flash a tight smile that is in no way an invitation to stay and chat, let alone play.

"Ah, sugar, do I look like I would give up that easy." He tries to lean in again but stops when he sees my eyes narrow to an inhospitable scowl.

"If you were smart, you would. So I guess that would be a no, you really don't." I carefully place my drink on the bar and wait until his eyes are fixed on me. "Look, how about I make it really easy for you. If you can turn me on, I'm yours." He sucks in a sharp breath, and his eyes widen as I pause for effect. "If not, you tuck that massive ego of yours between your legs and walk away. Deal?"

"You serious?" His voice catches, and he coughs roughly to hide the break.

"Absolutely." I can see Harry over this man's shoulder lightly shaking his head; his own shoulders are jiggling with laughter. I might as well have a little fun since my date is a no show.

"Oh boy," Harry mutters loud enough for me to hear.

"Damn right, oh boy." The man stretches his hand to my breast. Rookie.

"Nah, ah…no touching." I emphatically state my rule, and his hand halts, fingers stretching out in midair like a movie freeze frame. My words cause him to snap it back to his side, burnt but unharmed.

"What? How am I supposed to—"

"Please, don't finish that sentence. For the love of all the women in your future, *please* do not finish that sentence." I close my eyes and shake my head lightly.

"I'm going to need to touch you to tell if you're wet." His irritated tone would suggest I am the idiot in this exchange. I smile sweetly before mimicking retching into my own mouth, hand cupped for effect.

"Urgh, I think a little bit of vomit right there," Harry snickers. "Let's just say for the purpose of this exercise, we'll be looking for other signs?"

"Other signs?" he repeats, utter confusion on his handsome face, and he is handsome. Big, blond, beautiful blue eyes, and built, huge, wide shoulders and muscles pushing at the seams of his pale blue shirt. But it wouldn't matter if he was—well, it doesn't matter who he is, he's not Jason. I let out an exasperated breath.

"Yes, you know if my pupils dilate and my eyes darken. Of course, you'll have to stop looking at my tits for a second to notice that. Or if my breathing gets a little deeper, more rapid, perspiration might gather just here." I tap the indent in my collarbone and notice his throat struggle to swallow. "And if you're really lucky, I might get all perky in the nipple department." I give a sassy little wiggle that has my breasts once more the center of his attention.

"But no touching?" His voice has dropped an octave, and

his knuckles whiten with the curl of his fists.

"Nope," I clarify with a curt nod.

He pauses for a moment, his brows furrow with deep concentration. "Fine." He chews his lips, carefully selecting the perfect prose for seduction, no doubt. He takes his time, but you can't rush these things, so I wait. I'm getting good at this waiting thing. He draws in a deep breath, and I sit up nice and straight, fully attentive and eager.

"I'm gonna' stick my dick so far up your ass—"

"Okay, let me stop you there," I quickly interrupt, holding my hand up, flat palm inches from his nose. "Back up, big guy, back up. You're really gonna' start with that? No hi there, my name is Chuck The Wonderfuck? No kiss on the cheek? No—"

"This ain't no date, sugar," he adds gruffly, stopping my 'to-do' before you 'do' list.

"It's *always* a date." I roll my eyes and shake my head at this poor specimen before me.

"But you said no touching, so I'm talking," he grumbles.

"And you're gonna go straight for the dick up my arse—no gentle caress—just two strides into the room and hand straight down my pants."

"It works for me." He shrugs.

"For you, maybe. Okay, look, why don't you start again?" I encourage with a smile because his shoulders are a little slumped, his chest not quite so puffed.

"Right." He draws in a deep breath. "I pinch your nipple—"

"I knee you in the crotch. Seriously?" I can't help myself, but I do manage not to laugh.

"Look, lady, I can do this if you'd just let me touch you," he pleads, his fingers tapping anxiously on his arms, which are still crossed over his chest all tight and defensive.

"That's my point, *darling*." I'm not great with accents, but

I nailed that sweet endearment even if it was deeply sarcastic. "You shouldn't *need* to touch me. My man can turn me on with a glance. Hell, Harry here could turn me on with just one word." The man looks over at Harry for the first time since calling him a cab.

"Oh, really?" The man laughs out loud and sharp.

"Harry, if you wouldn't mind, would you give me just one word, please?" I ask as Harry grins and turns to face me. I click my fingers to get Chuck's attention. "And you, watch closely for those telltale signs. Because, even though I will be, you are not going to be sticking your hands down my pants to 'check if I'm wet.'" I air quote from Chuck's previous declaration. "Harry?"

"Jason," Harry says quietly, and I let that single word work its magic. Several long seconds pass before I choose to address the man still looking at my tits, which granted now look a whole lot more interested.

"I'm going to share this with you because I'm in a giving mood. Not for you, but for woman kind: Seduce her here." I lightly tap my temple. "Make love to her mind before you even lay a finger on her body, and remember this as if it was carved along the length of your cock, in *really* tiny letters." I hold my thumb and finger barely apart to indicate exactly *how* tiny, before I continue. It's almost sweet how he seems to be waiting with bated breath for my proffered wisdom. "There is nothing sexier than a well-placed kiss on the neck. Start there, Chuck, because then, when she's crying out, 'oh, God', it won't be for Divine intervention to help her out, it will be because you've brought her there. And you're welcome." I wave my hand, dismissing the mildly dumbstruck but perfectly harmless newbie. He turns back after a few steps.

"My name isn't Chuck, it's—" I hold up my hand to stop him right there, and he nods, his eyes barely hold my gaze, and his face is a perfect picture of sheepish. He had his chance to tell me that, and he knows it.

Draining my glass, saving the ice, I place it on the bar and stand, checking my watch. Over an hour late and I swallow back the lump recalling his last playful threat. I hate the speed of my heart thumping in my chest, the tightness, and the hollow pit deep inside growing bigger with each passing minute. I am no longer pissed, now my thoughts are wading through darkness and struggling with the worst.

"Marco, can you call me if you get a message, or if he shows." My voice catches, but I swallow it down before it breaks.

"I'm sure he's just stuck in traffic, Sam. Stay. He will be here. There's no fucking way he wouldn't show," he offers lightly, but his words chill me to the core.

"I know." I don't meet his gaze because I can feel the tingle of tears. I need to find Jason. I bend to pick up my briefcase of tricks, which now feels like a dead weight, and turn to leave, pausing to clarify.

"Call me if you hear anything." I walk away before I crumble; the worry in Marco's eyes is more than I need to break my fragile façade. His curt nod is enough to know he completely understands my meaning.

I take my coat from the cloakroom and dip roughly into the pockets for my phone. My fleeting feeling that I was, perhaps, being overdramatic flatlines. There are no messages, no missed calls…nothing. Jason doesn't do that ever.

The night air is damp and freezing drops of ice fall from the pitch-black sky. I haven't put my coat on, and the sleet is no doubt slicing at my skin, but I can't quite feel it if it does. A cab pulls into the curb before me without my signal.

"Where to, love?" the thick East End London accent calls

out. I open the door and sit back before I speak.

"Can you just drive for a bit?" I crumple over, my head in my hands, my insides in agony.

"Hey, if you're gonna hurl, you can get out!" the driver shouts in a panic.

"I'm not sick." I lift my head, and I can feel the first fat tear trickle down my cheek…that I feel. "I'm not sick," I repeat softly as the cab pulls away. *Not sick…I feel like I'm dying.*

My hand trembles, holding my phone, as I cut the answerphone message off for the millionth time on Jason's number. I press speed-dial number three and silently pray Leon isn't asleep.

"I wondered if you'd catch me before I boarded or whether you'd still be tied-up." His tone is playful and teasing.

"Leon, I—" My voice breaks, and his tone is instantly serious.

"Sam, where are you? What's wrong? Are you hurt?" he snaps.

"Jason…" is all I manage to say.

"Did he hurt you?" *No…God yes.* "Sam, talk to me baby?" he pleads.

"I can't get hold of him. Tonight, he didn't show for our *date.* He promised, Leon, and now I can't get hold of him… I'm…I don't know what to do." I'm a wreck, my tears are streaming down my cheeks, and I am only just containing the sobs that are bubbling under a very flimsy surface of restraint.

"Fuck." His tone is grave, and that is just what I didn't need. He is the only other person who knows me and understands how Jason feels about me. This isn't an overreaction. This is the only reaction. "When was the last time you heard from him?" His question makes me pause. It's almost midnight now. It's been hours.

"We spoke at lunch time. He said he'd text me before he left, but I went to the club early to set up and checked my phone at the cloakroom. I didn't think about it until…" I sniff and wipe my nose on the back of my hand. My face feels like it's melting; I'm a mess.

"Where are you, baby?"

"In a cab." I sniff, my voice barely audible above the dirty diesel engine.

"Where, baby?" Leon repeats with a much firmer tone that makes me narrow my eyes at the darkness through the window. The roads are empty, and I don't recognise the vista but the streetlights and shop fronts are bright enough for me to know we are still in the heart of the city. Just not an area I am familiar with.

"I don't know, just driving. Can I come to you? I don't want to go home." My fingertips press and rub the pressure point at my temple on the side not holding the phone. The sensitive spot throbs, and the pulse pounds without respite.

"Sam, I'm on the plane. I only took this call because the flight's delayed, and I hadn't switched my phone off. Shit!" I can hear the frustration in his tone, but I don't want him to feel bad. Especially when there is fuck all he can do about it sitting on a plane.

"It's fine. I'll be—"

"Shit!" he cuts in, but I couldn't finish the sentence. "I agree, don't go home. If he were there, he would've called. I think your best option is to go to his office. You never know? There might be a security lockdown or some such shit," he mutters. "You do that, Sam, and I'll check hosp—" He stops himself a little too late, and I squeeze my eyes tight as if that will make me unhear what he just said. But I heard it loud and clear. "I'll check around," he continues, rushing his words. "I have to switch this off now, babe. If you don't hear from me, it will only be until we reach altitude, and I can call again, okay. I will call you back." His words offer little comfort because they sound awfully like a promise I heard only earlier today.

"Okay," I reply softly.

"Sam. I'll be on the next flight back. You're not alone, baby." His calm tone is filled with love and affection, but I can't feel a thing.

"Without Jason, I am." My voice is flat, numb, and I embrace that feeling like I embrace myself. My arms cross and hug my body but I feel nothing. Nothing is better than pain. I'll take numb please, because I've had enough pain to last a lifetime.

I can take it, but I know I won't survive.

The night security guard at the Stone building is reluctant to let me in. At his initial refusal, my sadness evaporated into pure fury, and the young man quickly backed down, fearing for more than his life. I take the lift to the basement first and check the garage. Jason's private reserved space is empty, crushing my last hope that he might be here. The ride to the twenty-fifth floor is silent, swift, and as ominous as the dark cloud cloaking my thoughts. Jason's office is at the end of the corridor; his door is ajar, but even from this distance, I can see there is no light inside the room. More darkness and disturbing quiet greet me when I enter, and my feet fail to move another step. My stomach churns, and I suck in a steadying breath that does little to calm my rocketing anxiety and, not for the first time, I wonder why I am even here.

But then I remember: I don't have anywhere else to go.

My call to Bethany goes to voice mail, and I don't have a direct number for Daniel to check if he is working somewhere with Jason. I can't phone Will, he is too far away, and with the time difference he will still understand that it's late here in the UK, and late calls always mean bad news.

I don't know for sure it's bad news.

It's this grain of hope I cling to as I curl up on the sofa in the corner of Jason's office, gripping my phone like it's my *precious*. I don't feel the tears saturate my face; I only know that they are, because the pale blue material of the sofa darkens beneath my cheek. I am numb, empty, and exhausted, but I don't sleep; I wait.

My heart stops at two thirty two. I know this is because my phone has those digits illuminated on the screen in my palm, and that is when Jason steps into his office, not noticing me in the darkness.

I don't move, I don't make a sound, but with my next breath, I leap and run flat out toward him. A missile of pure utter fucking joy and relief hurtles toward a shocked and startled looking Jason. His arms wrap around my body on impact. I hit him hard, and he takes a steadying step back with the momentum. I bury my head in his neck and let the tears flow unchecked, big, huge, ugly sobs. Too much liquid is pouring from my face, but I just don't care, and I grip him so tight I don't think I will ever let him go.

"Hmm, okay not the reaction I was anticipating and not *where* I was expecting to find you, that's for sure." He chuckles...*chuckles*. I died tonight, and he chuckles. Pushing from his arms, I jump down, draw my hand back, and slap him hard across his beautiful face. He reaches to stop the second strike, his hand gripped tight around my wrist. "Now, that *is* the reaction I was expecting, but you only get one, beautiful." His tone is stern with a gravelly edge.

"I thought you were dead." I struggle to pull my hand

away, because I don't feel nearly done with my pent-up rage. We tussle, and he grabs my other fist with which I had managed to land a hefty punch on his rock hard pec. I am struggling hard to break free. My veins surge with adrenaline, frustration, relief, love, but also a shit-tonne of suppressed anger.

"What are you talking about?" he scoffs with a laugh, his face a picture of confusion, but his eyes are wide like I just said the craziest thing.

"You didn't call...nothing...no message." He deftly bends to the side as I snap my knee up to his crotch. He twists and spins us, slamming me hard against the wall and pressing his full body weight into mine. I can feel him hard against my thigh, and he rolls his hips and speaks with a low serious voice.

"Listen very carefully, and stop trying to kick me in the bollocks." He kicks my legs wide so my knees are no longer a concern. "I had an emergency. I had no choice but to deal with it. No choice, understand?" His voice softens, and his brows knit with concern, and I can see his eyes are pained at this clusterfuck. He shakes his head at the mess and continues to try and ease me down. "I left my phone on my desk, baby, look." He nods his head to the empty desk, but I take a second to glance and he's right. Some papers are piled in the corner and, just under one edge, the folded leather case of his phone. I didn't see that before. Stupid Sam, but it wouldn't make a difference, the net result is the same. His lips brush my forehead, and my eyes snap back to his. He draws in a deep, slow breath and exhales softly. The sickly sweet aroma of Red Bull is faint, but has obviously been effective at keeping him awake, when I needed no such artificial stimulant. "But I called the club and told Stephanie to tell you to go home...to tell you that I was sorry...that *I am* sorry, *Sam* ...because although it wasn't death that kept me from keeping my promise...it was important." He pauses, but my scowl is unchanged. "I left a fucking message, Sam." His tone is frustrated, but his words are pleading. He holds my gaze, searching my too-tired eyes for forgiveness. He can see firsthand what I have been through in these short but endless hours. "You didn't get the message." He sighs. It's not a question, but I shake my head all the same.

"Stephanie had her own emergency." I try to pull my arms free, but he keeps them high above my head. "I thought you were dead," I repeat, my throat raw from sobbing.

"A little dramatic, don't you think, beautiful?" His lips quirk, teasing me or waving the red flag. Yeah, the idiot waves a big fucking red flag. His grip loosens when I relax and exhale softly with a sweet smile. Instantly, I drop to my haunches and through his grip, I jab my sharp elbow in the back of his knees as I duck through the gap in between his legs and send him crumpling to the floor.

"Fuck!" he curses, hitting the ground hard with no time to brace. I scramble away, but he is on me, snatching my ankle before I can make a clean escape. He pins my foot to the floor and quickly immobilises the free, and more dangerous limb, flailing wildly, hoping to avoid capture...*inevitable capture*. With the stealth and speed of a seasoned predator, he crawls up my body, legs on either side of my torso, pinning my arms above my head but flush against the floor. He slides back down my frame, his full body weight crushing the air from my chest, his legs now wrapped like a vine around my own, constricting and effectively restricting any further movement and my ability to breathe.

"Calm the fuck down!" he growls, but I've lost it. His words have the exact opposite effect, and I buck and struggle with more strength than I thought I had left. He fights to keep control, and when I have no physical strength left, I scream with my last breath. An ear-piercing howl that fills the room and shocks him enough to let me go—completely. I scramble back and jump to my feet. My face is wet from a fresh slew of tears I didn't really feel.

"You don't get it!" I cry out, my arms hugging my waist as I watch him slowly unfold from the floor to his full height. His expression is wary, his eyes cautious and concerned.

"Don't get what, beautiful?" His softly spoken words try to soothe, but I can't feel their effect. All I feel is panic and sadness in huge waves, drowning me. I can't breathe; my chest is crushing my lungs. I fold over and crumple in on myself, sobbing. "Jesus, Sam." His voice catches, and I hear him step closer. I try to step back, but his hands pull me upright by my shoulders. "Talk to me, Sam…please, baby…talk to me." I curl my hand into a half-hearted fist and level a punch on his firm chest.

"You promised, Jason. I thought…you…you don't get to leave me," I sob, but my words are muffled into his hold, big strong arms capture me and lift me high. I slap his chest once more, but I've lost my fight. I cry out when he slams me against the wall.

"Never. I'm so fucking sorry, Sam." His mouth covers mine, swallowing the gasp he forced out with the impact. Hot urgent kisses then scorch my tears dry. "Sorry, baby," he murmurs against my neck, continuing to kiss and bite and mark my skin. I tilt away to give him more of me to claim. My fingers claw with wild abandon. His body covers me, consumes me, and I need him for my next breath and for my heart to take it's first proper beat. "I'll never leave—" he begins to say, but pulls back, his eyes wide with sudden and very real understanding, piercing mine, which glaze instantly. I am just too raw to brush this away even as I have him in my arms. "That's why you thought…"

"Jason, I'm not this crazy and unstable, but you promised

tonight was supposed to be special. You said only death—" I suck back a sob, gritting my jaw tight to keep it in.

"Fuck. I know. I know! Shit, Sam, I'm—" I shake my head to interrupt his apology.

"You were gone, and I couldn't find you. You can always find me, but I couldn't find you! I feel the same way about you, Jason, dammit, and I couldn't—" His eyes meet mine, and I know he understands, he gets it—he gets me. I drop my head into his neck, pressing my lips to the soft skin that smells like a sweet sweaty mix of musk and my man. I draw the comfort I need from that scent before I have the strength to meet his stare. Stray tears still fall, but not so many now that I have him in my arms.

"Please, baby, no more tears. You're right, and I'll fix this. I'm so sorry you were worried." His tender lips press against mine…once…twice. "I'm sorry I ruined our evening." He sucks in my bottom lip and drags it between his teeth. A million tingles dance across my skin, and the deeply erotic swirling sensation in my tummy is doing an admirable job at erasing my sadness. "I'll do anything to make it up to you." His sensual tone and tempting words make my body shiver from tip to toe at that very thought.

"Anything?" I drop my head back with a light thud against the wall. My legs constrict around his trim waist, and he must be able to feel my heat, if not my melting core at the possibilities. "What if my *anything* involved your brother?" I bite my lip to hold back a whimper that is bubbling at the recall that is always just under the surface of my ultimate *anything*.

"Well, after what you've been through, I think I would owe you that anything." His thick brows furrow at my request, but his almost black eyes darken further with equal desire.

"Maybe not, if it's going to cause that brow of yours to look like that." I purse my lips and check his expression for any hint of reticence. This may still be my fantasy come true, but not at any expense…not at his expense. I'll happily relegate it to a one-time thing, if that is the case, but looking into his eyes now, I know that's not the case. It's just an exception, but not a rule, because he makes the rules.

"I said anything, beautiful, and I meant it. I live to fulfill your dreams. The jealously is inevitable, but I'll deal. Trust me, it's not a hardship to watch you. I enjoy you, enjoying yourself." His grin spreads wide and wicked. "Fuck, how did I get so lucky?" He grinds his hips hard and holds me firm against his erection.

"I'm the lucky one. But since Will isn't here to make good on that *anything*, how about you drop and give me twenty?" I raise a brow, maintain his gaze, and hold my breath to see how he responds to a direct challenge, Mistress to Dom.

"Is this a little of what I missed tonight?" His eyes narrow; his voice is low and gravelly.

"A soupçon…a little taste." My tongue darts to wet the dryness and his eyes follow the movement before flashing me his most brilliant smile and dropping to his knees.

"Don't mind if I do."

TWELVE

Jason

MY HEART POUNDS PAINFULLY IN MY CHEST FROM THE broken expression on her face— heartbreakingly clear through her tear-soaked face. I had no fucking idea what was going on when she flew across the room and slammed into me...not a clue. But the instant that changed, I understood, and that fucking tore me up from the inside out. *I did that.* This may have been a simple case of miscommunication, but after what she's been through, I am not in the least surprised she had the mother of all meltdowns.

I never doubted how she felt about me, and I see it now, crystal fucking clear. If I have to put a fucking implant under my skin to ease her mind, I will, because I won't ever put her through that again. Ever. She needs to understand, I am never leaving, not while I still have a breath to give, because I will give it to her. But I guess that was the problem tonight. She knew that's how I felt, and she came to the only conclusion left.

I shudder internally as I drag my nails up her incredibly long legs, scouring her delicate skin until I get to the edge of her panties, under her sexy, skin-tight skirt. She trembles at my touch, and her breath catches when I yank the flimsy material to her feet. I tap her ankle, and she lifts for me to remove them completely.

I raise her leg and press it against the wall, my mouth waters at the sight and smell of her arousal—so fucking sweet. She's intoxicating. One of my hands supports her knee, while my other spreads her folds, wet and glossy on my fingertips. Her hands thread into my hair, and she grips for support; her whimper turns into a strangled scream when my tongue delves into her liquid heat. Her thigh muscles tremor as I take my sweet time devouring, sucking, and diving into her molten, soft center. Her little pants, and the tension in her grip, increases with every swirl of my tongue as I drive her incessantly toward her peak. The pad of my thumb rests on her clit, and I take the moment I hear her suck in a sharp breath to peek up through my lashes and watch her eyes squeeze shut and her tummy clench. She pushes out a steadying breath, and her head drops back against the wall. Her eyes fix on mine with such passion and fire, I know she's balancing on the edge. I drag my tongue flat and firm from her entrance to her clit where I rub in a steady rhythm…round and round…higher and higher. She cries out and comes so hard on my tongue, her essence pours over my lips; the muscles in her thighs contract and fight to snap around my head. I loosen my grip, and her legs do exactly that. They clamp tight around my neck. Scorching-hot, firm muscles in super soft silky skin engulf my head.

I stand and grab her arse cheeks, lifting her high, my mouth still glued to her core. I press her against the wall. Her legs constrict a little more, muffling any sound she might be emitting as I continue to devour. She tastes too good to stop.

The wall helps to support her, but she is gripping so tight I don't think she's in any danger of falling. *I'll never let her fall.* Her hips grind against my mouth, and her hands are trying to pull me this way and that. I growl low and scrape my teeth against her inner thigh. She tenses and gives this little squeal that I do hear, but her hands relax enough to let me do my job. She needs this, I know, but I do too, so fucking much. I need to take her there, my way. I will never get enough of her, and I will take whatever she is willing to give, because I know how damn lucky I am to have this precious gift in my hands.

"Oh, God, Jason, I can't…please, I need you…I really need you to…" She pants out a breathless urgent plea that nearly ends me. "Mark me, Jason. Make me yours. Make it hurt." I groan into her folds, sucking in the delicate flesh, as my cock feels fit to burst. *Holy fucking shit.* I want one more climax from her, then I'll gladly give her what she asks for, but she needs an overload of pleasure before pain. I understand her desire is an attempt to mask the hurt she felt tonight. I get that, and I am more than eager to mark what's mine, but first things first.

I swirl my tongue and suck my lips over her swollen, pulsing nub of nerves, and she screams. Not quite the howl that had me leaping from her a short while back, but a deep, sigh-filled, sensual cry that pierces the silence of the night and drowns the mere mortal sex noises that were prevalent just a few seconds ago. Her back arches, and her body jolts enough for me to lose my footing. I am seriously top heavy when I step back, so I swiftly let her drop from my shoulders into my waiting arms. The shock of the move obliterates any hope of coming down smoothly from that high, but it couldn't be helped. If I hadn't taken the evasive maneuver, we would both be sprawled on the floor and not necessarily in one piece.

I carry her over to the sofa and carefully place her on her feet. Her eyes are fixed on me, still a little dazed, but not for long. I sit on the arm of the seat, take her hand, and roughly pull her across my lap. Her feet skid on the carpet, and as they don't quite reach the floor, she is stretching both her hands and her toes to try and balance. Perfect.

"Hold still, beautiful, or this is going to be a very long night. You wanted me to mark you and since I only have my hand, and you have an exceptionally high tolerance for pain, I want to make sure you are absolutely satisfied with the result."

"I always am, Sir." She exhales, and her whole body relaxes under my caress. If I could bottle this feeling surging through me right now and sell it, I would give Daniel Stone and Bill Gates combined wealth a run for their money. Pure unadulterated power courses through me. She does this to me. Her unwavering trust and total submission give me that and so much more. I draw in a deep breath and stroke the curve of her backside once more before I peel the thin material up and fold it at her waist. Her skin glows in the fading moonlight, giving it a much paler pallor, ethereal and exquisite. My hand sweeps the skin, goose bumps dance under my touch, but I know she's not in the least bit cold. I lift my hand and hold it high, hovering. I love this bit the most—the anticipation—where her breath catches and her muscles tense and twitch expectantly. She forces herself to relax because she knows the pain isn't as bad when she does, but that first involuntary response gets me so hard I have to fight the urge to just spread her wide and sink balls deep for my own pleasure.

But this is all about her tonight; it's the very least I can do.

My first strike stings my palm but makes her sigh and sink a little heavier on my lap. The next makes her hips tilt, tipping her bottom higher, tantalising, teasing me for more. I'll oblige;

I'm in a giving mood. Again and again, I bring my heavy palm down on her soft flesh. The bounce and ripple of her arse with each strike makes my cock pulse, and the deepening rosy hue to her skin is making my balls scream in agony. Her skin glistens with perspiration, and her panting breaths have ratcheted up to a level that matches my own erratic heartbeat. She pinches her legs together, and it takes all my effort to not drag my hands between them when I just know how wet she will be. But if I do, I know this ends right now; I won't be able to hold off burying myself inside of her. If this was a normal session with a normal sub, I would happily leave my sub wanting. After all, this is not just a marking session; she hit me, bit me, and very nearly kicked me in the balls. This should be punishment, too.

I know marking her as mine is one thing, giving her the pain she needs is another, but any punishment that would involve me denying myself, well, that is just not going to fucking happen. She's my submissive, yes, but our situation is unique, and this punishment lesson is in theory only, because this is Sam, and I can't deny her a single damn thing. The red patch on her bottom has spread across both cheeks, down her upper thighs, and at the edges are the telltale prints of individual fingers. A perfect representation of my erotic appreciation; my applause is literally all over her backside. The final strike ends with a tender stroke all over her inflamed skin. She barely makes a sound, but she exhales softly now that my hand is resting on the small of her back: The signal that I have finished.

I help her up, and we switch places so she is now lying over the edge of the sofa, her gloriously red arse a far too tempting sight.

I nudge her legs a little wider and position myself between them. My hand makes light work of the material barriers before it is holding my raging erection at her sodden entrance. She twists to look at me, and her brows crinkle with confusion.

"You're going to fuck me?" Her frown deepens.

"You thought I wouldn't?" I raise my own brow, my expression otherwise deadly serious.

"I thought—" She swallows thickly and bites her bottom lip in an adorable display of trying to suppress her evidence of pleasure. "I'm glad." She gives a sassy little wiggle, but yelps when I swipe my palm heavy across both cheeks. I might choose to be soft with her, but I'm still fucking hard, and, boy, she makes my palm twitch. I push forward and sink my full length in one forceful thrust that causes her mouth to drop open in a silent gasp. Her eyes are wide enough to register both her surprise and the painful depth. Her fingers grip the leather edge of the armrest with white-knuckle pressure.

"Good idea, beautiful, I'd hang on tight." My voice is hoarse and deep, my throat dry from tempered desire. My tone is heavy with a mix of sensual promise and erotic threat. Her hands fist a little tighter, and she tilts her hips to take me deeper. *God, I love this woman.* It's enough, I lose it...whatever it was...it's gone...sense...restraint...my fucking mind. I slam into her—relentlessly—hard and fast like a fucking jackhammer. I can't stop. One hand grips her arse, my nails biting into the raised pink flesh and my other fisting a large clump of her sweat-soaked mane, lifting her head back and pulling her up to meet my punishing drives. Perhaps this is a punishment, after all? No, that's not it. This isn't about punishment. This is just wild abandon, souls imprinting, and raw, feral fucking.

"Come," I growl in her ear. I don't recognise my voice; it comes from such a dark, desperate place, but she does. She takes that spark of recognition, and it ignites her body like a touch paper. Her muscles tighten inside and out, taut and tense. Ripple after ripple, her body succumbs to the explosion of a lifetime. I can only make that assumption, because that is exactly what it feels like for me. Shots of pure agony and ecstasy in equal measure fire from the base of my spine, electrifying every nerve ending until with one almighty explosion, I release, riding with her climax as we come together as one. Fucking perfect. I collapse onto her, even my bones ache, and I feel so spent, so drained, and yet overflowing at the same time.

I roll onto the sofa and pull her into my arms, wrapping my body around her limp form. She offers absolutely no resistance. Sticky and slick, we slide and mould together and fall into a deep and peaceful coma.

Her shiver wakes me, but the light in the office might've had something to do with that, too. I kiss her hair, and she tilts her head to meet my stare. Her eyes hold a little of the puffy redness from last night, and I get a twisting pain in my chest at that sight. Her warm, tender smile goes some way to ease that feeling but only some way.

"Hey." She leans up to cover my lips with her sweetness.

"Hey, you." I give her an extra kiss on her forehead when she pulls away. "How are you feeling?"

"Good." She nods, and I search for any hidden hurt in her eyes, but there is none. There is something though, some trace of sadness I don't want to see.

"How about we cancel my parents this weekend and just spend the weekend in bed, marking each other like crazy people?" My tone is light and playful.

"I'd love that." She giggles, and her face lights up like a kid on Christmas morning. Jackpot. "But won't your parents be cross? Will your Mum have gone to lots of trouble?" She worries her bottom lip. I pull it free with my thumb and forefinger.

"Probably, she would've made up the spare rooms already,

but it won't be a problem. It's not a cancel, we're just postpon-ing. I think we need this after—" She nods so I don't bother to go over exactly what that *after* is.

"If you're sure?" Her bright grin is wide and relaxed. "Wait, you said rooms, who else is staying?"

"Just us. My Mum is a little old-fashioned." I raise a brow and wait for that to dawn.

"Really?" She snickers. "Separate rooms? You have to be kidding. You're nearly thirty!"

"I'm still twenty-nine!" I grumble indignantly. "Honestly, it's never been an issue before, because I've never taken anyone home, but I am definitely not kidding."

"In that case, then, maybe it is a good idea to postpone. I don't want to sleep without you." Her voice softens, and her eyes fill with liquid. I pull her to my chest, my arms so tight I hope she can feel what she does to me. How much she means and how fucking sorry I am.

"Me, too, beautiful, and I'm so—"

"Don't, Jason. No more sorrys, okay? You're forgiven, and I don't want to think about it again." She lifts herself from my em-brace and strides naked toward my office bathroom. "You made it up to me last night. Today, you have nothing to be sorry for."

"I think I do." I purse my lips and wiggle my brow; she frowns but follows my gaze to her backside. It is still tinged with red and mottled with tiny purple spots. My cock swells at the sight and gets so much bigger when she draws her hand back and loudly slaps one cheek.

"Not bad." Her tone is lightly mocking and deviously teas-ing. I stand and stalk toward her. Her gaze drops to my heavy, bobbing cock but snaps back to my eyes, which are on fire and ready to burn. She backs away, hands held up in a futile defen-sive gesture.

"Not bad?" I question, my sensual tone tinged with sexual menace. "Oh, beautiful, you haven't seen bad."

"I was so hoping you were going to say that." She spins on her toe and hightails it to the bathroom. Two strides and I am on her, and I have her in my arms. She didn't stand a chance, but looking into her eyes now, I know she didn't want one.

I wake to an empty bed and sunlight piercing the gaps in the heavy curtains. I rub the tiredness from my face and squint at my watch to try and gauge the time. We didn't get back home until the early hours. We narrowly avoided discovery by the night cleaners finishing their final polish of the reception area. We both looked fucked and dishevelled as we bundled into my car, but we escaped undetected. It's almost midday, and I can now smell something cooking. The sweet aroma wafting up through the house smells a lot like pancakes. My stomach grumbles with anticipation of the feast, but this isn't good. Despite some basic culinary tuition, Sam is a dreadful cook and never willingly cooks unless she's stressed—really stressed. Then out comes the ready-mix pancakes, comfort food enough to feed an army when she barely takes a bite herself.

I throw the bedcovers back and slip on my old, torn jeans, hopping from one foot to the other and running from the room as I do. I bound down the three flights of stairs and take a deep breath before striding into my very own International House of Pancakes.

I walk over as she pours more mixture into the ready pan, her concentration such that she hasn't heard me approach.

"Jesus Christ!" She jumps and jerks her arm, spilling a large dollop of mixture into the pan, drowning the smaller circles into one super-sized mutant pancake. She places the bowl of mixture down and tries to hurriedly fix the mess in the pan, but its too late. Her shoulders drop. "Oh, it's ruined." I step around and switch the heat off, taking the spatula from her hand and pulling her into my arms.

"That one maybe, but the other two hundred look perfect." I lift her chin so her eyes meet mine. Her nose and cheekbones have flour dusted in streaks, and she would look cute and adorable if her eyes weren't so damn worried. "Talk to me, beautiful." Her lips thin as she bites them together, holding back, but my mouth covers and coaxes with tender kisses. She's unyielding to begin with, but softens as the tension leaves her body, and she responds with more fervour than I had anticipated. I'm not complaining, but I also know her other method of coping is using this sexy little body as a distraction. I suck her bottom lip into my mouth and hold the soft flesh firmly hostage between my teeth. She whimpers and wriggles in my arms trying to climb up my body and take control. I bite down, and she freezes, her eyes widening, taking in my warning glare.

We need to talk, and the only time I'll accept her bottom to my top is when she's impaled on my cock. I narrow my eyes and emit a low grumbling noise from my chest. She pulls away, and I release her lip, tasting the trace of metal on my lip. She swipes her tongue and hums her approval, her eyes so fucking alive I have to check myself. Fucking temptress. "We need to talk." I state emphatically, more to myself and my raging hard-on than to Sam, who nods and now has the decency to look sheepish. Which is better than worried in my book, so I'll take it.

I lift her on to the counter and wedge myself between her thighs. We are almost nose to nose, but she has to tip her head slightly to maintain the all-important eye contact, and I wait. She holds my gaze, searching me as much as I am searching her. God, I love this woman, so much passion and fire dances in those deep brown eyes, so much hurt and hope and *love.* Yeah, there is a shit-tonne of love right there. My heart swells; I can feel it in my chest, beating just a little harder, a little faster, just for her.

"It was about me?" Her softly spoken words hit me like a sucker punch, because she's so fucking right. Everything is about her, but that's not what she means...not right now, at least.

"What was about you, beautiful?" I keep my intonation impassive, but she just slowly raises her perfect brow in query at my evasion. I concede a small nod of acknowledgement. "Yes."

She lets out her held breath, and her cheek dimples with a half smile. "Poisoned chalice that one—" She pauses, but she hasn't finished. "I'm glad it was about me that kept you from me, not something or someone else, I mean. But—" She hesitates for another long moment. "It's about me—" She leaves her statement hanging, and it's her turn to wait for me to fill in the blanks. But how much do I fill? She's smart, strong, and brave but she really shouldn't have to be all of those things. Not anymore, not with me in her life. *That is my job.*

"Did Richard have any siblings?" Her face pales, and her whole body becomes rigid under my fingertips.

"Shit!" She drops her head, but it snaps back with that familiar and welcome fire burning in her eyes. "What happened, Jason?"

I don't hesitate to answer. I don't want her to think I'm taking my time because I am censoring what she needs to know. I am, but she doesn't need to know that. Whether she would like that I am doing that is questionable, but protecting her is my job, and I take it very seriously. "I got an email, a threat of sorts, and it could only have come from someone close to

Richard— a brother or—" She shakes her head, interrupting my suggestions.

"He didn't have any siblings. He had a younger cousin, but I never met him. He lived in the States. Richard's family went to live near them when they emigrated. What was in the email exactly?" I don't clench my jaw even though I feel the tension in every cell. She is watching me like a hawk, and I have no intention of sharing this little nasty nugget of information.

"It was vague. It regarded you and Richard, but there was an undertone I didn't like. Did you see anyone you recognised while on the boat?"

"You know I didn't, Jason. What did the email say?" She repeats it, but doesn't give me time to answer. "Did it say something about Richard and me as a couple or was it about what happened on the boat?" Her back straightens, and her eyes are suddenly wild with panic. "They watched…did they make a recording?" Her voice is pitched with terror. I shake my head.

"No, not that. I promise it wasn't that." She visibly relaxes at my words, and I curse that I am feeding her half-truths. But her reaction alone is justification that I am doing the right thing, being selective with the information. I will protect her from this at any cost, and I will find the fucker responsible. I will happily cleave his chest open, cut his dick off, and place it where his heart should be.

"I'll forward you a copy." *Well, I will send something that resembles a copy of the email I received.* "I'm sure you'll read it and probably think I'm overreacting." I shrug off my comment, trying to make light of the situation for her benefit. Her eyes are searching every tick and twitch on my impassive face. Once satisfied, she exhales a long slow breath. I cup her jaw with one hand, and she leans into it. "This is you, Sam, and you are mine. You are my *only* concern." Her smile is fragile, and she loops her arms over my shoulder and pulls me into her embrace.

"Thank you." Her lips purse for me to take, and I do. My hand slides into her messy bun, and I grip her hard against my mouth, forcefully, urgently, and utterly proprietary. When I release her, she is grinning widely and a little breathless.

"You are most welcome." I lean into her tummy and hitch her over my shoulder, slapping her cotton-covered arse soundly, the noise echoing in the hallway as I stride through the house. She grips my loose jeans to steady herself, giggling and gasping for air.

"What are you doing?"

"You really want me to answer that?" My tone is derisive. I take the stairs two at a time.

"Aren't you hungry?" She grunts as each step exerts more pressure on her tummy.

"Always," I growl, and I hear her swallow down a whimper.

THIRTEEN

Sam

IBOUNCE BACK PRETTY QUICKLY AFTER MY MONUMENTAL meltdown and marathon baking session. I call Leon to fill him in, and Jason calls his parents to postpone our visit. In all honesty, I want to get that first visit out of the way, but I am not going to deny an entire weekend spent indulging in all things Jason. I happen to think a day trip is preferable to an overnighter in light of the separate bedroom disclosure. I still can't get my head around that, if Jason says his parents know about him, and I mean really know about him and it's not a religious requirement, I struggle to see what the problem would be. It's not like I'd leave the handcuffs still attached to the headboard or butt plugs in the sink...*hmm, well, I might.*

I lean back in Jason's mammoth bathtub; bubbles up to my ears and magical aroma oils infused in the water soothe my aching bones. My body is suffering on all levels of physical endurance, not just from trying to keep up with an iron/

marathon man hybrid, but we played newbie tourists all day. I loved every minute, from riding the top of the sightseeing tour bus, to the London Eye and lunch at the top of the Shard. We have walked from our home on the Southbank over the bridge toward Covent Garden, Leicester Square, Bond Street, along Piccadilly to Westminster, and back along the embankment. Fucking miles and I didn't notice the pain in my feet until I stopped. My poor toes are throbbing but are currently in tootsie heaven, submerged in the searing hot, scented water, and I wriggle them to try and get the feeling back without the agony.

Jason returns with an ice bucket and two glasses, but that's not what makes my mouth water. It's his toned, muscled chest, cut abs narrowing down to that divine muscle that is like a homing beacon to my libido. His snug boxer shorts just exaggerate all the goodness that muscle is pointing to. My mouth is suddenly dry, and I hold out my hand for the glass. His wicked grin widens, catching me red-handed staring at his cookie jar.

"See something you like, beautiful?" His lips twist into a smug smile as he nonchalantly pours the Champagne.

I blurt out a short laugh and shake my head. "Oh, the last thing you need is a stroke to that massive ego of yours."

"You're right, that's not what I want stroked." His voice drops a level, to a delicious and deeply salacious tone. "I have something else that is massive, that definitely needs that attention—if you're offering?"

I groan at the truly tempting thought, but my whole body revolts, and I sink under the water for refuge from his relentless sexual demands. *His blood must run thick with an equal mix of Red Bull and Viagra.* When I surface, I am faced with an ice-cold glass of liquid heaven, golden bubbles race for the surface as condensation trickles down the outside of the slim flute. My taste buds tingle. I sweep the wet hair back off my face and take the glass, raising it to clink with the one Jason is holding.

"What are we toasting? This is a school night, you know? We both have work tomorrow." I shake my head with mock disapproval.

"That is never going to be a reason to not celebrate what we have." He clinks my glass and, with his free hand, drags his boxers down his thick thighs, kicking them to the corner for the laundry fairies. *I mean that.* I have yet to see a dirty pile of clothes or heap of damp towels like Leon used to leave wherever he dropped them. "As for a toast, how about to health and happiness?" He holds a wry, sardonic smile.

"Ah, you're so sweet, I think I had a little bit of vomit in my mouth," I tease. He carefully steps in the tub, lowering himself and sending a wave of surplus water over the edge.

"Cute. How about to too much sex and even more orgasms?" he retorts and hums a sexy laugh.

"Oh, I like that." I pull my legs up to give him room, but the water is so high only my kneecaps are exposed. "I would've said there could never be too much sex where you and I are concerned, but seriously, I can barely walk. I'm going to look like I've been fucked by—" He holds up a warning finger to interrupt and his face darkens.

"Please, don't finish that sentence, even as a joke. I do not like to picture you being fucked by anyone but me."

"You, then. I'm good with that." I smile sweetly and watch his features soften.

"Me and Will, you mean?" His brow raises, but his tone is playful. His eyes give nothing away, and that worries me.

"Only if you're happy with that, Jason. The fantasy doesn't go away. That's why I said what I said last night, but I'm cool if you don't want to. I get it, really I do. This is not a deal breaker situation." My sheepish grin widens with his breathtaking smile. I add with a dismissive shrug. "Because I know for a fact I wouldn't be happy seeing you fuck another woman…a man on the other hand…Ow!" His fingers that had been trailing delicate patterns up my inner thigh reach forward and flick my nipple.

"Never going to happen, beautiful. So you can kill that thought right now." He holds my gaze and waits for me to acknowledge what he said. Even if I was joking, it is very clear he isn't. I nod and he gives me a wink, switching from stern to sexy so fast I get a little whiplash. "But I meant what I said, Sam. Christmas *was* a one-time thing, but the bottom line is, I make the rules, and my number one rule is to make you happy. I will do *anything* to make you happy. I'm happy when you're happy. It is that simple."

"You make me happy—very happy." I bite back the widest smile I feel begin to split my face, but it's pointless. Happiness is bursting from me because of him, and he deserves to see it. He really does.

"Good." He downs the rest of his drink and takes my foot in his hands, magically massaging the tiny tender muscles. "But not Leon," he states after a moment. I had let my head drop with the blissful feeling radiating from his touch and seeping through every cell in my body.

"Hmm?" I lift my head, but that champagne is working in tandem with his ministrations to send me to sleep.

"With Will, I know it's just sex. I mean he likes you, but it won't ever be more than sex. He's my brother, and I trust him, end of. With Leon, I'm not so sure. I won't pretend I don't hate that he has a connection with you, and I know there's nothing there on your end. But he loves you, and that line can get very blurred when sex is involved. Especially, phenomenal mind-blowing, out of this fucking world sex. So, I'm going to be selfish. Just thought I should make that clear." My heart beats a little harder at his words. I understand, completely, and the fact that he will share at all is massive for him. As much as I trust Leon, Jason isn't wrong. I know Leon loves me, and love complicates things even in the best of friendships.

"God, I love you." I pull my foot from his hand and slip my way up his body until I am wrapped and wedged around him, nose to nose, chest to chest, and heat to scorching heat.

"Good. Now, prove it." His cocky grin and hand on my shoulder makes me melt.

"Because nothing says 'I love you' like deep throating with champagne in the bath." I swipe my tongue enticingly along my bottom lip, fixing my gaze to his carnal glare.

"You got that right, beautiful." I sink down and wait for the sexiest sound known to woman—her man coming undone. I look up through my lashes as he drops his head back and lets out that gorgeous guttural sound as I take his length in my hand and squeeze. I swipe my tongue over the tip and feel him shudder. My lips hover just a breath away, and I relish his sharp intake of breath as I take him deep to the back of my throat, my fist making up the difference because he is just too damn big. *As if that's a thing.* I pump up and down, setting my own pace even as his hand threads under my hair and holds my neck with gentle pressure. I can feel every pulse of blood pushing through his thick veins with my tongue, and his salty taste is just as much an indication that he is close as is the constant twitch and tick of his taut thigh muscles. His fingers grip my neck, and I pull back and let him slide from my mouth.

I draw in a breath and look up to see two darkly dangerous eyes glaring back at me.

"You better have a good reason for stopping, beautiful."

"I do. I was thirsty." Before he can say, "State the obvious",

I reach for the champagne glass and take a large sip. I hold it in my mouth, only to place my lips back at the tip of his steely solid erection. I can't speak, but really I don't need to. His eyes widen as I slowly push him into my mouth. Trying my best to draw his cock inside without losing too much of the bubbly liquid.

"Oh, shit, that's…that's…Mmm." His hips surge forward, and I have to quickly swallow. Some Champagne sprays from my lips, but the lustful look in his eyes has me reaching once more for my drink and repeating the process. I can't think of a better way to get drunk. The third time I do this, both his hands wrap around my neck, supporting but not pushing, and I relax and let him fuck my face. His gentle hip action and the swell of his cock fills my mouth and throat, and I swallow like crazy when he jerks and empties down the back of my throat with a final thrust and roar. My lips are still wrapped around him when he pulls me up his body and kisses me hard.

"You're amazing, you know that?" I don't get to answer; his lips are on me again, his tongue diving in and stealing the very words from my lips. His arms wrap tight, and he twists our bodies so I am on my back, and he is looming large and lethal. The warm silky water swirls around me as I scooch back and give him all the room he is going to need. My mouth dries, and I lick my lips to moisten them; I am suddenly parched.

He reaches over to grab his glass and the bottle from the ice bucket. He tips the glass to my lips and, none to carefully, he pours the remaining champagne into my mouth, most of it spilling down my chin and onto my chest.

"Oops." He grins a wicked wide and not remotely remorseful smile. He replaces the glass but holds the bottle poised over my breasts. "You spilt some."

"I did." My voice is hoarse and hushed. His eyes bore into

me, so damn hot my skin sizzles until I jolt with the shock of ice cold champagne pouring onto my breasts.

"So did I." His mouth is on my skin, burning with wanton heat, searing where he touches from the sharp contrast of temperatures. I don't feel the bubbles, but my skin tingles as he drags his tongue and sucks on my body, licking it clean of the mess he made. His lips close around my aching nipple, and he sucks hard enough to make me cry out and arch into the draw of pressure.

"Oh, God," I pant out with fevered gasps of air. I hear the bottle thump to the floor and then his other hand is holding my other breast and pinching the nipple ready for his mouth. I am so damn needy, I fight to open my legs, but he has me pinned with his bent legs on either side of mine. I have absolutely no chance of getting off until *he* decides. I writhe beneath him. My hands pull his hair, and I moan for some sweet relief. "Please, Jason, please." He doesn't look up as I implore him, my eyes begging but to no avail. His focus is entirely on my breasts, and it feels so damn good, but fuck, I need to come. "Please, make me come. I need to come." I think I scream the last part, but the noise of swishing water and bodies sliding drowns me out.

He lifts me high into his arms and stands. I wrap my legs tight around his waist and cling for dear life as he steps from the bath and slams me up against the wall. His mouth is at my neck, his teeth scraping the soft skin and making me shiver. His breath cools the wet skin even though it feels scorching hot.

"You want to come, beautiful?" His deep tone is as rough as gravel, raw and sexy.

"Oh, God, yes, yes, please." I hold my breath, and the tension in my body is like a high wire when I feel his fingers between my legs, moving into position. I tremble and gasp when he thrusts his full and considerable length into me. So fucking hard and so very, very deep, my head drops to his shoulder, and I scream when he bites down on my exposed neck. I scream, and I explode. A million tiny sparks fire. Each and every nerve, and the individual hairs on my skin, peak with shots of electricity dancing across the surface of my skin. I cling to him as shudder after shudder wracks my body before they start to ebb, and I am able to breathe again. My heart is beating so hard, I see dark dots when I open my eyes. There is just not enough oxygen in my body to make me function like a normal human, but then that was far from normal. *I love our normal.*

"Wow," I manage to speak after some very deep and steadying breaths. I still haven't relinquished my hold, but Jason now has my bottom perched on the countertop with the sink, his forehead resting on mine. I get a warm, deep tingle of satisfaction that it is not just me who is affected by what we do together. He rocks my world, but together, we rock *us*.

"This isn't business, Jason. Are you sure Daniel is okay with it?" I take my seat in the Stone company jet. The large leather lounge chairs are absolute luxury, but I would've been fine flying commercial. Well, not fine exactly, I fucking hate flying, but I would survive.

"You don't like to fly, so I thought this would be better." He looks directly at me like I made the dumbest remark.

"It is, but I don't want you taking liberties and getting into trouble on my behalf." I try to argue, but his face just looks more confused until it changes and makes my core clench.

"Really, you don't want me taking liberties?" His lips turn up at the edges and carve a wicked smile.

"Oh, I definitely want—Shit!" The twin engines fire up,

and the noise drowns out my thoughts and my curses. Jason's hand covers mine; I turn my hand up and return the hold, although mine is more like a death grip.

"I don't have to ask permission, if that's what you mean, and there is no way Daniel will be leaving the country anytime soon, not with the baby due." Jason's tone is calm, his hold a comfort, but it's not enough to quell my anxiety.

"Oh yes!" I mutter, but my mind isn't engaged with this conversation. I press my head back and feel the pull of gravity as we hurtle down the runway and lift off.

"Shall we play the rapid-fire question game again? That seemed to work at keeping your mind off flying. At least until I can *take your mind off flying*." His tone drops with sinful, sensual intent, and I get a deep tingle that starts at the base of my spine and makes me clench in all the right places.

"Okay." I flash a tight smile that barely crinkles my lips. "You go first."

"What's your earliest memory?" He fires at me without hesitation.

"Oh, um..." My fingers release the hold on the armrest to tap my lips, thinking.

"It's rapid fire, Sam. You do understand the concept?" he teases, his thumb softly stroking the wrist of the hand he is still holding with a firm grip.

"Right, sorry. I remember my Grandfather. It might not be my very earliest memory, but it's the first that springs to mind. I used to sit on his lap next to the open fire, and he would tell me stories. I don't remember what they were, but I liked them." I absently rub my leg with my free hand. "I can still feel the rough scratch of his tweed trousers against my bare legs. He had this big dent in his nose from his heavy glasses, and he always had butterscotch candy in his inside jacket pocket. He would secretly give me a piece or two. I wasn't allowed sweets." I turn to see Jason staring at me utterly absorbed, like I am telling the greatest story ever told. I can't help but smile at the memory. I adored my Grandfather, and that is a beloved memory I haven't thought about in forever. "You know, like the sweets from that television advert? He actually gave me those, just like the ad. They were forbidden and tasted all the better for it."

"I don't doubt that for a moment." Jason smirks.

"My turn. What's your most embarrassing memory?" I shift to face him, relaxed enough to move, which is an improvement from terror-induced rigor mortis.

"Hell, no, I will take the forfeit," he barks out, shaking his head.

"No fucking way! You have to tell me now," I challenge, my interest clearly piqued if the memory has this type of reaction on Mr. Shameless.

"Not a fucking chance am I revealing that, and if you ask Will to tell you, just know I will cut his balls off if he so much as utters one word," he states, but I shrug off his threat until he clarifies. "So he won't be able to *play*."

"That bad, eh?" I laugh as he hangs his head, shaking it lightly.

"You have no idea," he groans.

"But Will does. Good to know," I taunt, mischief etched in the turn of my smile.

"He won't tell you—on pain of death, he won't utter a word." His emphatic tone, I think, is more for his benefit, because I just smile ruefully.

"Hmm, I'm sure you're right. After all, who am I to get someone to tell me all their secrets? I wouldn't know where to begin..." I lightly tap my lips at the non-existent quandary. It wouldn't even be a challenge. "It can't be worse than walking through town in your girlfriend's underwear," I add with a wry smile, biting back the shit-eating grin as his eyes first narrow and then widen with disbelief.

"Oh, he did not tell you about that?" His jaw grits tight and a deep rumble growls low in his chest.

"Oh, he did, and I didn't even have to use my whip." I laugh and shake my shoulders with a certain amount of pride. Jason's lips flatten with a smidgen of smugness. It only takes me a moment to recognise that look. "Dammit, that wasn't it, was it? Tell me. I really need to know now." I clasp my hands together to aid my plea, but it falls on deaf ears and a wider smile.

"Dream on, beautiful, but that secret is going to our graves. Try another." He waves his hand, moving the conversation on to safer ground.

"Fine! What's your happiest memory?" I pout, but only for a second because I am more interested in his answer than pursuing a topic I know he won't reveal unless he wants to.

"I have two moments tied at first place. Seeing you alive in the hospital." He pauses to swallow, and his eyes flash with pain we both share, but he shakes it off just as quickly. "And then seeing you come apart in my hands on Christmas Day. *That* was pretty fucking spectacular…definitely my happiest moments."

"Wow! Mine, too. Although, you walking through your office door the other day when I imagined the worst comes a close second, but how about before me?" I love that we share a favourite happy moment, but I am eager to hear what else brings him joy besides me.

"That's two questions?" he counters.

"Technically, it's still one. I'd like to know something before me. Our shared stuff I know about. Give me something more." I wiggle my brows suggestively, a playful grin dancing on my lips.

"You want more." His deep voice drops a little to a rough sexy timbre that makes my whole body shiver.

"Jason." My tone is a warning, despite being deliciously distracted.

"Fine." He holds up his hands in surrender, his bright smile dazzling, and I find I am a little more distracted. "Okay, it has to be seeing my Mum's face when my brother came home, clean. She'd been through hell, and to see her so happy after so much heartbreak, that definitely made me happy. Will and I both vowed that she would never again suffer the way she did with Will, well, with both of us really. I wasn't the easiest son. She's an amazing woman and deserves all the happiness in the world. She smiled that day, and she hadn't for so long. Yeah, that's my happiest memory."

"That's really sweet, Jason, and I'm sure she's super proud of you both. She did good." I playfully fist bump his chin and he flashes a shy, adorable smile.

"Her happiness is important, so I try." The pilot announces we are free to roam and Jason takes the first opportunity to scoop me onto his lap. His lips brush my neck, and I feel the shock of a million prickles kiss my skin. His breath scorches as he exhales a low whisper. "Tell me a secret so dirty it turns you on just to tell it?"

I drop my head to the side to give him all the access and more, then sigh. "Jason, you know all my dirty secrets. You fulfill all my dirty desires, and you own this depraved body and soul, but that wasn't a question."

"Maybe not, but that was the perfect answer." His mouth covers mine, his urgent hands explore my body, and I relish in his undivided attention and distracting tactics for the entire eight-hour flight.

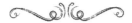

Getting through customs took a little longer than anticipated, due to my passport having a US stamp from leaving the country on my last visit but not one for entry. The officer looked highly sceptical at my explanation—and that actually gave me a disproportionate amount of comfort, that, thankfully, a kidnapping is still rare enough to raise an eyebrow or two. He did have to seek out his superior before I was allowed to re-join Jason, and we were both let through to the arrivals lounge, where Will was waiting.

Will leans against a column a few feet back from the welcoming crowd. His hair is perhaps a little longer, and he is wearing the scruffiest board shorts and faded T-shirt, which when he raises his arm in greeting, exposes his trim tanned stomach. His grin lights up the airport and having instantly clocked us, he is already striding forward to close the distance. Jason's arm, which was loosely draped across my shoulder, tightens, and I snicker and playfully jab my elbow in his side.

"What?" He just pulls me tighter so there is no room to poke him again. I raise a curious brow, but he holds my glare with impassive innocence. Before we take another step, I slip out of his hold and step in front of him, causing him to bump into me. His arms grab my shoulders to steady us both. His brows furrow with confusion, and I take that moment to reach up and softly kiss his lips, his cheek, and whisper in his ear.

"You own me…just you." I rock back on to my heels and watch his lips spread wide and deep into the most stunning smile, eclipsing his brother's grin, much like the sun outshines the moon.

"Damn right, I do." His gravelly tone is clipped, and he makes me squeal when he snaps to bend and lift me, caveman style onto his shoulder. I wriggle and reach, too late to grab my suitcase, as he strides away.

"Wait, wait, my case!" He slaps my arse, and I bite back a howl because, man, that stung like a bitch, but we are already making enough of an exhibition. Regardless of my cries, he continues to walk away from my worldly goods.

"Hey, man." Jason greets his brother with a shoulder press—his other shoulder. "Grab Sam's case, would you, Will? I kinda got my hands full."

Will barks out a laugh. "I can see that." He continues to laugh as he finally comes into my line of sight. I have one hand gripping tight to the seat of Jason's pants, partly for balance and partly to yank hard if he gives me any trouble—any more trouble, that is. "Hey, Sam, good to see you." Will has my case and is following directly behind Jason, grinning like an idiot as I bob uncomfortably on his brother's shoulder, grunting with the impact of each long stride.

"Yeah, you, too. Did you bring your car, or is he going to carry me all the way to your apartment, do you think?" I tease, but Jason doesn't break his stride.

"You honestly think you're staying with me and my flat mates? He hasn't even let me shake your hand yet, Sam." Jason spins so I am facing the sea of cars in the airport parking.

"Where are you parked?" Jason asks, completely ignoring our banter. I take that break in momentum to wriggle and slide down his body. He lets it happen; I would still be impaled on his bony shoulder if that wasn't the case, but he keeps his arms protectively around my waist even as I turn to face Will. I offer my hand for Will to shake. He stretches out, dropping the handle of my case. He takes my hand and turns it, and leans down to kiss the back. He flashes me a wicked smile and yanks me from Jason's hold. I hit Will's chest with a gasp. Will leans in and presses his lips against mine. I wedge them tight, but even without his tongue, the kiss still feels nice. He releases me, and I step back a little dazed and a lot apprehensive. I glance at Jason, expecting to see a shit storm brewing, but he is just standing there with his arms crossed. Muscles flexed on his forearm, his back ramrod straight, and a stern thin line behind which his full soft lips are lurking.

"Remind me why the fuck I decided to visit you, exactly?" His calm delivery belies the tempered fury I see etched on his face. "Do we need to take this outside so I can lay the boundaries out clearly in the form of kicking your sorry arse and painting a purple palette of bruises all over your pretty face?" His eyes narrow, and although his tone is not quite deadly, it's not exactly light and fluffy, either. I step between them, my palm placed flat on both their sculpted chests. I draw in a breath and lightly tap my fingers.

"Now, now…let's play nice." My soothing voice has absolutely no impact on the raging testosterone, but I persevere. "I *know* you both know how to do that. So how about we put our swords away until later and go grab something to eat?" I bite back my smirk, because as funny as I thought my double entendre was, I don't think Jason is quite ready for my jokes.

Will hold his hands up in an open display of surrender and laughs, instantly easing the tension. "Stand down, Jason. You can't blame me for trying, besides I never thought this day would happen, so I'm allowed a little slack in trying to get a rise out of you," he blurts out another belly laugh at Jason's disgruntled growl.

"Laugh it up, brother, but one more stunt like that, and Sam and I will find another playdate." Jason snakes his arm territorially around my waist, and I watch as Will's eyes widen with understanding at what he has just heard. I have to bite back a whimper. I really don't need to add anything flammable to his powder keg of testosterone.

Will swallows slowly, his tongue darts out to wet his lips, mirroring my own, but he is looking above me and directly at Jason. I don't see it, but I feel the shift, an understanding and acknowledgement of the balance of power. All in a silent exchange that makes me shiver and melt.

"I'm parked over here." Will breaks the burgeoning sexual tension, and I let out an exaggerated breath and mockingly fan myself. That makes Jason smile. In truth, there is very little mocking; I am off the charts horny and burning up, sandwiched, as I am, between my man and his mirror image.

Jason sits beside me in the back of Will's beat-up Jeep. This time of year, the heat isn't too bad, which is a blessing because this thing pre-dates air-con. I think it might pre-date the Ark. Jason's arm is a weighty reminder along my shoulder that he has yet to fully relax. I lean into his hold and place my hand on the buckle of his belt, my fingertips creeping under his thin sweater. His tummy tightens at my touch, and I can feel more than hear the low rumble of pleasure travel from the back of his throat. I rest my palm flat on his taut abs; his skin feels like it's on fire, or maybe that's just me. I look up to see him looking down at me; carnal desire so raw, I know for a fact it isn't just me.

"So what are your plans exactly?" Will yells over his shoulder, his bright enthusiastic tone momentarily drowning out the noise of the car's ancient engine.

"A few days at the Four Seasons and then we're heading down to the Keys for some privacy." Jason's disclosure is a shutdown statement if ever I heard one. I pinch his skin. It has little give so it stings enough to warrant a warning glare.

"Play nice," I mouth. Will has fallen silent, and I can see in the rear view mirror his brows are set in a deep frown. Jason draws in a deep breath and reaches his arm to nudge Will's shoulder.

"You're gonna hang with us though while we're in town right?" I can see from the crinkle in Will's eyes that the question has caused a big ol' smile, and I squeeze my appreciation tight around Jason's waist. Apart from Will's surprise visit last month, they normally don't see each other very often, and I don't want to be the one to make that situation worse.

"Yeah, I'd like that," Will calls back, his light tone evidence of his lifted spirit.

"Good. I've booked us a table at the steak bar for tonight, but then I've got nothing planned, so I'm happy for you to take the lead." Jason offers the olive branch.

"Oh, really?" Will's highly suspicious mocking tone makes my heart sink. Jesus, you just can't help some people. I snap upright and shuffle to the corner of the car.

"Right, call a truce, boys, or so help me, I will book myself into the nearest spa and you won't see me for the next seven days…either of you!" I bite out these words with utter conviction and seriousness, but I add just in case there is any misunderstanding. "I won't come between you…not like this. I mean it." Jason laughs and purses his lips like I have just done something incredibly cute. Will just snickers.

"Stand down, soldier. This is just Will being an arse hat. This has nothing to do with you. This is how we are." I narrow my eyes, because I have my doubts. Jason slaps Will's shoulder. "Isn't that right, dickhead?"

"Yeah, buddy, that's right." Will shifts to the side, twisting so he can look directly at me while we are parked in the heavy lunchtime traffic. "Look, Jason loves you, Sam, and I couldn't be happier, but he's also my brother, so I just have to take my shots when I can. It's sort of like the law, but I respect the shit out of what you two have, and I will only *ever* come between you two *if* I'm invited." His warm smile is genuine and heartfelt. I particularly like the way he emphasised the word *if*, because the *whens* would be entirely at the discretion of Mr. Possessive sitting beside me.

Jason sweeps his arm out and scoops me back onto his lap and as if reading my mind he whispers, "You green light the *if*'s, beautiful, but I decide the *whens*, understand?"

"Yes, Sir." My whispered response is more breathless because he does that with his words and his actions; he steals the very air from my lungs.

"I heard that!" Will yells over the noise of the car now that we are moving again. "And now I have a killer boner trying to rip my shorts in two. Cheers, guys." He groans and then starts this weird disgusting mantra, mumbling, "Genital warts and Granddad bollocks, genital warts and blue waf—"

"Okay, okay, we get the picture—you need distracting. How's work?" I jump in with my interruption before his list becomes even more disturbing.

"Work might not help. I fucking love my job, but I don't officially start until next month." He chuckles and tries to discreetly fix his predicament. "I'm kind of on a sabbatical between contracts. It's why I was able to sneak in that extra visit to you guys. I don't normally get this much free time." He grins like the cat with a bucket of cream. "How about I tell you what we're doing tomorrow?" His voice is pitched with infectious joy.

"Oh, yes." I bounce a little and lean forward, my hand gripping either side of the headrest. My tone is eager for information, my expression a picture of excitement. I flash a wink at Jason, but quickly turn back when Will starts to talk.

"I thought you might like to come see the center where I am going to be working. We have a compound at the back for the rescue animals. I'm more on the conservation side, but we do get calls where people don't know what to do with whatever they've found. We don't keep them there for long. We try to find suitable homes straight away, but yesterday we got a call to pick up a white tiger cub that was in a crate on one of the boats that was impounded at the dock. "

"Really? That's awful." I mutter.

"It is, but I've seen worse, and this little fella is one of the lucky ones." Will shrugs, clearly not wanting to dwell on that aspect of his job. "He's pretty cute, but he gets picked up sometime tomorrow, so I thought we could drop by before we go to the lake."

"The lake?" I look back at Jason who shakes his head and shrugs, because this is news to him as well.

"Thought we could take the jets out for a race, if you're up for it?" Will's smile is as wide as his tone is challenging. *Bring it on…although…*

"Oh, I'm up to it, but I've never actually driven a Jet Ski, so—"

"Then that would be a *no*," Jason interrupts with a look of disbelief blazoned on his face.

"What?" I cry out.

"You just said you've never driven a Jet Ski, but you are happy to have a go at racing my brother!" He rolls his eyes, and his condescending tone has my hackles rising.

"And?" I snap and lean back as far as the back seat and sitting on his lap will allow, but I think he gets me.

"You must have lost your mind somewhere over the Atlantic if you think I'd let you do that." He chuckles. *Maybe he doesn't get me.*

"You don't get to tell me what I can and cannot drive. You are not the boss of me," I state flatly. My eyes fix him with my sternest stare, but he is unfazed. In fact, that spark and flash of heat I see means, if I'm not mistaken, that he is turned on.

"Wrong!" He grabs the back of my head and smashes my face to his, crushing the sass right from my lips and melding me to him. I twist and crawl so I am now straddling him because this kiss is all fire and lust, and I can't get enough. He breaks and fixes me with eyes burning with passion and love.

"We will race, but you will be wrapped around me when we do, okay?"

"Spoilsport." I playfully poke my tongue before I grab him right back, kissing him with a fever I feel in my soul and pray will never fade. Not even when I hear Will moan.

"Fucking brilliant!"

I barely notice the rest of the drive until we come to a complete stop under the shade of the large canopy overhang of the Four Seasons Hotel Miami. Arrangements to meet in the bar tonight are quickly made, but he has no intention of sitting around as third wheel for the afternoon. Will dumps our bags with the bellboy and waves us off.

FOURTEEN

Sam

"WILL'S WAITING IN THE BAR DOWNSTAIRS," JASON calls out from the bedroom. He opted for a quick shower that could've happened five minutes or five hours ago. I am in heaven, drifting in and out of a bubble-bath-induced daze, soaking aching muscles and soothing sun-kissed skin not used to exposure this early in the year.

"And I'm still in the bath," I yell back but make no movement to remedy the problem. My eyes are closed, the lids too heavy, or maybe I'm just too relaxed, but I feel him watching me. I peek through one eye and smile. He is dressed, but his stealthy approach meant even his shoes made no sound on the marble tiled floor. I open my eyes, and at the first sight, I find myself sitting taller, leaning toward him because he does that; he draws me in, and he knows it. I drag my stare so slowly up his immaculately suited form. I am not at all surprised by his knowing grin, spread wide and wicked across his handsome face.

"Keep looking at me like that, beautiful, and see what happens." He pulls his cuffs free from his jacket sleeve, adjusting the platinum links I bought him for Christmas—puzzle pieces to match my tattoo.

"You can't be serious? I can barely walk!"

"If it's only barely, then I think you know the answer to that one." He steps farther into the cavernous bathroom, which suddenly feels claustrophobic and a little too hot, but I hold his heated gaze. He towers over me, blocking the overhead soft lighting, all dark and dominant. So fucking hot, but I wasn't kidding about the sex. He may very well be half man, half machine, but this human needs to skip a service.

"Back up there, Tony." I hold my hand up and sink down into the deep water up to my neck; a mass of silky bubbles cloak my nakedness. But the way he holds my gaze, it doesn't matter, he sees me, *all of me.*

"Tony?" He queries with a wry smile.

"Stark, you know as in Iron Man, never mind—"

"Oh, I get the reference, but if you're going for Marvel superheroes, I think I prefer Thor." He smirks.

"You do have a very impressive hammer, but you're not the only one that can pick it up, are you?" He steps back away from my wet arm and dripping hand as I make a grab for his magic tool.

"Cute, but I meant demigod," he states without a hint of irony, and I shake my head. He's so full of himself, even if I do happen to agree. "And if you get me wet, beautiful, I'm joining you in that bath right now." His tone holds a light warning.

"Fine!" I snap my hand back and hide it under the blanket of bubbles. "Look, you go down to the bar. I'll follow in a bit. I am not quite recovered from this afternoon, or the flight."

"Really?" His sinful tone and the playful wiggle of his thick brow make me snort a short loud laugh.

"Really. Don't look so surprised. If I died tonight, they would have to bury me in a Y-shaped coffin. You're relentless." I roll my eyes at his salacious grin.

"You make me relentless. I can't take all the credit."

"Jeez, you're incorrigible."

"I really am." He steps back to bend closer, his hand cups my cheek and his fingers slide to pinch my chin. He swoops down to plant a tender kiss on my expectant lips and hovers just millimeters from me. The sexual charge between us fires like a lightning storm, and my skin prickles despite the heat. Endless erotic seconds tick slowly by until he breaks the hold, pulling back to speak. "If you're sure. I don't mind keeping him waiting." I puff out a breath I didn't realise I was holding and regain my senses enough to respond.

"I'm sure. Please go. It will give you a chance to catch up and maybe we can drop all the willy-waving and actually have a nice evening together." My comment is playful, but I am only half joking.

"I don't willy-wave. It would imply there is some sort of competition. There is no competition." He punctuates his matter-of-fact statement with a cocky wink.

"No, there isn't. None at all. So let's have some fun." I reiterate my feeling for the umpteenth time.

"Fun we can definitely do." He blows me a kiss from the doorway.

"Perfect." I close my eyes and lay my head back; the light curl of my lips spreads to rival the Cheshire cat when I hear his parting words.

"Yes, yes, you are."

"Reservation under the name Sinclair," I tell the pristinely groomed male host on the spotlit podium at the front of the restaurant. I don't think I have ever seen a goatee trimmed with such precision, and each hair on his head is sleek and styled to GQ cover perfection. The young man is Philippe, according to his gold-plated name badge. He swipes at the concealed screen, his haughty expression barely cracking a courteous acknowledgement of my presence. "I'm a little late. I was supposed to meet them at the bar, but they might've gone to their table by now," I offer to fill the awkward silence.

"The table would not be kept empty, I can assure you. Wait here while I check." He gracefully dismounts his stage and disappears behind an embossed, opaque glass screen. He returns almost instantly with a flush of colour to his cheeks.

"I am sorry to have kept you waiting, please follow me." He is quick to usher me inside, and I follow behind, only to freeze immediately after I enter the room. At the far end of the restaurant, a long sleek bar stretches the length of the room. Low level lighting and not an empty table means the room is alive with atmosphere, buzzing with animated chatter, and oozing glamour. All of which pales into insignificance at the sight ahead, in the center of the cocktail bar.

"Oh, my," I exhale quietly.

"I know." Philippe looks directly at me. His eyes twinkle with mischief, and, thanks to my six-inch heels, we are closer to eye-level so I can actually see the reaction up close. His prior implacable expression softens, and I snicker at the resurgence of that flush to his cheeks, as he, too, clocks my man—*men*. A cursory glance around the room and it is all too evident that the Jason and Will combination is attracting more than its fair share of attention. From furtive fluttered lashes to actual jaws dropping, it would be comical if it weren't wholly justified.

They are both perched on bar stools, facing each other, and at this moment, laughing. Each is dressed immaculately. Jason, I know, is in a navy tailor-made jacket and trousers. I like him in navy. He has a matching dark tie and crisp white shirt. Will looks to be wearing the same style, if not from the same tailor. The cut and quality of the cloth only serves to enhance the packages beneath. Fine Italian fabric shifts over broad shoulders as they both reach for their beers, mirrored and synchronised movements that are too fluid to be staged. Will drags his hand through his hair, which is longer and a shade lighter than Jason's. Even from this distance, I can see he is still sporting his five o'clock shadow from when he picked us up. Christ, they look hot. I swallow back an inaudible whimper and, as if sensing my presence, they both turn. Strike that, they don't look hot, they look absolutely lethal.

"Oh, shit." That exclamation wasn't quite so inaudible.

"What a waste." I turn to see Philippe holding his beating heart and playfully dropping his shoulders, his bottom lip protruding in a playful pout. I laugh and lightly pat his cheek.

"Oh, trust me, Philippe, there won't be any waste." I blow him a kiss, which is my only concession to waste this evening, and I make my way over to the bar.

The heat emanating from these two is palpable and my legs tremble from the effect, but I hold Jason's scorching gaze and draw in a steady, fortifying breath. With each step closer, I feel his burn like a brand on my fevered skin. Tonight, there is no doubt I will be playing with fire. Jason stands before I reach them and sweeps his arm around my waist, molding me to his body and claiming me for all to witness. Urgent powerful lips crush mine, and he doesn't stop until he is ready. I'm in no hurry. I relish the dance and duel of tongues, sweeping and demanding, taking and tasting each other as if we were starving. He releases my mouth, but holds me tight, which is a blessing, because my legs are no longer capable of supporting my weight. He lifts me onto the bar stool and removes his jacket, placing it over my shoulders.

"I'm not cold, Jason. You've just spent five minutes devouring me. I am off the charts turned on, but I'm not cold." I try to shuck the jacket, but he pulls it farther across my body. I slap his hand away when he tries to do the button up.

"I know." He still crosses the front panels as best he can.

"I'm not wearing this all evening." I scowl.

"We'll see." He flashes a self-satisfied smile, pleased with my modified appearance.

"I'm not." I straighten my back and raise a challenging brow. "This is a sexy dress, and the whole swamped in a suit jacket isn't the look I was going for," I quip.

"But giving everyone in the building an erection was?" he retorts.

"Well, duh!" I tease and wink at Will who has remained quietly amused by our exchange. "How about I wear this until I am a little less pointy, hmm?" I smile sweetly, offering my only compromise.

"Sam," Jason grumbles, and I respond with a teasing impression of his stern warning.

"Jason." My attempt to recreate his deep tone causes me to cough and splutter. He reaches over to offer me some water, and when I finish sipping, he nods his agreement to my suggestion.

"That dress is wicked sexy, Sam," Will adds, and I brace, waiting for Jason to pull out some sort of balaclava jumpsuit to hide me in, but he just steps to my side, sweeping my long hair over one shoulder. His featherlike touch makes my whole body shudder, maintaining a chill that ensures I remain covered, *sneaky*. He brushes his lip along the nape of my neck and rests his hand on the bottom of my spine, against my bare skin. The loop of the red silk backless dress barely hugs the curve of my bottom. Thin spaghetti straps hold the floaty material that skims and exposes tantalising amounts of skin. I have it secured discreetly in all the right places and it hangs a modest length just above my knee, but I don't kid myself…it's a fucking sexy dress. Even so, I still needed my killer heels, because looking at these two? They set *that* bar very high.

"Why, thank you, Will, you don't look too dusty yourself." I lean over to kiss his cheek as Jason orders more drinks.

"But it's not *me* giving everyone in the room a boner." He raises his glass like this statement was a toast. I clink my glass to his and take a large sip.

"Philippe, the maître d', would argue that point." I *call* his argument and *raise* since this feels like a high stakes games we are playing. "And judging by the death glares I'm getting, I think you will be responsible for a wet pair of panty or two."

"But there is only one wet panty that is of any interest." Will takes another draw from his beer and holds my gaze as I hold my breath.

"Oh, I forgot to say, Will, Sam can't come out to play today." Jason takes my empty glass for a refill and raises a brow at my dropped jaw. *He has to be kidding?* Dressed like they are, looking like they do, and knowing what I know…He can't possibly be serious. "You're over an hour late, Sam. I take it you fell asleep because you never take that long to get ready."

"I may have had a nap, but—"

"Nah-ah," he interrupts, placing his finger across my lips to silence me. I start to bare my teeth to take a bite of that digit when his words stop me. "You're clearly exhausted, beautiful."

He traces his finger along my jaw. I might've thought for a moment he was teasing, but I can see the genuine concern in his eyes.

"Jason's right, Sam." Will adds his opinion with just as much thoughtfulness in his tone. "You need to be fit and healthy. There's no rush."

"I am fit and healthy," I grumble, leaning back into Jason's hold. I look directly up to his face, which is smirking down at me.

"And utterly shagged…you said so yourself. You need to take it easy for a day or two before we wreck you," he states calmly as a matter-of-fact.

"A day or two?" My indignant cry is cut short. "Wait, wreck me?" My breathless words transform Jason's smirk into the familiar nefarious curl of his soft lips.

"Hmm, hmm." He slowly nods, and I tingle from tip to toe, shiver, and melt all with one sharp intake of breath and clarity of understanding.

"Shall we?" A voice behind me speaks.

"Oh yes, please." My eager response makes Jason laugh out and shake his head.

"Your table is ready, Mr. Sinclair." That voice again…not Jason or Will, but our waiter. My heart drops, my cheeks flush with embarrassment, and my tummy rumbles.

"First things first, beautiful, food, then rest, then—"

"Wrecking?" I slide off the stool and thread my arm through Will's offered crook of his arm. Jason still has his arm wrapped around my waist.

"Yes, beautiful, then you get wrecked."

"If I was wearing any panties, they would be soaked right about now," I mutter low, but loud enough.

"Oh, fuck!" The brothers exhale together, and their

whispered exclamation sounds a lot like a plea.

"You know where to find me when you think I've had enough rest." I smile sweetly as I take my seat in a semi-circular booth, flanked by the sexiest men on the planet. My tummy may rumble, but I am not in the slightest bit hungry for food.

The meal is amazing and delicious enough to take my mind off every woman's wet dream seated on either side of me. Even with Jason absently stroking my thigh, the only groans of satisfaction leaving my mouth are entirely due to the melt-in-the-mouth steaks and triple-cooked chips—sorry, fries. But I am also vocal with my disappointment at the size of the key lime pie. I thought everything was supposed to be super-sized in this country. The delicate biscuit disc in the center of the plate holds a petite tower of pale green mousse and an elaborate curl of chocolate filigree on top of that; it looks very much like a work of art, but it is tiny. I finish mine in fewer than three bites and can't help but covet Jason's untouched order of the same. He doesn't even glance my way, engrossed as he is, talking to Will, but he skilfully switches our plates, and that is why I love this man.

I clean that plate, too, and just wonder if requesting another would be *bad* when Jason excuses himself. I nod my understanding when he mentions the men's room, but I felt the vibration of his phone along the shared seat, and my heart sinks. If it were work, he would say so, and *that* is a worry.

"I'm sure it's nothing." Will covers my hand that is fisting the napkin into a tight ball. He picks my fingers free and threads them with his own.

"You felt that too, huh?" I take comfort from his offered hand and squeeze it in return.

"It was either that, or you're packing more than a killer

body under that dress." He wiggles his brow playfully, and I bark out a dirty laugh.

"You think I'd need any more stimulation sitting between you two," I scoff, but my humour is short-lived.

"Did he tell you?" I ask quietly, searching Will's face for secrets shared.

"Tell me what?" Will's eyes narrow, and I answer his ridiculous question with my silently raised brow. He lets out a heavy sigh. "He told me what he told you, Sam." Will's dark brown eyes hold all the compassion and honesty of his brother, and I feel the warmth of that in my bones. "He worries about your safety, that's not surprising considering...Look, he told me he received an email. But cut him a little slack, he is trying to protect you. You're his life, and he nearly lost you. I know how deep that fear runs in him."

"I know, but protecting me can feel a lot like hiding stuff, and if it's about me, I need to know. I may not like it, but I deserve the chance to make up my own mind."

"I'm sure he knows how you feel." His claim feels very much like a brush off, and I get an uncomfortable feeling there is something more.

"Well, if he doesn't, you two are pretty tight. How about you remind him." I push my point, but he shakes his head before I even finish my sentence.

"Fuck, no, I am not getting in between you two...not like *that*." His grin is utterly wicked but softens to a smile filled with concern. "You're his world, Sam, and he is just protecting his world."

I puff out a deep frustrated breath. I get what Will is saying, but this trust thing goes both ways and sneaking off to take calls doesn't feel like trust.

"So dodged the bullet meeting the in-laws, I see. Really,

Mum's not that bad." Will throws his head back in raucous laughter that completely stuns me.

"What?" My face crinkles with confusion. "What do you mean? I don't understand. Jason said your Mum was cool."

"Really? He said those exact words?" Will runs his hand through his hair front to back and repeats the move. His agitation is doing little to calm my rising anxiety.

"I don't know, now. Yeah, he definitely said I wouldn't need to worry. He said she would be thrilled he was settling down with someone." My words are a rush of nervousness. "He said she wouldn't care what I was, I mean." I pull my hand out of his hold and wrap my arms around my waist. I've never cared what people think about me, so why should I now? I know exactly why…because this is Jason, and this is his Mum, whom he adores. This is a big deal.

"Hmm." Will looks pensive but doesn't try to make light of the conversation, which sends me reeling into full on panic mode.

"Will, is she going to care what I do, what I *did* for a living?" I can feel my tummy roil, and I now challenge the wisdom of Miss Two Desserts.

"Kind of—" He grimaces out a tight smile. *Shit.*

"Why would he tell me different?" I almost screech, the panic rising in my voice but my gritted teeth manage to keep the volume to that of my indoor voice.

"Probably because he loves you and didn't want to freak you out. That's just a guess given that we are over four thousand miles away, and you are, in fact, freaking out." He passes me a glass of water that I snatch and down in one long unladylike glug. I let out a slow breath, but feel the prickle of tears behind my eyes. Will is silently focused on my every move.

"She's going to hate me, Will." I pinch the pressure at the

bridge of my nose and squeeze my eyes tight.

"No, she won't." Will reaches for my hand and pulls it free from my waist. He clasps it between his and shakes his head, emphasising his resolve.

"This is not good. Jason adores her. He told me very recently that he would do anything to make sure she's happy."

"And?" Will's dark brow furrows like he is not following the problem...that *I* am the problem.

"Believe me, Will, her son marrying a sex-trade professional, albeit an *ex*-professional, is not going to make her happy."

"I haven't lived in the UK for years. She's probably lightened up a bit." Will has the decency to look embarrassed at his statement that, given his own admission that he hasn't actually spent much time in the same country, he has absolutely no foundation for.

"Really?" I splutter, my tone thick with sarcasm. "You're sure about that? Because isn't this the same woman that won't let her twenty-nine year old son share his bedroom with his fiancée for one night?"

"Ah, I see your point. You're totally fucked." He pinches his lips together in a shy grin, which morphs into a much larger smile. He's right, but it's hardly his fault, and that face looks far too much like the man I love to stay mad. I screw up the napkin and hurl at his adorable grin.

"Thanks." I let out a resigned sniff and join his smile.

"Who's totally fucked?" Jason slides in beside me.

"Me. Your Mum is going to hate me." Jason scowls at Will, who holds his hands up.

"I was trying to steer the conversation away from your not-so-suptle disappearing act."

"And that's what you came up with? Genius." Jason rolls his eyes at his brother, but quickly turns his full attention to me. His hands cup either side of my face, so we are almost nose to nose. "My Mother will love you because I love you, end of. And what she doesn't know won't hurt her. I won't hurt her any more than I would hurt you. She can be a little judgmental and protective of her boys, but what mother isn't?" I tense in his hands, but he looks mortified. "Ah shit, I didn't mean that. Look, beautiful, I just didn't want you getting all worried. It's not like you ever introduce yourself like 'Hello, my name is Sam, and I'm the best ex-dominatrix in London. Would you like to see my impressive whip collection'?" There is an awkward cough.

"Would you like some coffee or brandy perhaps?" Our waiter is trying desperately hard not to look at me and failing *magnificently*.

"I don't need to introduce myself when you do it *so* well." I flash a tight smile at Jason and address our poor waiter. "I'll have a peppermint tea please and a ball gag, if you have one." The waiter's wide eyes haven't left my face, but his cheeks flush with an adorable splash of dark red.

"I'm sorry, ma'am," he stutters.

"Two espressos and a mint tea will be all, thank you." Jason curtly dismisses the waiter before he starts to drool. "Behave," he grumbles at me.

"*Me* behave? After *that* introduction?" I retort with mock indignation, pulling away from his hold.

"I did say you were the best, and I did say ex. Now, play nice when our waiter gets back." His stern tone is tinged with humour, and his eyes crinkle with the wide smile spreading across his gorgeous face. He shakes his head lightly. "There is no way he will be getting our order right. He couldn't take his eyes off your lips."

"They're very nice lips," Will adds his two cents. I try to smile, but the spread of these 'very nice lips' barely makes a full curl.

"Hey, you have nothing to worry about." Jason threads his hand around the back of my neck, and his hot palm brands my skin. He holds me fixed; his eyes bore into me with a heart melting mix of love and concern. It takes the edge off my worry to some extent, but his mother isn't my only concern.

"And the phone call?" He stiffens and flashes a look at his brother. I can't see the exchange, but his eyes soften when they return their fix on me.

"It was an update, nothing to worry about." He drops his forehead to mine, but I nudge him back up so I can see his eyes.

"Okay, that's all right then, I won't worry…said not me!" I try to pull away, but his hold is strong; his tone is resolute.

"Tomorrow, I will tell you everything, which, by the way, is nothing, but I will tell you tomorrow. Let's have tonight." His voice drops to a sensual whisper that has every hair on the back of my neck dancing.

"But I won't be able to think about anything else," I mutter my objection like a brat.

"Oh, I think we can help with that." His voice is barely audible by every cell in my body heard it in Dolby HD.

"You said no playing." My voice cracks; my throat is suddenly parched.

"I changed my mind." Jason's dark glare is utterly carnal, and I absolutely melt from its intensity.

"Check, please!" Will shouts out, not sure if it was a twin thing, but he certainly read *my* mind.

I'm going to internally combust. Let me paint the picture that's causing this very real crisis inside me right now. We left the restaurant and took the lift to the Presidential suite. Jason and Will stood behind me, silent the whole way, but I could feel their eyes on my back, my legs, my neck, my hair, and definitely my butt. We entered the room, and Jason told me to stand in the lounge area, eyes forward, legs wide, and he warned me not to move while he fixed drinks for himself and Will. They took their sweet time coming back into my line of sight, but damn when they did. Will had lost his shirt completely, and Jason had his loose and open, neither of them had shoes or socks. They each take one of the armchairs facing me and relax, iced drink in hand. Gorgeous—no, that's a wholly inadequate adjective. I wrack my dazed brain, but I don't think there is a word in the English vocabulary to describe this picture of perfection. Two pairs of impossibly dark eyes smoulder and sear my body, from the painted toes of my feet to the tousled hair fallen around my face; carnal, raw and so damn intense. I ache to move my legs together; they twitch enough to make Jason pull his bottom lip through his teeth and raise a knowing brow. This anticipation is pure agony. I'm in heaven, and this—this is sweet hell. I am so ready to burn.

FIFTEEN

Jason

"Lose the dress." I'm impressed my voice sounds as calm as it does, because she looks so fucking beautiful. My throat is bone dry, and my lungs have all but seized up, fighting to get some much-needed oxygen inside. Her hands instantly, but, oh, so slowly, slip the thin straps from her slender shoulders. The weight of silk glides the dress to the floor, revealing the single most amazing view on this planet: My girl, almost naked, and in killer fuck-me heels. Her eyes dip to her thong and then meet mine. She bites her lips tight in an impish grin.

"Tsk, tsk, Sam, you lied about the panties." I shake my head lightly. "Teasing like that deserves its own punishment, don't you think?"

"I think making me stand here looking at you two, all hot as hell, is punishment enough," she grumbles, and I can see her thighs tremble with the effort to keep them parted. I can smell her from here, and my balls are in fucking agony; that aroma is sent from the gods to drive me crazy.

"Oh, I don't think it is." Her eyes widen as I loosen my belt and unzip my pants. Will follows my lead, and I release my straining erection into my waiting fist.

"Oh, shit," she gasps and drops her chin to her chest.

"Eyes on us, beautiful." A deep groan escapes her pursed lips, but she obeys. Her face is flushed, and her jaw is clenched, as her greedy eyes devour each languid stroke I administer to my rock-hard cock. Not for pleasure, mind, I just need to relieve some of the unbearable pressure building in my groin… and, perhaps, to return the favour. Her 'no panties' comment meant this evening I endured a hard-on from hell, at least until the main course was served. Now I think on it, this is definitely to return the tease. I continue to stroke my length, but I am far from getting the relief I crave, because what I crave is just a few tortuous steps away. For a moment, I wonder whom this is teasing exactly.

"Jason," Will mutters beside me, and I can hear the strain in his voice. It would match mine if I spoke. I stand abruptly and kick my loose pants to the side. I turn and nod for Will to do the same. He doesn't need to be told twice. Sam's breath catches when I face her, but she holds it with a pained expression and thin lips when Will and I step closer. She pants out some sexy little puffs of air when we stand on either side of her trembling body, close enough to feel the electricity fire between our bodies, but not touching, not yet.

"Jason, I can't breathe." Her soft voice breaks into a whimper that I feel in the base of my spine.

"Burning up, beautiful?"

"So hot," she gasps, and I don't know if she's referring to the situation we are in or her personal body temperature. It doesn't matter, because she's right. *She is fucking hot.*

"Shower," I state and watch her whole body shudder before she manages a heartfelt, ball-aching moan and replies.

"Oh, God, yes."

Will strides off and opens the door to the en suite, and I scoop Sam into my arms, my erection bobbing and stroking the curve of her arse with every step I take. I walk us both straight into the cavernous shower and wet area and hit the rainforest downpour dial on the control panel. The water is instant, heavy, and hot. The lighting in the room dims with spotlights of blue and green, and there is a soft background sound of a rumbling thunderstorm, which is apt. I am consumed with uncontrollable pent-up lust and tempered desire poised to unleash, just like a storm…a wild force of nature.

We are all instantly drenched, and despite the hot water, Sam's nipples are tight peaks begging for my attention. She cries out when my eager mouth covers and sucks, twirling my tongue around the stiff little pebble. My hands hold both breasts up for my pleasure, and I take turns teasing and squeezing, nibbling and grazing with my teeth. One of her hands fists my hair, and I look up through soaked lashes to see she is leaning back against Will, her other arm reaching high and back behind her, her hand cupping his neck. He is leaning forward, kissing along her shoulder and up to her ear; his other hand wrapped around her waist, holding her tight as she writhes and undulates between us. The moans and groans echo off the tiled walls, but they are soft and no competition for the Amazonian soundtrack playing through the hidden speakers.

I pull back and stand tall, pressing my body against hers. The water aids the glide of skin on skin, but I'm surprised it hasn't sizzled or turned to steam; her body is so damn hot, and we three are all on fucking fire. I tip her chin up, and her lashes flutter with heavy drops of water. Her lips part and are full and wet.

"Thirsty?" I ask, releasing her chin as she tips her head fully back and opens her mouth. The downpour quickly fills her, spilling over her lips. She lifts her head and her wide smile lets the water fall back out. She doesn't swallow...*yet.* I place my hand on her waist and twist until she is sideways between us; her palms are pressed firmly on our chests. I can feel Will's eyes on me, waiting, but mine are fixed on her. I raise a brow, and she instantly drops slowly to her knees. Dragging her nails down our torsos until her tight fists grab a cock in each hand. She looks up at me, then Will, but she always returns her gaze to me; those heavy lids and the utter raw desire alive in her eyes is the fucking sexiest thing ever. Oh, and she's on her knees with my dick in her hand, yeah, that too. She tilts her head like she is weighing her decision, the wicked curl of her lips almost makes me make that choice for her, but I keep my hands flat at my side. She might like to tease, but she's not stupid. I slam one palm hard against the wall to steady myself when her tongue flicks my essence clean off my sensitive crown. Her lips quickly follow, and her tongue works its magic as she eases me into her mouth. Her nimble fingers help to push me farther as she swallows more and more. *Fuck!*

My head drops, and I watch her work me with her lips, her hand; her whole fucking body moves with the rhythm she sets, and her other hand is just as attentive. She groans, and I have to fight not to come; the vibrations at the back of her throat are very nearly my undoing. She switches just in time, and I let out a stuttered breath filled with timely relief. Her smirk and raised brows makes me think she *owns* me. She literally has me by the balls, and I fucking love it.

I can't take my eyes off her. She presses the crown of Will's cock against her lips and looks up to his eyes and then to mine; her smile is short-lived as she sinks her mouth over his length, never breaking her heated glare with mine. *God, I love this woman.*

She repeats this once more and is about to switch again, but I have had enough and judging by the fierce expression on Will's face, he feels the same. We both reach a hand under her arm and lift her to her feet. She sways a little, but we have her.

"Head or tails?" I growl. Sexual tension is coiled so tight, I am one big fucking trigger, and she is the hairpin. Her cheeks are an adorable pink, flushed and wet, her lips are swollen, and her breath is short and rapid, but her perfect brow pitches with confusion.

"Hmm?" Her eyes flick between Will and me for clarification.

"Do you want my cock in your arse or your pussy?" I calmly state. Lady's choice, and I don't really care which, but I told Will he's not allowed anywhere near her pussy, so this decision could suck for him, literally.

"Shouldn't the question be cats or dogs? You know as in cats are pussies and doggy from behind. I think that would work better, don't you?" She snickers at her own joke, but there is way too much tension and testosterone to filter in any humour.

"Sam." My tone is thick with lust and warning.

"Heads," she blurts, and I spy Will's widening grin, his lucky night. Sam turns to face me, between my arms, bouncing on the spot. I make the most of the move and lift her high on to my hips. "I want your head." Her hands clasp my face, and her lips kiss a thousand kisses all over my face, playful at first, but like I said, too much sexual tension. I fist her sodden hair and yank it back. Her head tilts, she gasps, and I thrust my tongue into her open mouth. It's ferocious and wild like the storm brewing in the speakers, crashes of thunder as her hands grip and pull my hair. She parries each move of my possessive tongue with her own demanding moves. My cock nudges against her entrance, and I brace my legs. I feel some cool liquid and foreign fingers move skilfully around her entrance, barely touching me…barely. One tilt of my hips and I bury myself to the hilt. Her arms tighten around my shoulders, and her whole body tenses at the intrusion. I'm not surprised; I don't think I have ever been this big—well, maybe once, not so long ago.

"You're going to need to relax a little, darling," Will whispers in her ear, but my ear too, since we are all so close. Sam pulls back and breaks the kiss, her eyes wide and alive. She gives a little nod and lets out a deep and steady breath.

I feel the pressure first against my cock and see the recognition and wince of pain flash in her eyes.

"Relax, beautiful," I coax, and she nods. Her eyes glaze, but I can still feel the tension in her frame. "Look at me." She does, her bottom lip is gripped between her teeth. *So much for relaxing.* "Breathe with me, baby, feel me, hmm?" She nods, and her lips soften. "Feel how deep I am. How good does that feel?" My tone is deep and gravelly, but I keep it calm, like a soothing wave to wash her worries away.

"So good." She sighs, and I roll my hips once more, making her gasp when I hit that sweet spot. "Oh God, so good." Her voice catches and her mouth drops open on a silent cry.

"More?" I exhale and wait for her to nod, which she does. Her eyes are fixed on me, deep, dark pools of liquid lust.

"More…please." She lets out a deep breath and all that tension, and it's enough. It's more than enough, and Will pushes past her tight barrier; the thinnest of membranes separates us, and she doesn't flinch. She is floating; her lips part with something unspoken and an inaudible whimper. We all take a moment… a heavenly moment as one, arms locked tight, skin on skin on skin. So fucking erotic, but I want more. My hips start to move, and Will and I quickly find a perfect rhythm of push and pull, in and out, but always keeping her full.

Driving her higher and higher.

She does her bit, lifting her tight, little body and dropping down hard, but I'm setting the pace, and it's me that will take her there. My lips seek hers, and she is ravenous for the contact.

"Jason." Her cry is an urgent plea as her body starts to take over.

"Come for me, beautiful." My lips are pressed against hers, my words soft, but she hears them loud and clear. She throws her head back, every muscle in her body clamps down, constricts, and she comes like a fucking freight train all over my cock. I can't ease her down gently; I no longer have that level of control. My hips piston into her, and I don't stop until she is screaming once more, and I am coming with her second and equally impressive orgasm. I step back and am thankful for the seat, which stops my body sliding down the tiles from hitting the floor. Sam's head is resting on my chest, her heart hammering the same beat pattern as mine. It's only after a few long moments when the blood is no longer rushing in my ears that I look up to see Will standing with his back to the water and a very angry-looking erection.

I tap Sam's cheek; she's all floppy and pliant. She tilts her head to look up into my eyes. "You got a little feisty and slippery when you came," I add, but I don't think it really needed an explanation. She had two cocks inside her, and now she just has me. She looks over at Will and back to me for permission. I tip my chin, but before I can agree verbally, Will speaks.

"Only if you're up to it. I can finish myself; I just thought I'd ask." Will shrugs like this offer isn't killing him, and I appreciate his attempt at least to be gracious. Sam shifts in my lap and off my cock to face him, but she leans back in to my chest. I wrap my arms tight around her waist.

"Heads or tails?" Her words are breathy and sexy as all hell and I can't see it but I can feel the grin.

"Oh, definitely heads." Will's tone drops an octave as he drops to his knees and wedges himself between mine and Sam's legs. Hers are draped over mine. Will's hands sweep along her thighs but rest at her hips, part gripping her arse cheeks, part holding her thigh. He freezes when he catches my scowl. I don't need to have this fight here...now, he fucking knows.

"Sorry, man, heat of the moment." He stands up and takes a slow step back, cupping himself.

"Right," I drawl. My hands drift down Sam's stomach to the top of her thighs that have instinctively tried to close. I press my palms flat against the taut muscle and pull them wide again. "So now you're just going to have to watch." Sam tenses in my arms but wisely remains quiet.

"Damn it, Jason." Will's jaw is clenched, but he's in no position to argue. He's my fucking guest.

"My rules, Will. There's the door, if you want it." Sam's back arches when I cup the apex of her legs possessively with a growl heard deep from my chest. She turns her head and has a flash of concern in her eyes. That's not what I want. This isn't a problem, but I won't let the heat of an encounter undermine my rules or me.

I take one hand and grab her jaw, pulling her open mouth to my lips. My tongue plunges into her softness and takes ownership, as if that was ever in question. Her arms thread around my neck, and my other hand grips and holds her steady, as her hips want to roll against my hold. She thrummed under my touch, and I want to take her there...just me. I spread my legs wide and as hers are over mine, hers are much wider. I guess Will has a great view, but I couldn't give a fuck. Sam is with me, her eyes never leaving mine.

I reach for the edge of the seat and hook the slim lightweight chrome showerhead. She shudders against my body and my cock strains against the small gap of her arse.

"Up you get, beautiful." I sit up straight so she lifts herself and pitches forward. Her hands rest on my knees, her arse lifts, and she positions herself just above my cock. I grab the base and push the tip firmly against her tight ring of muscles. "Ease back down, baby, but take all of me. Don't stop until I say." Her muscles clinch tight, and I catch a breath. Jeez, that is tight… shit! She relaxes and drops a little more. It's clearly taking effort on her part as short sharp breaths are being pushed out with equal force as her hands grip at my knees.

"Jason," she gasps, and I steady her with one hand on her hip, my other still has the showerhead that is pulsing a steady stream of water down my leg.

"Nearly there, beautiful, nearly there." I swallow the thick lump, my eyes fixed on her tight arse sliding slowly down my cock, perfect round swells of smooth skin, slick and shiny from the steam or sweat, it doesn't matter. It's fucking perfect. Her thighs tremble as she holds her weight, and she lets out a pained groan that filters out into a sensual sigh, finally sinking. All. The. Way. Down. We take a moment, and I let out a deep satisfying groan that I feel in my balls. *Damn.*

She starts to move her hips, rolling round, up and down, pressing her body to mine, using one arm around my neck for leverage. She tilts her head so our lips meet, frantic and urgent, and she squeals into my mouth when I press the fierce jet of water between her legs. The needles of the individual jets prickle the base of my shaft when she lifts her arse, but the bulk of the spray is directed right at her clit. The fingers from my other hand push into her entrance and pump gently to match the thrusts I am driving into her from behind. I am so fucking deep, and she is pounding hard, wanting more. My hands are wedged between her legs, one hand holding the shower head and the other with three fingers curled inside her, feeling the torrent of water rushing past my fingers and filling her as I pump and push the water back out. She's drenched.

Her own fingers grip my hair as her back arches away from me with the intensity of building pleasure.

"Touch yourself, beautiful," I groan against her lips, but I'm not sure she hears me; she takes a while to respond but then moves. Her hand drifts down her body, and she squeezes her pert, heavy breast, pinching the hard peak, before dropping it to join mine.

Our joined touch sends a jolt through her body that makes her arch and tense and cry out all at once. Her nails in my hair grip, and she holds so tight as my final thrusts take us both barreling, unstoppably, to the crest of a euphoric wave all our own, *mine*. She slumps against my body, dragging in frantic breaths and shivering despite the heat. I lift her off my cock and maneuver her until she is tucked up in my embrace, molding perfectly to my body. Her expression sated and satisfied, her heavy lids struggling to open, but they do, and the smile that spreads softly across her face is breathtaking. Happy in my favourite place, and I all too easily begin to drift off.

"Fuuuuuck." Will's distant voice breaks through the haze of my climax-induced daze. I drag my eyelids open and see that he is supporting himself on unsteady legs in the corner of the shower. *So he decided to stay after all.* "Fuck!" he repeats, dragging himself upright and hitting the button to stop the water.

He rests his head against the wall and takes deep breaths, making his chest swell as he slowly recovers. I take my own moment to come back to Earth before I try to move.

I shift Sam into my arms and carry her out. Will already has a warm towel and wraps it around us both.

"Definitely wouldn't be doing *that* if we stayed at Mum's." Will grins, roughly dragging a towel through his hair.

"Ya' think?" Sam can barely keep her eyes open, but she still has a little sass in her tone and the snort-laugh.

"What she doesn't know won't hurt her and this...this would kill her," I quip and stride off to our bed. I lay Sam down and climb in beside her. Will is about to climb in the other side.

"Are you staying?" I ask, and he freezes mid-climb and rolls his eyes at my curt tone.

"Yes, because if I don't, I will end up feeling like a fuck toy. I have feelings, too." His mirth has a tinge to it, and he tries sliding a little closer to Sam.

"Now who has the vagina?" I laugh but stop him snaking one arm around my fiancée.

"You do, you lucky son of a bitch." He lightly kisses Sam's shoulder and closes his eyes. Sam sighs, she nuzzles close into my side, molding her body flush to mine. I kiss the top of her head.

"Yes, I am."

"Fuck off!" I whisper grumble. A sharp pain at the top of my ear is getting fucking irritating. I squint one eye open and see Will leaning up on his elbow with a finger bent and poised to flick me again. He tilts his head and motions with his agile brows that he wants me to move. I start to curse, but Sam shuffles in my embrace, and I fall silent. She is still dead to the world, so obviously whatever Will is so fucking desperate to discuss only involves me. I slide my arms free and roll her on to her side, swapping my body for the warm pillow I was sleeping on. It's no substitute, but she coils around it all the same.

Will eases himself off the bed. I drag my boxer shorts on and stumble after him. The breaking dawn might be peeking through the blinds, but I am nowhere near done sleeping. I fail to mask my grouchy tone, but then I'm not really trying.

"What the fuck, Will?" My clipped question is masked by an exaggerated yawn. He doesn't reply until we are near the bar area of the suite and he finished pulling the rest of his clothes on.

"I have to leave, get a change of clothes before I pick you guys up later." Will keeps his voice low in a hushed whisper so I do the same, but my tone is a little more irritated.

"I would've worked that out, arse-wipe. You did not need to wake me for that earth-shattering revelation."

"Jeez, you're grumpy, and it's not because you woke up on the wrong side of the bed because you had Sam all fucking night," he quips.

"Damn right I did, and I'm grumpy because for no fucking reason you've dragged me away from that," I retort.

"Not for no reason…What was that call about last night?" His voice is no longer whispering, but is quietly serious.

I drag my hand down my face, feeling the tiredness in my brows, cheeks, and jaw, but I am fully awake now. "Put some coffee on while I grab a T-shirt, would you?"

"Sure."

The coffee machine makes a hell of a noise, but Sam doesn't stir as I sneak back into the bedroom to grab my top. Will is seated in one of the two chairs in the corner of the room overlooking the ocean now that the blinds are open wide. I blink, adjusting to the bright Florida sunshine, the sun having fully risen above the glittering calm of the endless horizon. I take the offered espresso. Looks like I'm up for the day now.

"It was James, my IT guy. He, I mean, I got another email that he tried to trace." I puff out a breath, barely containing my own frustration.

"And?"

"And jack-shit!" I snap, but shake off my anger, or its misdirection at least. "Whoever is sending this is smart enough to stay hidden. But I don't get it, because if its money, why doesn't the fucker just ask? This isn't about Sam. It is, obviously, but they contacted *me*. They want something from me. I just wish they'd fucking ask instead of all this playing games bullshit." I rub my thumb in small circles against the instant pressure pulse in my temple. Will waits a while before speaking.

"What did the email say? The new one, I mean?"

"Nice try."

"I'm just asking—" He holds his hands up, offended at my brush-off, but I wave him down and interpret.

"No, idiot. The email. It said, 'nice-try.'" He tips his head in understanding, and I continue to explain, my tone choked with doubt and impotence. "I can only assume whoever it is, now knows we've got the laptop he was bouncing the email from."

"Did you get anything off of it in the end?" Will leans forward, fingertips pressed together in contemplation or prayer maybe. It seems that's what is needed…Divine intervention.

"No, it was pretty much an empty shell. James is still checking, and he's going over the old emails to see if there was something, some code, or some shit that he missed."

"You want to send it to me and I'll get my FBI flatmates to have a look?" Will offers.

DEE PALMER

"James is the best," I snap, and my tone is too harsh for his best intentions, but I put that down to the lack of sleep.

"I don't doubt that, but a fresh pair of eyes can't hurt." He holds up his hands, palms out in a show to calm my open hostility. I let out a slow breath and give a light nod. I'm just damn tired.

"No, it can't. I hate the fucking waiting though, but until the fucker lifts their scumbag head above the parapet, I can't take a proper aim. When they do, I am damn sure going to be the one to take that motherfucker out."

"Take whom out?" The soft voice from the bedroom warms and chills me in equal measure. Shit, I flash a worried glance at Will, who winces with the same dread I feel in my gut. How much did she hear? Her feet pad softly across the floor, her hair is loose and wild—a little like her, and she looks *fuck-me* gorgeous in my dress shirt and nothing else. She slips onto my lap and snuggles into my protective hold. Her voice is sleepy, and her eyelids flutter closed when she yawns. "Are we going somewhere now?"

I release the breath I seem to have held since I heard her voice, and I notice Will do the same.

"No, beautiful, not right now. Will is going home to get changed, and then he's coming back to pick us up. Late morning though right?" Will stands and walks around the small coffee table and towers close to my seat.

"Yeah, late morning. I have to check with work that it's okay to drop by and load up the Jet Skis. Maybe pack a lunch if I get time." I'm not sure if his long list is trying to gain him favour or make me feel bad, but after last night, I feel neither.

"Are you trying to avoid the walk of shame, Will? It's okay to admit it," Sam teases, tugging his trousers in a playful manner.

"No fucking shame here, darling. I'd wear a T-shirt with

pictures if Jason would let me." He winks mischievously at Sam, who giggles; her whole body jiggles in my arms with mirth. Will leans down and holds her chin. I suck in a breath through my teeth and hold it for the second time this morning. He pauses millimeters from her lips when she smirks. This is like an ultra-high definition torture scene playing out right in front of me.

"You have a death wish, Will?" Sam asks calmly, but her eyes flick to mine, and Will's follow. He turns her head to face me and gently kisses her cheek.

"Just dickin' with my brother, darling." He stands and swiftly steps out of reach as I swing my clenched fist to administer the rightly deserved nut punch.

"Hey, don't be doing that." Will grabs his precious package with one hand. "You might be needing these later." He wiggles both his brows and roughly shakes his handful.

"Don't fucking count on it," I grumble, sinking my face into Sam's sweet ginger and orange blossom scented hair, inhaling my fill. Everything about this woman calms my mind and fills my soul.

"Never do, brother, never do." His wide grin is as bright as the sunlight streaming through windows. He grabs his jacket and slips out of the door, calling out, "Later," before the suction seals the door closed and silences the room.

"I like your brother." Sam looks up as I look down, her dark brown eyes impossibly large and wide, her smile breathtaking. She is absolutely flawless, seriously sexy with a surprising mix of innocence that owns my fucking heart.

"Yeah?" I lift her into my arms and walk back to the bedroom. Her lids are heavy, and her face is still crinkled with sleepiness that seems reluctant to yield its hold just yet.

"Hmm, yeah." She sighs and conforms around my body

so there is no distance—none at all—and it is perfect. I kiss her hair and climb into the bed, still holding her tight to my chest.

"Me, too, beautiful, me, too." I kick the bed sheet up enough to partially cover our entwined bodies and instantly fall into a heavy sleep. *Fucking perfect.*

SIXTEEN

Sam

I AM SO DAMN EXCITED. JASON LET ME RIDE SHOTGUN IN Will's jeep, and we just pulled up to where Will is going to be working starting next month. A single story modern office block set back from the main road on the edge of town. Don't get me wrong; it's completely horrific and disgusting that people deal and trade these precious exotic animals. But today, I get an up close and personal visit with a two-month-old white Siberian tiger cub, and that is something that just doesn't happen, so I am off the charts giddy. Jason and I sign in, and Will gives us a brief tour of the fairly standard offices: one large open room with too many desks for the space, an old drink machine in the far corner, and a very sad looking potted palm tree by the main door. Very different from Jason's elegant office overlooking the Thames, but Will beams with pride, and there is certainly no hint of jealousy between the two on a professional level, or any level for that matter.

There is a small kitchen, a conference room, and two small private interview rooms, and we poke our heads in before Will leads us into a large open backyard with a variety of small caged pens.

Most are very basic, but some have dug-out pools. Will explains is mostly for the Crocs and Alligators, but today, they are empty of water and prehistoric man-eaters. The pen at the far end is much larger and has a cozy-looking kennel with several blankets scattered all around. There are colourful toys strewn, balls, chewed up rope pulls, and a sagging fluffy bear draped half in and half out of the kennel, effectively blocking the entrance. I gasp as we get close enough to see the saggy bear is actually the fluffy bundle of white and grey fur of the baby tiger, dead to the world in the midday heat. Will goes to open the door to the enclosure.

"No, don't wake him!" I grab Will's arm, and he turns back with a confused look on his face. "He's a baby. Don't wake him just for me. If he wakes while we're here, that's different, but if he doesn't, I'm happy just to be this close." I keep my urgent plea in a soft, hushed tone, but I fix my steely glare on Will so there is no misunderstanding.

"Really?" Will screws up his face, incredulous at my comment.

"Really!" I emphasize my commitment with a sharp nod of my head. "No one really likes being woken up, Will." I crouch down on my haunches to get a closer look.

"Ain't that the truth," Jason chides, punching Will in his arm. They both stand behind me chatting, but I am engrossed with the little fella asleep just inches away from me. Tiny round ears peek out of the mass of white fluff, twitching occasionally with unseen disturbances. The stripes on his head are closer together, dark and more defined than those on his body. His paws stretching out in front of him, on the end of his little legs, are disproportionately large, giving a telltale indication of how big he is going to get. I look back up at Will.

"He's got a proper home, right?" My voice is still soft, so Will leans in to hear me.

"Yeah, darling, he's off to a big cat reserve and rescue center." He smiles softly at me, and I notice his lips carve a bigger curve when they check out the cutest cub ever.

"Do you get many cases like this?" I can't hide the sadness in my voice. This little fella is just a baby.

"We get enough." His somber tone speaks volumes, and I turn back to stare at the adorable creature still napping. I sit there transfixed until my bum starts to get numb.

"Are you sure you don't want me to give him a prod? Kinda feels like a waste of time," Will mutters as Jason helps me to my feet.

"No, I do not want you to give him a prod." I roll my eyes, and he has the decency to look a little apologetic.

"Okay, if you have finished gawking and really don't want me to wake him, let's head out to the lake. I've packed some food, but it's nothing fancy. I made some rolls, got some fried chicken, brats, chips, and beer." He beams and pats his very flat, fit tummy. "Oh, and watermelon," he adds a little louder, making me jump. His grin widens as he mentally checks off his lunch list, satisfied he has remembered everything.

"Sounds perfect. I'm starving," I gush and slip my arm around Jason's waist and through Will's arm. "Is it far to the lake? I wasn't joking, I will need feeding ASAP."

"It's about an hour drive, but I suppose I could let you have a roll to tide you over," Will muses.

"You are too kind. Unlike your brother, who made me skip breakfast," I remark with a little attitude and a lot of sass.

"That's harsh," Will goads, his tone filled with mock sympathy.

"Isn't it though?" I sigh, wearing my wounded self in the full curl of my pushed out bottom lip, sad doe eyes, and clutching my aching heart, all very melodramatic. A low grumbling sound rumbles from Jason's chest.

"I believe I told you exactly how much time we had until we needed to leave, and I believe I even offered to order room service, which you declined." His tone is stern and reprimanding, but tinged with humour. "Care to tell Will why you declined?" I shake my head and bite my lips into a tight, thin line to stop from smirking. "No? Care to tell Will what you chose to have instead of breakfast?" He fixes me with his dark brown eyes that scorch a path straight to my memory bank and alight my blood like a wild fire, melting my core and leaving me a liquid mess of wantonness.

"I didn't think you were serious," I mutter, but my defense is very weak and the timbre of his voice drops to a deep and serious rumble.

"What on earth gave you the idea I *wouldn't* be serious about making you come...again?" His tone is light but holds that erotic undertone that makes me tingle in all the right places.

"Not a single thing and I'd happily forgo my morning muffin for my muff—" I am cut off mid *overshare.*

"Yeah, all right, guys, I get the picture. In fact, I'm getting the IMAX version and these shorts are not up to hiding the aftermath of this conversation, so zip it." Will jumps in with his rushed interruption. "And I still have to show my face here, and I'm kinda like Jason in mixing work and pleasure." He flashes me a scowl that darkens his features for a moment.

"Sorry." I beam my widest, most innocent smile, which

makes his face crack with a loud belly laugh.

"Tell me another, why don't you, because that is not the face of contrition." His face tries to hold a modicum of seriousness, but it's tentative at best.

"Oh, Will, what big words you use! Someone else who is not afraid of a mouthful, hmm?" I drag my bottom lip in slowly, and he freezes for a second before he catches himself and shakes his head at the lost cause that is me and strides off in front.

"You can't help yourself, can you?" Jason leans down, snickering at his flustered brother, who is not so discretely adjusting his flimsy shorts.

"I really can't." I giggle as Jason pulls me tighter into his side now that his brother has stormed ahead, eager to leave his place of work and take refuge in his Jeep.

"Behave. You might want to cut back on the teasing, though, because I have no intention of sharing you again so soon," Jason states as a matter of fact. He looks into my eyes for something, maybe a reaction, I'm not sure, but I am more than fine with his statement. This thing we have, this thing we *do,* may be my ultimate fantasy, but it's only fun if it's fun for him, too. He has to be completely happy, so I am more than happy to follow his lead—on this, at least.

"I only do it when he's getting you all riled up. It seems only fair," I clarify my position with a light pitch and drop of my shoulders.

"Ah, beautiful, that's sweet, but I can handle my brother." He taps my nose, and I can't help myself; it's too damn easy.

"So can—" I snap my mouth shut mid-taunt at the instant cloud distorting his handsome face and the scary draw of his dark brows. I puff out a petulant breath of air. "Fine," I huff as we reach the car. Will is already seated in the front, and Jason opens the door for me. "You're no fun," I mutter but slide into the back seat on my own.

"That's not what you said this morning." He slams the door before I can retort or most likely agree.

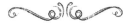

The drive down to the lake seems to take no time at all, and I spend most of the journey with my head resting on my arm, hanging half out of the window. Letting the warm sun saturate my skin and the wind whip so hard, I have to close my eyes, even behind my sunglasses. We turn off the highway and head inland and then hit a dirt track that leads almost to the edge of a stunning lake. Will backs his Jeep and trailer onto the slipway next to the jetty, and Jason and I unpack the supplies. Gorgeous soft sand surrounds the lake, from the water's edge right to the trees that offer some much needed shade. But looking around, you could be forgiven for thinking you were at the ocean with the expanse of water and no sight of the opposite shore line. Kids off in the distance are squealing in the water, motorboats racing in the distance, and there is a waft of burgers cooking on portable barbecues. But there is no cooling salt-laden sea breeze licking my skin. The air here is hot, probably not for a local, but certainly for a Brit in February.

We unload and set up a cute mini camp, close to the water, but secluded enough from the throngs of families, almost private. By the time we have finished though, I am no longer hungry, but I am a ball of sweat and desperately need a dip in that nice cool lake. I peel my thin sweater over my head and shimmy out of my loose jeans, kicking my Vans off as I do. Jason and Will freeze and stare, jaws dropped so wide they look hysterical.

"Do I have something in my teeth?" I drop one hip and quirk my lips, hiding my knowing smile. The bikini I was hiding under my clothes is super cute, white crochet, with string ties and tiny crystal beads sewn in the material, which catch and reflect the sunlight. But it is teeny tiny, so I know it's not the sparkles that have caught their attention. Jason drops the case of beer, narrowly missing his brother's foot, and strides over to me, hauling his T-shirt over his head as he goes. I see the look of determination in his eye, so before he gets too close, I spin on my toes and dart into the water. Two ungainly hop-steps and I am deep enough to spring forward into a dive and submerge myself in the crystal clear and not surprisingly, cold water. I gasp when I surface—shit, that's freezing. I start to swim just to warm up and possibly to allow that mountain of furious male on the shore time to cool down.

I call out. "I'm not coming back in until you stop clenching your jaw and put your clothes back on."

"You better be a strong swimmer then because I was going to say the same," he yells back in a grouchy grumble and folds his arms over his naked chest, all hard lines and soft tan. His forearms are pumped with tension, and the muscles swell to that delicious taut roundness that I just want to sink my teeth into. He's so damn sexy when he's mad. I quite like him mad. I splash a wave toward him, blow him a cheeky kiss, and swim off.

My legs start to ache after my second large loop of this little area of the lake, and I head back into the shore. I have cooled down and warmed up. I near the edge of the lake and notice that Jason is still standing there with his T-shirt in his hand; he hasn't so much cooled down, as stewed. I find my footing on the sandy lakebed and stand; the excess water glides down my body, and the air chills my skin. Jason's eyes are pretty much the size of saucers as they drag slowly up my body. I peek down; my bikini is lined, so I know it's not translucent like white swimwear can be, but it is now slick to my rather perky body.

"Jesus Christ," Jason seems to say without moving his lips, but then I realise it's Will's voice. Jason's lips are fixed in a strained grimace. I smile my widest and lean up to kiss him as soon as I am close enough.

"Calm down, caveman, it's just a pair of tits." I chuckle.

"Wrong. It's *my* pair of tits." He reluctantly returns my kiss, his full but dry lips slide against my wet ones, and he releases a soft groan. With stealth like efficiency, he quickly dresses me in his T-shirt that swamps me and hangs to just below my knees. I roll my eyes, but accept his chivalrous offer to protect my modesty.

"And this is mine, but you don't see me hiding you away. Quite the opposite. Everyone can gawk all they want, because I love that it is *all* they can do. Because all *this*—" I crawl all my fingers up his torso and link my hands together once they are around his neck. "*This* is all mine."

"Damn right, beautiful. It's not that I don't understand where you're coming from, but we're gonna agree to disagree on this one." He grabs my arse cheeks roughly in each of his sizeable hands and lifts me high. I wrap my legs around his waist and he carries me back to our picnic spot. "And I'm not hiding you, I'm protecting."

"You know I'm quite capable—" My objection is interrupted by a low growl.

"I know you are, beautiful, but I wasn't talking about you." He nods over to the jetty where a group of young lads are hanging off the side of a speedboat. "I'd rather spend the week with you than in a cell explaining why I beat the crap out of some horny teenagers."

"Careful there, brother, I didn't pack enough plasters for your knuckle-dragging activities," Will teases, and I snicker.

"Laugh it up, Will, but you'll be exactly the same when you find someone like Sam." Jason's voice drops to a soft whisper, and his eyes fix on mine with absolute adoration that makes my chest ache.

"There *is* no one like Sam," Will states, but when I flash a glance his way, he turns away, and I miss his expression.

"Ah, guys, you'll make me blush," I mock sweetly, jumping down from Jason's hold.

"That makes you blush, never mind being all wet and naked," he scoffs.

"I'm not naked." I sigh, exasperated.

"Semantics. You *look* naked," Jason grumbles, stubbornly hanging on to his grouchy mood.

"Yeah, she does." Will grins.

"Fine, I look naked. I'm not naked though, and just as this conversation is now wearing on my last nerve, I am in fact wearing *your* T-shirt, so unless you want me to take it off, let's just eat." I flop down in an angry flounce, cross my legs, and fold my arms.

Jason lowers himself beside me and tentatively rolls to sit a little closer. He leans over, and with a hushed, calming tone, starts to speak.

"It's just—"

"Nah-ah!" I interrupt and hold my finger against his lips in case he feels inclined to continue to explain. With my other hand, I make the universal sign of lock your lips and throw that motherfucking key away. "Agree to disagree." He nods and opens his mouth wide capturing my finger in one swift grab. He holds it between his teeth and swirls his scorching tongue around the captured digit before slowly releasing it in a seductive reverse pull of his lips.

"Hungry?" That tone is temptation from the devil himself,

and all I can manage in response is a strangled whimper and a lot more liquid pooling in my bikini bottoms.

I thought Will had packed enough food for an army when it was all finally laid out on the picnic table. But, after an hour of picking at the variety of dishes and drinking beer, we have collectively decimated the feast. All that is left is a few sad-looking watermelon slices and more beer, and until we've been out on the skis, I'm the only one drinking.

"You fancy a spin round the lake then?" Will sucks his fingers clean from the last of the fried chicken.

"Do I get to drive?" I ask excitedly but am shot down in stereo.

"No!"

"Well, unless you want a visual recap of my lunch, I would suggest giving me an hour. You two go get all that showboating shit out of the way." I wave them off.

"You sure?" Jason frowns, but Will is already walking to the jetty and Jason is half turned, clearly eager to ride.

"Very sure. If I go now, the first wave we hit, you'll be wearing that very lovely lunch I've just eaten, and believe me, it won't look quite so appetising all over your back." I stick my tongue out as if my explanation needed further clarification.

"Thanks for the visual." He wrinkles his nose and laughs.

"You're welcome." I swipe a blanket from the top of the cooler box and go to lie in the sun. My British body may be in shock at being exposed this time of year, but I am going to make the most of the Florida sunshine. I yank Jason's T-shirt over my head and watch his eyes narrow and his lips thin. Ignoring the rising levels of testosterone, which seems to correlate with my skin exposure, I screw the material up to fashion a makeshift pillow and lie down. I pull my shades from the top of my head over my eyes, sink into the soft fibres of the blanket, and bask. Bliss.

"Ahhh!" I scream and wildly flail my arms, but the damage is done. Drenched, I jump bolt upright from utter shock that instantly turns to blind rage. "What the fuck! You fucking... fuckity, fucking arsehole!" I shake off the excess, freezing cold water and angrily snatch the towel that Will is holding out to me at arm's length. *Very smart.*

"I told you she wouldn't find it funny." Will wisely steps back.

"No, *she* doesn't find it fucking funny. I was asleep, you shithead." I roughly dry my stomach and legs. My head snaps up to Jason's uncontrollable belly laughs. He waves his hand slowly up and down, and I find my blood boiling. If he's going to say what I think he's going to say...

"It's just a bit of water, calm your tits." I notice Will wince and brace, but it isn't him that needs to brace. I push off like an Olympic sprinter on the start block and fly my full body weight and considerable momentum into Jason's middle. Utterly shocked and wholly unprepared for my surprise attack, Jason falls flat on his back and grunts as I knock the wind right out of him. I quickly try to fortify my position and as strong as I am, my attempt to pin him to the ground is laughable. And he does laugh, but only once. He instantly has me flipped, and our positions are reversed, then he continues to laugh and laugh and laugh. I am so fucking mad. I don't know why I was mad in the first place but, boy, that smug grin makes me pine so hard for my trusty bullwhip.

"Wishing you had your tool bag, beautiful?" His eyes sparkle with mischief, and he flicks his head to move the hairs of his damp fringe that are obscuring his view. Although why he needs a perfect view when he can so clearly read my mind, I'm not sure.

"Something like that," I grate out through gritted teeth, bucking wildly beneath his immovable frame.

"Would you just—"

"If you tell me to calm down one more time, I swear to fucking god—"

"Well, would you maybe stop wriggling, at least, you're making me hard." He snickers, and I lose it. I lift my hips with strength I didn't know I had and knock him off balance, enough to swipe my elbow wide and whack him in the side. I twist and scramble away, but he snatches my ankle and hauls me back. As I fight his capture, and we tumble and tussle together rolling, grabbing, and each struggling to gain the upper hand, something changes. We both feel it, because it's like a fucking tsunami of pure unadulterated lust. I've never actually fought anyone, not like this, and by the wild and wanton look in Jason's eyes, I'm not sure he has. He holds his face inches from mine, but his body covers mine, his weight and power absolute. I let out a stuttered breath, but not because of his heavy frame crushing me, because I can't breathe from want so raw...so primal.

"Sam?" Jason's voice is low and tentative. He must know this should have triggers flying left and right for me, but it doesn't...not at all...not with him.

"Can we do this again?" My voice a breathy plea, my mouth is bone dry, and my tongue has little success at moistening my lips, but I drag it along my lips all the same.

"Fuck, yes." He crushes his mouth to mine, owning my words, my thoughts, *owning me.*

"Ahem." I hear Will's exaggerated cough, but only after the third maybe fourth attempt does Jason relinquish my lips and slowly turn his head to his brother. "Um, public place, guys. I take it we are done for the day?"

"No!" I yell. Jason flinches because his head had turned but hadn't moved away and his ear was right where my mouth is. "No, I want to have a go on the Jet Ski," I repeat, but this time with my indoor voice. Jason lightly kisses my nose.

"Your wish is my command." He pulls himself to his feet with me in his arms and carefully places me on my feet, but keeps me wrapped in a tight embrace.

"Oh, I do hope so," I whisper back and feel him shudder at my words.

I know he can't hear my squeals of terror and joy over the roar of the engine and thump, thump of the ski as it drops against the endless waves that he and Will are creating and circling back on. But my throat is hoarse from yelling, and my fingers are numb from gripping so tight. *This is so much fun.*

We have raced the length of the lake several times and messed about for ages in the heat of the afternoon, but I don't want it to end. Every time Jason asks if I've had enough, I grin like a kid on Christmas morning and shake my head. I unclip the front of my life jacket because Jason did it a little tight, and I am seriously hot, but I keep it pulled close and press against Jason's back. Will is tucked in behind us, riding our wake, but I only chance the odd glance back over my shoulder because even the slightest movement tips the balance of the ski, and we wobble, or at least I feel that we do.

We hit a massive wave created by arsehole behaviour from the young guys in the speedboat racing too close. Jason yells *motherfuckers,* and we hit another crest, but this time it is on a sharp turn, and I lose my grip and am thrown high off the back. I know it probably happened in a split second, but the next few events seem to play in front of me like I am standing just outside of them, breath held, hoping it won't play out quite like it's going to.

I tumble in the air, spray and white angry water swirls below me, and my scream is sucked back as I snap my mouth shut preparing for the water. It doesn't come, not when I expect it. My head smashes against the hard yellow rim of Will's Jet Ski, but I feel the slice more than the impact. I hit the water before I can dwell on what that means. I think I gasp for air or cry out, but my lungs are burning to breathe, and the weight of the water is crushing me. My head feels heavy, my legs, arms…the hairs on my arms; everything is so very, very heavy. My eyelids are the worst; they must be bleeding from the weight because all I can see is red…so much red.

SEVENTEEN

Jason

THE LONGEST FORTY-EIGHT HOURS OF MY LIFE. NO, WAIT, Sam was drugged and kidnapped, and I couldn't find her…that was the worst. But sitting beside her bed while she is in an induced coma because of the swelling on her brain comes a pretty fucking close second.

"Here, drink this." Will holds a grey liquid that I suppose is coffee by the aroma assaulting my nose. I shake my head, but he lifts it close to my face and holds it there until I take the damn cup.

"How's the wife?" Will raises a brow and sits in the chair beside me. His comment makes my lips twitch; I fail to form an actual smile, but the intention is there.

"Semantics, brother…she's gonna be my wife and the sooner the better." My eyelids close briefly. It hurts to see her like this, but it's agony to tear my eyes away. "I was not putting that fucker Leon's name down as next of kin one more time.

She's mine," I grit out through a clenched jaw, my frustration and fear morphing into impotent rage.

"I get it." He places his heavy hand on my shoulder and rests it there. "So how's she doing?"

"They did a scan this morning, and the swelling's gone down. The doctors were pleased, and they stopped the drugs keeping her in the coma a few hours ago. It's now just a case of waiting until she wakes up." I let out a long slow breath, failing to hide the fear those words hold. His hand squeezes tight on my solid, tense shoulder muscle.

"Is there any damage? Will she be okay?" His voice catches, and that causes a pain through my chest that makes me double over. *Fuck, this is killing me.* "Shit, sorry, Jason. I didn't mean... shit." He lets out a stuttered breath, and the room falls silent. We are both silent; Sam is silent. Only the machines that monitor her life are screaming an unbearable sound to my ears. *Nails down a chalkboard.*

Will takes my full cup of cold coffee and mutters something about getting a fresh brew and something to eat. My stomach groans at the mention of food but churns with sickness at the thought of actually eating. Nurses and doctors come and go, kind words of comfort barely register, but I manage to nod my appreciation. I hold her warm hand and talk to her as if we are alone. I whisper, recalling our erotic playtime. I tease and make sinful threats, hoping my words will bring a flush of colour to her cheeks, as they do to the few nurses close enough to hear what I'm actually saying. "Dammit, Sam, it's been hours. Wake-up!" I drop my head and growl out in frustration. My angry tone fills the vacuum of desolation and hangs heavy in the air. *Nothing.*

"Jason." Will calls behind me, but I don't have the strength to lift my head.

"Hmm?" I stretch my neck to the side and wait for the pop, so much tension even my bones ache.

"Jason." His tone is urgent, and my nerves are that frayed that I snap my head round and shout.

"What?" I scowl at his wide eyes and open mouth. I take a moment to register his stare is fixed over my shoulder. My head twists back sharply to see what has him speechless. Those eyes…those beautiful, soul-stirring eyes are smiling at me. I stand and step close, still holding her hand. My other cups her face. I can't breathe.

"Hey." Her voice is croaky, but her lips spread wide. Her eyes are fixed on me, and I join her sweet smile. I let out a strange strangled sound that is a mix of utter relief and happiness, a laugh and gasp all in one. My lips fall to her forehead, and I close my eyes and breathe her in. The clinical covering of antiseptic masks her scent, but I can still find her essence in the breath I draw deep into my lungs. I pull back and cover her mouth. Her monitors instantly bleep a discord of their disapproval to my kiss, and I couldn't care less. This is fucking heaven because for the first time in nearly three days, my girl kisses me back.

"Mr. Sinclair, would you please step back." The nurse that has been mostly in charge tries to pry me away, but I won't be moved. She huffs and manages to squeeze in between the bed and me, but I am right at her side. I let her because she's checking shit, but I'm not letting go—not now—*not ever.*

"How are you feeling, honey?" The nurse asks Sam after taking a note of all her vitals.

"Tired." Sam gives a tentative smile that lights up my world.

"Well, you're in the best place. So get as much rest as you need." She steps away and walks around to the other side of the bed to fiddle with and take notes from the various machines still attached to Sam. She clutches the clipboard to her chest and starts to leave at the same time the doctor enters the room. I look over to see Will still standing in the doorway, but he is now sporting a wide grin filled with utter relief and joy. *Snap.*

"Mrs. Sinclair, good to have you back." The elderly Swedish doctor beams at Sam, and seems genuinely pleased and not at all surprised, which is a comfort.

"Mrs. what? I'm married?" Sam's face registers confusion, her voice piqued with shock. I cringe.

"Yes, Mrs. Sinclair, you are married. Your husband hasn't left your side for a moment, he has talked to you the whole time you've been asleep." The doctor takes the chart from the nurse and falls silent as he reads the new information.

"Boy, did he." The nurse behind me breathes out in a whisper that makes me chuckle. Sam tries to pull her hand free, but I squeeze a little tighter, not ready to relinquish my hold. Her brows knit together and she fidgets; she looks uncomfortable.

"What is it, beautiful? Are you in pain? Can I get you anything?" I ask softly.

"I…I don't know. I don't remember." Her eyes glaze with water, but before I can reassure her that this is an administrative issue, the doctor interrupts asking her name, and my whole world implodes with her reply.

"Grace," her voice waivers. "My name is Grace Cartwright." As much as I feel like I have been hit with a fucking anvil in my chest, *she* looks so much worse. Colour drains from her face and fat tears roll down her cheek. I squeeze her hand, and her eyes meet mine. That look nearly breaks me, so unbearably sad, vulnerable, lost. *My girl is lost.*

"Is that wrong?" She roughly dries her cheek; her tone flips from uncertain to sharp and irritated.

"No beautiful, that's not wrong." My voice is soothing, my thumb brushes her wrist, but even I can feel her pulse jump erratically beneath the skin. I turn to the doctor.

"Would you give us a moment?"

"We need to do more tests, Mr. Sinclair." He tries to argue, but I stand up to my full and not inconsiderable height. I am effectively blocking him from even seeing Sam, let alone getting close enough to administer more investigations.

"Just one moment," I state, brooking no other response. The doctor nods and leaves the room with the nurse. Will still hovers, and honestly, I don't mind that he is there, but Sam looks over to the door and back to me as if waiting for me to finish clearing the room. I turn, but Will has already taken the hint. The door closes, and it's just us. I should be elated, but I am suddenly terrified. The last time she was Grace was over ten years ago, before me, before The Club and Mistress Selina, before Leon even. I have no idea who Grace was, but I doubt she'd love a kinky fucker like me. *One step at a time.*

I sit on the edge of the bed, and she shuffles to face me but also moves a little further away, confusion etched on her face. *Fuck this.* I climb onto the space she's made, clearly aware that wasn't her intention when making it, but I settle back and pull her half onto my body. Tugging her arm to rest across my stomach, I gently press her head to rest on my chest. I finally tuck her limp hair away from her face and cup my hand around her jaw and hold her to look directly up at me, no escape.

"Hey, beautiful," I whisper, and my heart clenches when her lips carve the most amazing smile across her face. *Score one.* I don't care if she's remembered that is the name I call her all the time or not, it's made her smile, and I'll take that.

"Hey," her smile doesn't quite reach her eyes, and she lets out a sad stuttered breath.

"Hey, it's okay." I kiss her forehead and hold her close. I can feel her tremble and break with sobs. My shirt dampens under her head and I just hold her for endless minutes until she's ready. I soothe and hum, stroke her back and squeeze her as tight as her injuries will allow.

"I don't remember getting married." She lifts her head and her sad eyes almost break my heart.

"That's understandable since you aren't married." I keep my tone soothing but her brows shoot up with shock all the same.

"What?" Her face screws up with confusion and tension that I can feel radiate through her body.

"What do you remember?"

"Jason, I don't understand. What do you mean I'm not married? The doctor said Mrs. Sinclair, what—"

I cut any further questions as I instantly scoot down and cover her mouth with mine, my tongue forcing an easy path between her soft lips and diving in to taste her again, my Sam. Urgent kisses, tongues dancing, no…duelling as I feel her come back to me. She breaks the kiss, breathless and on fire. Her face glows, her eyes pierce mine, her hand fists my shirt, and she pulls me back for another kiss. *Fuck, yes.* She moans into my mouth, and her hand drifts from my waist to my pants. Her fingers curl over the waistband, and I can feel my cock strain behind the material to try and make contact with that light touch. My hand, the traitor that it is, rests over hers and prevents this situation from deteriorating out of my limited self-control.

"Sam," I warn, my voice a low, friendly grumble. Her eyes flick to mine, and I can see the cogs turning, processing, as her brow furrows, and she takes her time to pick through the fog that must be her memory.

"We are getting married, though?" She purses her lips in

a playful pout, and I let out three days of anxiety and fear in a loud liberating laugh.

"Yes, beautiful, we're getting married." I plant an aggressive closed mouth kiss on her lips. "I told the hospital we were married because I am still not your next of kin, and when they brought you in, there was no fucking way I was going to give them the opportunity to deny me access."

"Oh." She nods slowly. "Leon is my next of kin."

"Yep, but not for long, and after the last three days, the sooner the fucking better," I grumble.

"Such a romantic...what happened to me having my dream wedding?" she teases.

"It will still be a dream wedding, but you will just have to step up the date that's all." I poke the end of her nose. A cute set of wrinkles appears on the bridge as she scrunches her face. "So what do you remember?"

"Red and water...we went to the lake with...is Will all right?" She looks over at the door as if he is still standing there.

"Will is fine—just worried, that's all. But he got the air ambulance to you in record time. You lost a lot of blood, your head was a fucking mess, but they patched you up quick and *that* definitely saved your life." I struggle to swallow the lump in my throat and watch her eyes register my nightmare. Her hand presses against my cheek, and I lean into her touch. *So damn grateful.* My eyelids close, and I savour her touch, her warmth. That time waiting for the ambulance, watching the life literally drain from her body I don't ever want to replay. The scar will heal, and she is back, but that nightmare will be forever etched in my brain.

"It was bad?" she asks when I open my eyes.

"The worst, beautiful. I thought I'd lost you when you went under like a fucking stone, and there was so much blood, you turned the lake red." I kiss the single tear tracking its way down her cheek. The salty water so sweet on my lips. *Mine.*

"Water and red," she repeats softly.

"But 'Grace' nearly gave me a heart attack." I'm deadly serious, but my face is a picture of relief and joy.

"Grace?" She sniffs and flashes a knowing grin. "Ah, yes, that *would* be a worry, not sure why I recalled that name, but having to teach her all of Sam and Selina's tricks would've at least been interesting."

"If she wanted to be taught. She might not like this kinky fucker as much as you do." I raise a perfectly valid point with a raised brow. She bites back a sensual smirk.

"Oh, she'd love this kinky fucker almost as much as I do." She tilts her head as an open invitation to kiss, consume, devour. R.S.V.P Abso-fucking-lutely

The next day Sam undergoes more test and endless questions, which establish she hasn't actually lost any memory, but the severity of the head injury and risk of repeat swelling on the brain means under medical advisement she shouldn't fly home for at least a fortnight.

"I can stay at the hotel, I will be fine," Sam argues for the umpteenth time. I hate that I will have to return to the UK without her. It's out of my hands with Daniel on paternity leave. This trip was only ever supposed to be a few days.

"I'll get a nurse to look after you." My angry tone is a reflection of my frustration. I have back-to-back meetings all week, or I would work from here dammit

"Oh, make sure he's really hot, would you." She grins, and that wicked smile is enough of a distraction.

"Cute." I narrow my eyes, and she sticks out her tongue. "If you're well enough to be waving that thing around, then I have just the place to put it to proper use." Her eyes sparkle, and I swear my cock groans.

"*I* never said I wasn't well enough." She licks her lips and kneels up on the bed almost as eager as I am but slouches back when the doctor enters the room, followed by Will.

"How are you feeling today, Sam?" Dr. Eriksson asks brightly.

"Well enough for anything, doctor." She swipes her lip wet with a flash of her tongue, winks at me, and bites her smirk back when I scowl. She'll pay for that.

"Good. Your tests are fine, and I understand you've agreed not to fly back to the UK just yet. I really think it is for the best." She nods but doesn't look happy. That makes two of us. "Do you know where you will be staying? Do you have family here?"

"She does," Will answers. "She can stay with me. I have some time owed from work, so I can take care of her too." The muscles in my neck tighten at this news. It might be perfect, but it's the first I've heard of it, and I don't like to be kept in the dark.

"She's not staying in your fuc— your shared apartment, Will." I correct myself, but he knows what I meant to say.

"She won't be. I'm house-sitting for my boss. He has a place just down the coast. It's a beautiful beach house, private, and perfect for resting. She'll be fine. I promise to take care of her," he adds, but I know he will, I just hate that he can when I can't.

"*She* would quite like a say in this," Sam huffs, and we all turn to face her and wait quietly for what she has to say. "That sounds lovely, Will, but you don't have to babysit. I will be fine reading and whatnot in the daytime. I'll most likely sleep all day."

"Yes, he does, or it's the nurse. I'll let you make that choice, but you are not staying home alone after a head injury," I answer for Will, who will soon share my frustration at herding cats—or getting Sam to do as she's told.

"Fine. There probably isn't a nurse as sexy as he is anyway." She snickers at my sudden frown.

"You're so funny this morning. Just remember it's your head that's injured, not your arse." Her face colours a fantastic shade of red and my palm twitches to match that colour on said arse cheek.

"I can't believe you just said that!" She slaps her hand over her mouth in shock, but the good doctor barely looks up from his clipboard. Will snickers, and I let out a deep belly laugh at her mortification.

"Okay, then." The doctor hands over his clipboard. "If you can sign these discharge papers, and wait for the nurse to bring you your meds, you are free to go." He holds out his hand and Sam shakes it, as do Will and I. They have all been amazing, and I happily tell them as much.

Sam is sitting on the bed with Will one side and me the other when a young nurse we haven't seen before bounds into the room with two large paper bags. She skids to a comical stop when her eyes flick wildly between Will and I. Sam groans and rolls her eyes. I shrug and flash a killer smile at the nurse that makes her jaw go slack.

"Jeez," Sam mutters with justified exasperation. Sometimes, I can't help myself. "Are those for me?" Sam holds out her hand, and the nurse snaps her mouth shut and offers a shy smile.

"Oh, yes, sorry. These are for pain, but only if you need them, and they are obviously safe to take in your condition." I take the bag from Sam's hand and pass it straight to Will to carry. "And these are your antenatal vitamins." I reach to do the same with the next bag, but my hands freezes mid-air and all air leaves my lungs in a puff.

"What?" Three voices of varying pitch and panic have the poor nurse looking like a deer in the headlights.

Not quite…The End

ABOUT THE AUTHOR

I met my husband when I was sixteen and I feel for him because there is no way I am the same person he fell in love with but after twenty ahem… something years perhaps I'm not so bad. He now has a wife that can name her favourite porn star…research of course, never says no…and knows a thing or two about … probably too much ;). He may not 'get' what I do but he is a little more tolerant of the voices in my head because now they appear on paper. I love, love writing and hope to be able to do this until I am very old and grey…growing old disgracefully.. and dee-spicably, always…xdee

Stalk me On Facebook, Twitter and Instagram

Join my reader group…it's not all books ;)

www.facebook.com/
groups/902682753154708/?ref=bookmarks

If you haven't already signed up to my newsletter now is a good time. I don't spam but you are the first to learn of new releases, freebies and extras

Click here for the password: http://eepurl.com/biZ6g1

Printed in Great Britain
by Amazon